Titles by Peter Duchin and John Morgan Wilson

BLUE MOON
GOOD MORNING, HEARTACHE

BLUE MOON

A Philip Damon Mystery

Peter Duchin
and John Morgan Wilson

BERKLEY PRIME CRIME, NEW YORK

This is a work of fiction. Names, characters, places, and incidents either are the product of the authors' imagination or are used fictitiously, and any resemblance to actual persons, living or dead, business establishments, events, or locales is entirely coincidental.

BLUE MOON

A Berkley Prime Crime Book / published by arrangement with the authors

PRINTING HISTORY
Berkley Prime Crime hardcover edition / October 2002
Berkley Prime Crime mass market edition / November 2003

Copyright © 2002 by Peter Duchin and John Morgan Wilson.
Cover art by Jill Boltin.
Text design by Kristin del Rosario.

For information address: The Berkley Publishing Group,
a division of Penguin Group (USA) Inc.,
375 Hudson Street, New York, New York 10014.

ISBN: 0-425-19306-3

Berkley Prime Crime Books are published
by The Berkley Publishing Group,
a division of Penguin Group (USA) Inc.,
375 Hudson Street, New York, New York 10014.
The name BERKLEY PRIME CRIME and the BERKLEY PRIME CRIME
design are trademarks belonging to Penguin Group (USA) Inc.

PRINTED IN THE UNITED STATES OF AMERICA

10 9 8 7 6 5 4 3 2 1

*For all the mystery writers we've enjoyed so much
and the dedicated booksellers and librarians
who've kept them on the shelves.*

ACKNOWLEDGMENTS

The authors wish to thank the following for their invaluable contributions: Sgt. Robert A. Fitzer, director, San Francisco Police Department Museum and Archives; Samara Diapoulos, director, public relations, the Fairmont Hotel; the San Francisco Public Library's History Center; Katherine E. Atkinson, Director of Cemeteries, Catholic Archdiocese of San Francisco; and James E. Cornett, Special Projects Coordinator, Holy Cross Cemetery. We also wish to recognize three very helpful books: *The World of Herb Caen, San Francisco 1938–1997*, by Barnaby Conrad; *The National Geographic Traveler: San Francisco*, by Jerry Camarillo Dunn, Jr.; and *How to Enjoy 1 to 10 Perfect Days in San Francisco*, by Jack Shelton, published in 1962 and discovered at a garage sale in 2001.

Individually, Peter Duchin wishes to thank his wife, Brooke Hayward Duchin, and three special friends: fellow author Howard Kaminsky; San Francisco architect Sandy Walker; and Charlotte Schultz, for showing him San Francisco as only she could.

John Morgan Wilson is especially grateful to Pietro Gamino, his companion of many years; his agent, Alice Martell; the Berkley Publishing Group staff, in particular Natalee Rosenstein; and two organizations so supportive of mystery writers: Sisters in Crime and the Mystery Writers of America.

Chapter 1

I WOKE ON the morning of October 20, 1963, with Duke Ellington's "Sophisticated Lady" playing in my head.

It was one of those disorienting moments between waking and sleeping when you're not quite sure whether you're still dreaming or back in reality—or if there's a difference. I lay alone in the big bed I once shared with my wife, Diana, hearing the lush melody as it mingled with the early morning street sounds of midtown Manhattan drifting up through the open window. Wondering why that tune, that moment.

Then I recalled that I'd been practicing "Sophisticated Lady" on the piano exactly two years earlier when the call had come telling me that Diana was dead.

* * *

A horn honked down on West 57th Street, bringing me back, grounding me again in my surroundings. My apartment was perched high atop Carnegie Hall, between Sixth and Seventh Avenues, affording me spectacular views of Central Park, the Hudson River, and the Upper West Side. Two legendary stores—Patelson's for music, Steinway Hall for pianos—were located just down the block. Bobby Short, the wonderful cabaret pianist and singer, had the place across the roof, which made for great parties when we jointly opened our apartments to let our guests mingle. My rooftop perch was home, even if the bed beside me was empty now.

I bounded out of bed, happy to leave my reverie and focus on business. In my case, that meant music—mostly swing, the way it was played back in the thirties and forties when a new kind of rhythm got people up and dancing like never before. Late October, of course, was the height of the fall social season—charity balls, cotillions, private debutante parties, corporate events—always my favorite time, my busiest and most profitable. The weather was gorgeous in New York that Sunday as I jumped in a taxi for Idlewild Airport and the six-hour flight to San Francisco.

Not exactly my idea, to be sure. A few weeks earlier, I'd attended the theater with a small party of close friends—Jackie Kennedy, the authors Truman Capote and George Plimpton, and Joseph Kraft, the syndicated political columnist. At Jackie's invitation, we'd gone to the Alvin Theater on 46th Street to see *A Funny Thing Happened on the Way to the Forum*, a wonderful hoot that had Truman giggling unabashedly, which became infectious. I soon found myself laughing genuinely for the first time since Diana had been taken so abruptly and violently from my life.

After the theater, Jackie had us up to her suite at the

Carlyle for supper. She seemed awfully pale and somewhat distant that night, but still looked quite lovely in a no-frills red dress by Oleg Cassini, with a matching full-length coat but no hat, and a tasteful Pierre Cardin handbag. The First Lady was in from Washington for the evening and some appointments the next morning, while the President stayed behind at the White House, handling press interviews on the first anniversary of the Cuban missile crisis. Although they were now America's royal couple, Jackie had confided to me that, as a Catholic, she always felt a bit the outsider in certain stuffy social circles. It didn't surprise me that she often seemed more comfortable among other quasi outsiders, like those who comprised the group that night: Joe Kraft, a Jew married to a painter, who'd managed to gain acceptance as a Washington political insider; Truman Capote, with his literary genius, eccentricities, and offbeat private life; George Plimpton, the patrician writer who'd started *The Paris Review* in France in the fifties, before returning home from self-exile; and me, born to a Jewish mother and a Catholic father, but taken in almost as an orphan and raised in the most upper crust of Protestant homes, among the Eastern political aristocracy. It made for an interesting mix, four quite different men and a remarkable woman who regularly worked and mingled in "high society," yet always with the sense that they would never fully belong, because of who they were and where they came from.

During an otherwise grand meal, Truman had a bit too much fumé blanc, as he tended to do, and began quizzing me about Diana's murder. I did my best to change the subject, asking if anyone at the table had seen *Tom Jones*, the big movie of the moment, for which I'd performed at a special opening not long before.

"I didn't mean to be nosy," Truman sniffed apologetically, speaking in his childlike voice that stumbled along over an endearing lisp.

"Of course you did," Jackie chided, and the rest of us laughed.

"But it's been two years, and we've heard so precious little!" Truman poured himself more of the white wine, cocking his balding head and pouting mischievously. "I think we deserve just a teeny update. The newspapers have certainly been no help."

"Philip will talk about it when he feels he's ready," Jackie said, in her customarily gracious manner. Then, almost as an aside, she slipped in some wisdom no doubt forged from some of her own personal anguish: "Of course, verbalizing it sometimes helps exorcise one's ghosts. Or at least face up to them."

"I quite agree," Plimpton said in his stentorian voice, sitting tall in his gray suit, his long legs crossed beneath the table. "Best to get it out, I say."

"As painful as it might be," added the rumpled, bespectacled Kraft.

I caught their eyes discreetly connecting and began to suspect a benevolent conspiracy at work. They'd all known and liked Diana, and were familiar with the broad strokes of our relationship: the exhilarating courtship in San Francisco before I brought her back to New York to begin the three happiest years of my life. The moment not quite two years ago, on my thirtieth birthday, when she'd surprised me with the fantastic news that she was pregnant. The awful night soon after when I was on the road with the band and someone entered our New York apartment and strangled the life out of her. It was a booking in Atlantic City that I could easily have turned down, to spend more time with Diana in her early pregnancy; I still blamed myself for not being with her that fateful night.

"There's really not a lot to tell." I kept my eyes on my plate and the remnants of my veal cordon bleu. "You know the essentials. Someone found a way in, although there were no signs of forced entry. Diana died struggling. Our place was ransacked but nothing was taken, at least not that I could see."

"Highly unusual," Plimpton said. "Didn't all the papers make a big deal of the fact that 'Blue Moon' was playing on the hi-fi?"

I nodded, shuddering at the irony. "That old swinging Anita O'Day version, the one Diana listened to so often. The turntable was still spinning when"—the words bunched in my throat—"when the cleaning lady discovered her body."

"Awful," Joe said, his dark eyes somber behind his black horn-rims. "I'm so sorry, Philip."

"The papers got most of the details right." I forced a smile. "Except for the *Post*, of course."

Kraft chuckled at that, until Truman grimly recalled the *Post* headline aloud: "BLUE MOON" PLAYS AS BEAUTY MURDERED.

I cleared my throat with a sip of pinot noir, then went on gamely. "No fingerprints or other evidence of any value. No witnesses who heard or saw anything. The police questioned a few suspects from Diana's past, but they all had ironclad alibis. Or so the cops told me—I was more or less in shock and seclusion when all that was going on. I wish now I'd been more engaged, more involved." I looked up, shrugging. "The case remains open. That's all I know, all anybody knows."

"Except for the wretched person who did it," Truman said.

"Yes," I said, "he'd be the only one."

"You're presuming it's a man," Plimpton said.

"That's the police theory. Diana wasn't a small woman, and she was in pretty good shape—all that tennis and horse riding. Someone would have to have overpowered her. Anyway, it's all in the past, isn't it?"

I glanced around the silent table, attempted another smile, desperate now to steer the conversation in another direction. "So, has anyone read *The Feminine Mystique*? This new Betty Friedan book seems to be making quite a splash."

"That woman desperately needs some hair and wardrobe advice," Truman said, splashing yet more fumé blanc into his Waterford goblet.

"No, that would be me," Joe said, slump-shouldered in frayed jacket and button-down shirt, well past his last trim. Jackie chuckled, and Joe gave her a wink.

"I'd say Friedan's on to something," Plimpton put in. "How long do we honestly expect women to knuckle under, for God's sake?"

"I saw Jane Fonda quoted in one of the entertainment columns the other day," Kraft said, looking bemused. "She declared flatly that marriage is obsolete."

"Who's Jane Fonda?" Truman tittered. "All right, I know who she is. But she's only twenty-five, and everyone knows she'll never amount to anything."

To my surprise, Jackie turned the subject back to Diana, resuming Truman's initial probe. She was gentler and less direct, of course, and had my best interests at heart. Truman, maybe not so much. Ever the writer, he couldn't resist a good story line—one that had a beginning, a middle, and an end. The problem with this one was that it still needed a final act. The killer had never been identified, and my life remained frozen in that numbing moment when I'd first learned that Diana and our unborn child were gone forever. I know it sounds maudlin and self-pitying, but I missed Diana beyond description, and moving on often seemed impossible.

So I talked a bit more about the case and answered my friends' questions the best I could. By the end of supper, as the men sipped cognac and Jackie took Perrier with lemon and ice, they were encouraging me to return to San Francisco. It was the city where Diana and I had met—she as a graduate student in classical languages at nearby Berkeley, me playing a gig at the Starlite Roof of the Sir Francis Drake Hotel. Going back, they all assured me, would be therapeutic.

"To embrace Diana's memory," Plimpton said.

"To exorcise those ghosts Jackie spoke of," Kraft added.

"So you can begin to let go," Truman lisped.

"And finally say good-bye," Jackie concluded, ever so gently.

Returning was something I'd resolutely resisted for two years, possibly because I had other ghosts in my past that I'd never quite faced up to; my nature was to put on a smile, surround myself with people, have a good time. Yet my dinner partners were insistent, Jackie most of all. I suspect that part of me wanted to go back, if only to revisit the city Diana had loved so much, while another part dreaded the feelings it might stir up.

As it happened, a few days later the band was offered a booking in San Francisco, an engagement too good to pass up. Gritting my teeth, I accepted.

Chapter 2

" MR. DAMON, WE'LL be landing shortly."

The purring voice belonged to the stewardess, the one with the nice legs, perky hair, and Pepsodent smile, which pretty much describes all the stews aboard that day. Surrounding me on the DC-8 were several members of the band; the rest I was picking up from local musicians around Frisco with whom I'd worked before. As usual, I'd had to pay an extra half-fare for my bass player, whose cumbersome instrument was strapped into the seat beside him—with a ticket issued to Mr. Bass. The stew asked me to fasten my seat belt, then for an autograph, and I obliged. I scribbled Philip Damon into her autograph book, with an exaggerated flourish on the P and the D. Then, with two or three quick strokes, I sketched the outline of a grand piano. It was something I must have done a few thousand times for other fans since starting the Philip Damon Orchestra in the early fifties, after my education at Eaglebrook, Hotchkiss, and Yale and two years of military service as the Korean War was winding down.

"You're even better-looking than on your album covers," the stewardess said, sounding well rehearsed but nervous.

I offered her my best coy look as I handed back her little book, just flirtatious enough to soften the coming rejection. "You've obviously got great taste," I said, doing my best to come off as suave and self-effacing, but not quite pulling it off.

She laughed, thanked me for the autograph, then hesitated for an awkward moment while our eyes danced a bad tango. Finally, growing flustered, she moved on. In the old days, before Diana, I would have tried for a phone number and probably gotten it. I'd been in my mid-twenties then, cocky as hell and shamelessly randy in a world filled with enticing women. An American Airlines pilot, an old pal, had even given me a book filled with the addresses and phone numbers of all the American stews. Without the slightest flicker of conscience, I'd managed to work my way through the J's before a close friend introduced me to Diana Larocque. It had happened over cocktails at Andy Wong's Chinese Sky Room in San Francisco before my evening gig at the Starlite. That was the night when I'd finally started growing up and begun to see women as something more than lovely objects of pleasure—the night, at twenty-seven, when I'd finally met the woman I knew I was meant to be with forever.

*   *   *

MY father, by the way, was Archie Damon—as in the more famous Archie Damon Orchestra of the thirties and early forties, the favorite band of high society in those days. Sometimes people get the names confused, mixing us up.

Dad had been one of the prominent front men of the Big Band Era, not quite in the pantheon of the greats—Duke Ellington, Louis Armstrong, Benny Goodman, Count Basie, Glenn Miller—but a famous orchestra leader nonetheless. He never played much swing, like they did, after it became wildly popular in 1935, when Goodman introduced it to white America long after blacks had embraced it as part of the jazz lexicon. Dad had a classical background and liked jazz, but his trademark was what they called "sweet" music, smooth and elegant, more in the style of Guy Lombardo and Hal Kemp. Dad was a good-looking guy who starred in a few movies, playing himself, before dying suddenly of an aneurysm when I was twelve. Hollywood even made a film about him in the fifties, *The Archie Damon Story*, although I always felt Montgomery Clift was a bit too melancholy in the title role. Maybe Clift had seen something in Dad that I hadn't, or hadn't wanted to.

I formed my own band in '53, as my military service was ending, a decade after Dad's death and twenty-two years after the passing of my mother, an exceptionally bright and beautiful woman who died three days after my difficult birth. Unlike the Archie Damon Orchestra, the Philip Damon Orchestra *did* swing, along with playing some of the sweeter music for which Dad had been famous. My band was just well enough known for me to make a comfortable living and have a good time, and successful enough in its own right that I had no problem performing in my father's shadow. Other things about our relationship troubled me—

after my mother's death, Dad had slipped into a deep depression and virtually abandoned me to doting nurses until my godparents, Barclay and Isabel Harrington, took me in. As a kid, I'd never really gotten to know him before he passed, and it left me with a confusing emptiness, too many unanswered questions, maybe even a lingering bitterness I kept well beneath the surface. But I cherished the musical legacy that was my inheritance, the opportunity to sit at a piano with the band swinging behind me, watching people out on the dance floor having a great time. I lived for that, now more than ever.

"I guess it's that time, isn't it?" Gloria Velez stood beside me in the aisle, dress bag slung over her shoulder, nearly a foot shorter than me at five-three. She was a real knockout—dark-eyed, shapely, sultry-voiced—but Gloria was also a fine vocalist who could bring down the house with a great ballad or torch song.

I applied a smile like a Band-Aid. "Just another city. Just another gig."

"Sure," she said, glancing at me sideways. "Now maybe you'd like to sell me the Golden Gate Bridge."

AT baggage claim, we collected our luggage, which included trombone, trumpet, and saxophone cases, one or two of which probably had a little marijuana tucked away in the lining.

We were met out front by Charlene Mitford Hogan Statz, a pal of my mother's who'd become a dear friend to me in the years since Mom's death—the same friend who'd introduced me to Diana. Charlene's hubby, Reinhold Statz, owned the legendary Fairmont Hotel, where we'd be playing that night. But he was out of the country on business, so Charlene had brought along Joe DiMaggio, a buddy of Dad's back when Joe was playing with the Yankees, on his way to the Hall of Fame. Joe was dressed impeccably in suit and tie, as low-key and courtly as always. I hadn't seen him since Diana's funeral; I'd missed the service for Marilyn Monroe the previous year, unable to face Joe's grief while my own still felt so fresh.

He stuck out his big hand, smiling a little, his eyes surprisingly soft and shy for one of the most celebrated athletes in American history.

"Hello, Phil. Welcome back to The City." He glanced at the musicians. "Hello, fellas." Then at Gloria Velez, with the slightest bow. "And, you, young lady."

They knew each other—through Marilyn—and Joe offered Gloria a brief embrace that she awkwardly accepted. Marilyn's death, coming so soon after Diana's, had linked the three of us in mourning, and our meeting now felt tinged with sadness. But Charlene Statz was having none of that. She flicked her Benson & Hedges to the curb and embraced me with both arms, squeezing me like a tube of toothpaste while welcoming me with her hospitable Texas drawl.

"It's about time you returned to pay your respects to this great city!"

Charlene was a fifty-something platinum blond, tall and voluptuous, with curling lashes over bright green eyes and more energy than a bottle of seltzer. She'd been a Texas beauty queen—Miss Watermelon, out of Austin— before marrying well and engineering a remarkable self-transformation into one of San Francisco's foremost civic leaders and philanthropists. She'd survived her first two older husbands—a banker and a senator, respectively—and by marrying her current spouse, a man she adored and treated like a king, she had made the luxurious Fairmont her queenly domain, along with much of San Francisco itself.

She stood back, looking me up and down, taking in my lanky frame, my still collegiate-looking face. She glanced approvingly at the tweedy Brooks Brothers jacket, less appreciatively at the chinos that needed pressing and the rubber-soled sneakers with laces that needed washing. I'd started wearing my hair on the shaggy side, and Charlene reached up to brush a few loose strands off my forehead.

"You could use a haircut, honey, but you're still the sexiest goddamned bandleader since your old man—even if you do get your looks from your mother."

WE rode back to the hotel in a vintage trolley car, one of numerous vehicles that made up Charlene's sizable collection of motorized toys.

Joe stayed in the back with the band, signing autographs. Charlene and I sat up front while the old trolley lumbered north with the Sunday afternoon traffic. All around us were gas-guzzlers as wide and long as small boats, with gleaming grillwork and ascending tail fins, competing for freeway space with tiny Volkswagen bugs and gleaming Airstream trailers. The San Francisco skyline gradually loomed, dominated on the northeast side by the blocky skyscrapers of the financial district and, just beyond, chimney-like Coit Tower rising from Telegraph Hill. It was a bright, clear day, brilliant blue sky and scudding white clouds, with a lively breeze coming off the bay—the kind of San Francisco day that could turn dark and chill in an instant, its weather as deceptive and unpredictable as life.

"Looks like the same old town," I said, "the same old Frisco."

Charlene patted my knee. "Try not to call it Frisco, sweetie. Frisco's a little town in Texas. You're in The City now."

AS we entered its metropolitan heart, I recognized neighborhoods that had been favorites of Diana's, and memories tumbled over me in a bittersweet blur: a park here, a shop there, a little bookstore where she'd bought me a W. H. Auden collection I carried with me now. A quiet restaurant where we'd often returned to the same window table to watch the light change outside or the fog roll in. On a side street, a theater with a fading marquee where we'd seen our first Bergman film.

Charlene held my hand but left me to my silence and solitude. We rolled through the Civic Center and past City Hall, where Joe had married Marilyn in 1954. I spotted the cable car turntable at Powell and Market, where Diana and I had hopped aboard for our first ride together, climbing an unbelievably steep hill, holding each other tight while I wondered how the hell the brakes worked on an eight-ton machine essentially unchanged since 1873. Diana had laughed at me, in the best way; as elegant and sophisticated as she'd been, she could let her hair down when she was with me, unafraid to be herself, the way it is between two people who've found the real thing.

The trolley made a turn, and we were passing through the seedy Tenderloin and bustling Union Square. The magnificent spires of Grace Cathedral rose into view, more than twenty stories high, along with the rooftops of exclusive Nob Hill, where the calamitous fire following the earthquake of 1906 had destroyed the great mansions, and the city's finest hotels had risen from their ashes. As we climbed toward 1 Nob Hill and the lavish Mark Hopkins, the sight of it gave me a jolt. It was in the hotel's rooftop bar, Top of the Mark, that I'd proposed to Diana. Bobby Short had been playing that night, and as I popped the question, he'd broken into "Come Rain or Come Shine" right on cue. He'd performed it slow and bluesy, causing Diana to cry while she laughed and looked into my eyes and nodded yes. Then Bobby had segued into "Blue Moon," the Rodgers and Hart tune that had sputtered to life in a couple of Hollywood films before Hart had reworked the lyrics and turned it into a huge commercial hit. *Blue Moon, you saw me standing alone/ without a dream in my heart,/without a song of my own. . . .* As Bobby sang and Diana wept, I'd slipped the ring on her finger, knowing I was the luckiest man in the world.

"How you doing, kid?"

It was Charlene Mitford Hogan Statz, bringing me back to a pleasant autumn afternoon in 1963.

"Not bad, all things considered." I winked, trying to blink away the past. "Thanks for asking."

WE pulled up under the burgundy awning at the main entrance of the Fairmont, which faced a quiet section of Mason Street. Except for its new twenty-four-story tower, the stately Renaissance Revival structure was unchanged from my last visit, rising like a great palazzo to encompass nearly 600 rooms and suites and occupy an entire city block.

The doorman approached, a young Irish fellow in a long

black coat with gold piping, and uniformed bellhops scurried out with their carts to handle our bags.

"Mrs. Statz," the doorman said, tipping his cap and bowing slightly.

Charlene knew most of the staff by name and introduced us in her charming drawl. But I barely heard what she was saying. My head was light, my senses numb, overwhelmed from processing too many memories too fast. As I stepped down, the solid feel of the pavement almost startled me.

It was no dream, this return to San Francisco. I was back for real, come what may, in search of something I couldn't name. I felt Charlene slip her arm through mine, and Joe lay a hand on my shoulder, never more grateful for their company.

Chapter 3

"I'VE PUT YOU in the Tudor Suite on the fourth floor," Charlene said. "Stocked the bar with Dewars and the fridge with lots of those chopped vegetables you like to munch on."

"No Nero Wolfe, in case I feel sleepless?"

"I'll have a few sent up from my personal library." She raised a finger playfully. "First editions, mint condition, so treat them nicely."

We stepped with Joe DiMaggio through sliding glass doors into the Fairmont's opulent lobby, where a pianist in a tux nested among potted palms, tinkling a pleasant rendition of "It Had to Be You."

"The views are better from the upper floors, where we've got the band," Charlene said. "But the lower rooms are more comfortable and have more charm."

"Sounds fine." I watched the musicians troop across the big lobby to check in at the front desk, wishing I were with them on my way to a nap. But Charlene was suddenly in a chatty and expansive mood. She paused at the edge of the central sitting area, where smartly dressed guests lounged on sofas and chairs of red velvet while waiters served them drinks from trays.

"We're thinking of doing a major restoration," Charlene said, raising her eyes twenty-two feet to the ornate, gilt-coffered ceiling. "We'd keep all the gold leaf, of course, but we'd lose the dark backgrounds, returning to the original creamy whites and buttery yellows." She leaned close, as if confiding. "The architects have made some wonderful discoveries. Two domes in the Laurel Court hidden by ceilings, and some beautiful alabaster and mosaic floors beneath this old carpet."

I glanced down at the thick carpet—a deep red floral pattern against black—that ran up stairways and along corridors, through the Laurel Court and into the Venetian Room. Throughout the lobby, Corinthian columns of Marezzo marble soared and crystal chandeliers sparkled. The effect was bold and sumptuous—one of the most impressive hotel lobbies in the country.

"But I'm not so sure," Charlene added quickly. Her clear green eyes came keenly around to mine. "You start tearing things apart, digging around, who knows what problems you might run into?"

If any hotel deserved restoring, I thought, it would be the historic Fairmont. Designed by the famous architect Stanford White, the monumental structure had been erected on land once owned by James "Bonanza Jim" Fair, a Comstock silver king. But before the Fairmont could welcome its first visitor, flames had engulfed and nearly destroyed it, along with much of the city, following the catastrophic earthquake of 1906. Architect Julia Morgan had overseen the Fairmont's resurrection a year later, when it opened among the fire-ravaged mansions of Charles Crocker, Leland Stanford, Mark Hopkins, and Collis P. Huntington. These were Nob Hill's "Big Four"—the unscrupulous robber barons who'd joined to engineer one of the shrewdest business deals in U.S. history, financing the railroad that would eventually become the Central Pacific. In the process, they'd come to control California politics, monopolize transportation, and crush anyone or anything that got in their way. Their vision and greed had transformed San Francisco from a sleepy coastal port into a booming trade and banking center, a bustling metropolis ruled by the city's wealthy elite.

Now, Nob Hill's most prominent hotels—the Fairmont, the Huntington, the Stanford Court, and the Mark Hopkins—stood as timeless symbols of luxury and tradition. The Fairmont, of course, was the grande dame, the residence of choice for visiting heads of state and royalty, including John and Jacqueline Kennedy. Yet for all their stature, the four great hotels also stood as a reminder of the two industries—mining and transportation—that had irreparably corrupted and polluted the region. My godfather, Barclay Harrington, the former governor of New York and now a U.S. diplomat, once told me that behind every great city lies a history of graft and injustice, threading itself inevitably through the decades to become intertwined with the present. Most people, he said, prefer to ignore the shame of the past, unwilling to disturb their comfort and their conscience. Yet I could sense that dark history now, just below my feet and that luxurious carpet Charlene was thinking of lifting.

"Valentino!" She called out across the big lobby, waving to a slender gentleman in a waiter's uniform who was emerging from the Laurel Court stairway that led to the downstairs restaurants. As she beckoned, he moved nimbly in our direction, seeming almost to waltz as he weaved through the staff and guests. Moments later, I found myself facing a sleekly handsome man with an olive complexion and slicked hair going gray on the sides. Charlene offered her hand, which he kissed while bowing slightly, before turning to Joe.

"Mr. DiMaggio," the waiter said grandly, "always an honor to see you, sir."

Charlene introduced him to me as Valentino del Conte, and suggested I ask for him whenever I took my breakfast or lunch in the Squire Room downstairs.

"There's not a better waiter in San Francisco," she said. "He turns every meal into a fine-tuned performance. Don't you, Val?"

Del Conte bowed more formally, spreading wide his hands. "For you, Mrs. Statz, I'd recite Shakespeare if it pleased you."

Charlene wagged her finger at him. "But I couldn't get you for our table tonight, could I?" She turned to me, winking. "Valentino only works days. His evenings are mysteriously taken. Aren't they, Mr. del Conte?"

"One has to have a private life, Mrs. Statz." His dark eyes were lively, his manner unabashedly effete. "Even a tired old waiter like me."

"Tired, my ass," Charlene said, and they both laughed.

"And if it's gossip you're after, Valentino knows this town better than anyone except Herb Caen."

The waiter winked slyly. "You might say I cover the waterfront." Then he bid us adieu and sashayed away, as slim and graceful as a debutante.

"Interesting fellow," Joe said, sounding utterly bewildered.

"He's a dear," Charlene said, "even if I can't convince him to work the dinner shift."

I suddenly felt exhausted and wanted very badly to be upstairs, introducing myself to my new bed. I thanked Joe for the kind welcome and told him we had to get together for dinner, preferably where the tortellini was top notch. He suggested Ernie's and I said fine, even though Ernie's was expensive—close to ten bucks for a three-course dinner with a good bottle of Chianti—and I knew I'd be picking up the tab, as one always did with Joe. He may have been the greatest baseball player of his era, but when his $100,000 salary set a new record for athletes in 1950, it hardly put him in a league with kings.

I gave Charlene a kiss and we agreed to meet later for a drink, to go over the program for the dinner dance that night. She suggested La Ronde, the Fairmont's rotating cocktail lounge, and I told her the merry-go-round would do just fine.

BY the time I checked in, most of the band was upstairs, no doubt kicking off its collective shoes. Following routine, two of the guys were going out for vodka, tomato juice, and the fixings for Bloody Marys, while the others warmed up a pack of cards. They invited me up, but I begged off.

A small stack of messages was waiting for me, from my friends back in New York and a few more down in Hollywood, as well as a telegram from France, where my godparents, the Harringtons, were on a diplomatic mission for the State Department. They'd been hush-hush about the trip, but I suspected it had something to do with this unpleasant Vietnam business, which seemed to be getting more complicated. I tucked all the messages in a coat pocket and turned toward the elevators, which were manned by sleepy-eyed old men in uniforms.

Upstairs, on the fourth floor, I followed a Negro bellhop who pushed a cart with my bags down a wide, carpeted hallway as quiet as a funeral parlor. He stopped at the hotel's northeast corner, inside a small foyer where a door was marked 490, Tudor Suite. As he turned the key, I heard a voice behind me, husky but female and familiar.

"Philip."

It was Gloria Velez, my vocalist, her face clouded by something indecipherable. She told me she was going out for cigarettes and wondered if I needed anything. I asked her to pick me up a tube of Ipana; she said she would.

Then she stepped closer, lowering her voice and speaking with an odd intensity. "Something good's going to come out of this trip, Philip. I'm certain of it. Something Diana would want."

Back in New York, Gloria had been one of Diana's closest friends, almost like a sister though sharply different, as dark and fired by passion as Diana was blonde and elegantly cool. Diana's death must have been a terrible blow for Gloria, although I was so distraught at the time, I'd barely paid attention.

She touched my face and kissed me on the cheek, which

she'd never done before. I realized then that this trip must
have been nearly as important for her as it was for me.

She turned without another word and disappeared
quickly down the hallway.

I tipped the bellhop three bucks as he left, then made a quick
survey of my suite: in the central room, sofas arranged cozily
around a coffee table and facing a fireplace, with a well-
stocked wet bar along the back wall; in the bedroom, ample
closet space and a king-sized bed, long enough to accommodate my six-two frame; a tiled bathroom gleaming with
new plumbing, which suggested quiet pipes in the morning.
The complimentary rooms were one of the best perks when
we played a class joint like the Fairmont, which was strictly
five-star and didn't come cheap: singles were running eighteen to twenty-five bucks a night, with doubles starting at
twenty-three dollars.

Good booze was another perk, at least in the bandleader's
suite. I poured a short Dewars over ice and carried it to the
window, which I unlatched and opened. I sipped the Scotch
for a minute or two, listening to the sounds of the city—
the clanging bell on a cable car climbing nearby California
Street, the doorman out front blowing his whistle for a taxi,
a siren somewhere over the hill, from the direction of Chinatown and North Beach. I ticked off in my head what I
needed to do before taking the stage that night: make sure
the Steinway had been properly tuned, check the sound system and lights, shower and shave, slip into the tux, make
certain all the band members were reasonably sober. Somewhere in there, after meeting with Charlene, I had to put
together a vague outline of the show—how many sets we'd

play, what tunes, along with a few special numbers I wanted Gloria to sing, favorites of some of the people who'd be there.

I was about to turn back into the room for a nap when a taxi caught my attention as it pulled to the curb across Mason Street. The driver hopped out and opened the rear door facing the hotel.

That's when I saw Diana.

At least that was my first, startling impression. From my fourth floor window, the passenger stepping out bore such a striking resemblance to my late wife they might have been twins. She was dressed in an evening gown of shimmering blue satin with a matching stole, white gloves buttoned to the elbow, and silvery pearls at her throat. Like Diana, she was on the tall side for a woman, with shapely, tapered legs, a narrow waist, somewhat wide shoulders, and breasts that appeared to fill her gown fully and firmly. But it was her striking Nordic face and blonde looks that I found so disconcertingly familiar: the high cheekbones, the delicate, up-turned nose, the perfectly pointed chin, softly dimpled. The platinum hair was cut full and flowing, swept dramatically to the side, in the old Jean Harlow style. Exactly the way Diana had often worn hers, in defiance of the carefully coifed look of the fifties and early sixties.

As the young woman strode across Mason on high, narrow heels, she even moved like Diana: brisk but graceful steps, strong and confident, with her handbag clutched securely under her left arm. Exactly the way Diana had always carried hers.

I very nearly called out to her, using Diana's name. Then she was under the hotel awning, out of my view.

*   *   *

I'M not sure how long I stood there, staring down at nothing. When I finally looked up and across the street, the ice in my glass had turned to water and the taxi was gone.

I remained there several minutes more, gazing at the empty curb, wondering if I'd really seen anything at all.

Chapter 4

AT 8 P.M., in the Fairmont's Gold Room, I sat at a polished black Steinway, my fingers poised above the keys.

As usual, the piano was set in the center of the lowest riser on the stage, putting me closest to the audience, with the orchestra behind me. To avoid blinding glare, the band played under subdued lighting, with a broad spotlight on me, the lighting designed to create an island, separating us visually from the rest of the room. My tenor saxophonist raised his instrument, I nodded the downbeat, and the ten-piece orchestra broke into "Make Someone Happy," the infectious number by Styne, Comden, and Green that we'd opened with for the past couple of years.

Within seconds, most of the guests had abandoned their tables, along with their bubbling champagne flutes; the open floor in front of the bandstand was quickly crowded with dancing couples dressed in their fashionable and formal best. With the band swinging behind me, I'd all but forgotten the woman in the blue satin gown I'd earlier seen step from a taxi. I was in my element now, grinning like a kid at Christmas—lost in the music, the energy, the motion, transported by the great feeling of abandon and freedom that always comes when the band is tight and the tempo just right.

I almost never look at the keys when I play, and that night was no exception; my eyes were on the audience and the ballroom, which was magnificent. The rectangular Gold Room was the most precious of the Fairmont's twenty event spaces: Beaux Arts in style, hinting of Versailles, its ivory walls and ceiling set off by an excess of gold leaf and brocade. The carpeting was gold, along with the plush, upholstered chairs; so were the trim and sashes on the curtains draped at the tall, arched windows along the south side. The long room featured more than a dozen hanging chandeliers and as many faux candelabra festooning the walls; these were now dimmed, yet their muted light—reflected in a series of recessed mirrors—gave the Gold Room an added sense of dimension and grandeur. Each round table, seating ten, was set with the hotel's finest linen, crystal, and gold plate, with a lavish floral arrangement of yellow and white roses at the center. Even the champagne was a bubbly gold—Roederer Crystal—and that night it was flowing freely. The affair was to benefit the Catholic Youth League, a favorite of Charlene's that provided funds for some of the city's poorest kids. Most of the city's socially elite were set to attend, at a hefty hundred bucks a pop, while Charlene and her husband donated the room and the alcohol and covered the fee for the orchestra. There was a local saying that nothing ever got done in San Francisco because everybody was too busy attending fund-raisers, and maybe that was true. If it was, they sure knew how to do it in style.

We followed our opener with a couple of up-tempo Cole Porter tunes—"Anything Goes," "I Get a Kick Out of You"—before Gloria Velez stepped out front to sing "Stormy Weather" and give the dancers a breather. From the orchestra's position at the back of the house, nearest the service kitchen, I spotted Charlene sitting at a table midway, where she could keep an eye on all the tables around her. She was wearing a black satin gown by Patou, with a ruffle extending around the neckline and down the front, her hair done up and fastened with a diamond tiara given to her by a heartsick oil sheik decades ago. Joe DiMaggio was with her, looking less comfortable in his well-tailored tux. They were chatting with the famous *Chronicle* columnist, Herb Caen, a good pal of Charlene's (whom he always called Tex, with great affection). Herb had come with a shapely model just back from Hollywood, where she'd landed a small part in the latest Rock Hudson-Doris Day movie. After a while, Charlene got up to work the room, which was filling with familiar faces: Cary Grant, Kim Novak, Carol Channing; the film director Alfred Hitchcock, who'd shot parts of *Vertigo* in the Fairmont a few years earlier, with Kim as one of his stars; Willie Mays, the Giants' great center fielder; Melvin Belli, San Francisco's famously flamboyant attorney; George Christopher, the city's grinning, gap-toothed mayor. Too many others to keep track of—famous, wealthy, powerful, or simply beautiful—as Charlene greeted new arrivals and the band played on.

Then—as we picked up the pace again with the two-beat tempo of "Just One of Those Things"—my eyes were drawn

to the main doors at the front of the house. It was the woman
in the blue satin dress, sauntering in with her chin held
high, slightly remote, as if getting her bearings, just the
kind of entrance Diana would have made. I fixed my eyes
on her, faltering with the beat, feeling as if all the oxygen
were being sucked from my body. She was on the arm of a
handsome older man—tall, trim, white-haired, dapper in a
striped gray dinner jacket with a showy white carnation. I
vaguely remembered him from dates we'd played previously
in The City; I recalled that he especially liked to fox-trot,
and was quite good at it. Despite his grand smile, there was
an unmistakable air of arrogance about him, as if everyone
in the Gold Room were a subject in his kingdom, at least a
notch or two beneath him. But it was the woman—looking
and behaving too much like Diana for it to be accidental—
to whom I quickly returned my attention.

From the corner of my eye, I saw that Charlene had taken
notice of the new arrivals. She followed my gaze to the
woman in blue, then glanced back in my direction, looking
concerned. I performed dazedly through several swing standards—"One o'Clock Jump," "Tuxedo Junction," "In the
Mood"—then signaled the orchestra to take a break. It was
then I realized that several members of the band also had
their eyes aimed at the Diana look-alike; one or two had
even turned to me in confusion. Gloria Velez, in particular,
seemed stunned and troubled by the presence of someone
who looked so uncannily like her late best friend. I told them
tersely to be back in twenty minutes, then busied myself
putting the next set together while I tried to make some
sense of what was happening.

Most of the dancers drifted back to their appetizers and
bubbly. A few dropped scribbled song requests into the Bac-

carat bowl on my piano, which was quickly filling up. Several others approached to introduce themselves, ask for autographs, or reminisce about my father. I must have seemed badly distracted, even rude; all I could think about was the woman in blue. I watched the white-haired gentleman escort her to a table near the front, not more than thirty feet away. He greeted the mayor and his wife as if they were old friends, along with several other couples who had money and power stamped all over them. The woman on his arm was introduced around, smiling stiffly each time she stretched out a long white glove to shake another hand.

Charlene hurried across the empty dance floor in my direction, looking uncharacteristically uneasy.

"Who is she?" I demanded.

"Let's get you a stiff drink, Philip. I could use one myself."

She took my arm, but I didn't budge. "Not until you tell me what's going on."

Together, we turned our eyes back to the group where all the handshaking was taking place. The tall, white-haired man was volubly holding court, clearly enjoying the attention.

"Terrence Hamilton Collier III," Charlene said. "Great-grandson of the famous real estate tycoon."

"Collier Avenue?"

She nodded, then informed me that the older Collier had made his fortune in real estate during the gold rush of the late 1840s, when the city's population had grown fiftyfold during a three-year stretch. "You know the saying, Philip—gold created San Francisco. Which tells you something about the lingering wealth and clout of his principal heir."

I took a deep breath. "And the woman?"

"Lenore Ashley, a local poet."

"Is that a profession?"

"I don't know much more about her. I understand she was an actress with the American Conservatory Theater, but I believe she's given it up."

"The resemblance to Diana is remarkable," I said dryly.

Charlene smiled with effort. "It *is* quite a coincidence, isn't it?"

Waiters passed through one of the two swinging doors behind us, stage right, coming from the service kitchen with heavy gold tureens of lobster bisque; the menu that night was French, prepared and donated by Fleur de Lys, thanks to some charitable arm-twisting by Charlene. She stopped a passing waiter, straightened his collar, then sent him on his way again.

Her eyes found me sheepishly. "Terrence Collier knows about Diana, about her resemblance to Lenore Ashley. He was aware that you'd be performing tonight, how upsetting it would be for you."

"How did he come to know that?"

"Because I told him, dammit." Charlene seized my arm sympathetically. "I'm so sorry, Philip. I begged him to come with someone else, or show up alone. You have to believe me."

"Of course I believe you." I offered a weak smile. "That doesn't make it any easier." I studied Lenore Ashley's flawless profile. "It's like seeing Diana all over again."

Charlene's eyes flashed in the direction of Terrence Hamilton Collier III. She stamped one foot angrily, drawing the attention of a passing waiter.

"I could kill Terrence Collier," she said, spitting the words.

"Let's go get that drink," I said.

*   *   *

TOWARD the end of the break, the members of the band drifted back to their positions. Rosamund Kelly, the matronly president of the Catholic Youth League, was on stage with the microphone, attending to business. She was a large, auburn-haired, well-powdered woman in a décolleté lavender gown that looked like a museum piece, amply covering her broad shoulders and bosom and every inch of ankle. As she spoke, her face reddened, the color seeping down into her extra chin and fleshy throat, just above a sizable jeweled brooch that looked heavy enough to serve as a paperweight.

As I took my seat at the piano, Mrs. Kelly was thanking Charlene and several others for helping make the evening such a success. Her final act was to formally introduce the Philip Damon Orchestra, calling us "America's premiere dance band" and mentioning the three-week engagement we'd be playing at the Venetian Room, starting Wednesday night. I took a small bow to the applause while waiters moved among the tables, removing the remnants of the appetizers and soup before delivering the *salade de saison*.

As the band resumed playing, we changed to a tempo more suited to dining and conversation, running through several easygoing instrumentals. Next, Gloria took her turn with a couple of ballads—"Embraceable You," "The Man I Love"—then slipped out for a smoke, which she generally did as often as the playlist allowed. Now and then, between announcements and speeches, couples would get up to slow-dance. All the while, I tried to keep my eyes off Lenore Ashley, which became more and more difficult as the evening wore on.

I was itching to get back to some swing music, to shake the place up. Finally, the *suprême de volaille* and the *grenadin de veau grand dufour* had been served and eaten and the plates cleared away, and waiters were trouping out with *tartlette bonne-femme* for dessert. As the coffee was being poured, along with snifters of Remy Martin, Gloria took the stage again, singing "I Can't Escape from You," in her husky contralto.

As she neared the song's end, I reached for the crystal bowl on the piano and began sorting through a couple of dozen requests. As always, "As Time Goes By" was the big favorite, but it was slow and sentimental, and I wanted to kick things into a higher gear. Someone had asked for "Rock Around the Clock," possibly as a joke, since I never played such nonsense. Then I found exactly the right number: "Just in Time," another tune from Styne, Comden, and Green that's great for dancing because the tempo sets up just right. The request was written in a delicate, feminine hand on a folded slip of pale pink notepaper. Instinctively, I raised it to my nose, and found it heavily scented—dabbed with one of those popular sweet perfumes like White Shoulders or Shalimar that was potent enough to make a strong man queasy.

I hollered the tune to the band and went into a simple four-bar intro on the piano. By the time we'd played the third bar, at least a hundred couples were on their feet, threading their way through the tables in our direction. From his place near the front, Terrence Hamilton Collier III led Lenore Ashley by her gloved hand, maneuvering her until they were dead center on the dance floor. He launched into a lively fox-trot, agile and adept, with moves that would have had Arthur Murray clucking with admiration. Lenore Ashley, who couldn't have been more than thirty, was less comfortable with a dance far more popular in her parents' era than in her own. But she was graceful and game, and soon began moving in time to the music, following Collier's commanding lead. He kept them right at center stage, more animated than any other couple on the floor, clearing space around them until he'd made himself the star attraction.

The place was jumping now. Charlene was spinning with Herb Caen, a big fan of Benny Goodman and the Dorsey brothers who cut quite a figure on the dance floor himself. Willie Mays was stepping out on the arm of a gorgeous black woman in a vivid green gown that looked like Dior. Kim Novak got the rotund Hitchcock to his feet, despite his protestations. Cary Grant was fox-trotting cautiously with red-faced Rosamund Kelly, making her the envy of every woman in the room and probably a few of the men. The mayor was dancing with his wife, who was sneaking a glance at the tall and debonair Grant, while the mayor had his eyes on Kim.

Then, just as my drummer launched into a wild eight-bar break, the Gold Room went dark.

AS one might expect, a chorus of gasps and exclamations followed the unexpected blackout. I stopped playing, and the other musicians followed my lead. Murmurs and nervous laughter punctuated the stillness.

Then I heard one of the doors to the service kitchen swing open, followed by quickening footsteps—high heels, by the sound of them—and the rustle of an evening gown as someone moved across the dance floor. Here and there, cigarette lighters flickered on ineffectually. I glanced at my Bulova, which glowed in the dark: 10:32 P.M. I stood, finding the microphone.

"No need to panic," I announced. "Everyone please sit tight, until they get the lights back on. If you're so inclined, now's the time to steal a kiss."

A ripple of laughter followed, and a few more lighters sparked, casting the room in jumpy light that further confused things. I heard someone whisper sharply, like the hiss of a snake, and sensed a flurry of motion fifteen or twenty feet from the stage. After that came a loud groan, then a flurry of footsteps as someone made a hasty exit through the doors stage left. Just as the doors closed, a bone-chilling scream cut through the darkness from the direction of the dance floor.

Fifteen or twenty seconds later, the electricity came back on—the crystal chandeliers overhead, the faux candelabras along the walls. The Gold Room was faintly aglow as before, but this time the party wasn't so pretty.

The screaming woman was Lenore Ashley. She stood with a gloved hand to her gaping mouth, her eyes wide in shock. Terrence Hamilton Collier III lay sprawled at her feet, his jacket lapels spread, an ice pick thrust deep into his chest. A red stain on his pleated white dress shirt appeared to be coagulating, rather than spreading, which meant that his heart had stopped pumping blood.

The sight set off a wave of hysteria and stunned exclamations. Cary Grant stepped over to Miss Ashley, wrapping a comforting arm around her. Mayor Christopher knelt to check Collier's neck for a pulse, and Rosamund Kelly and Melvin Belli stooped expectantly beside him. The mayor glanced up and solemnly shook his head, eliciting more gasps and cries and several outbursts of tears. Then the shock set in more deeply and a hush fell over the room.

Not surprisingly, it was Charlene who broke the silence.

"My God," she muttered, staring down at the body. "We haven't even gotten to the raffle!"

Chapter 5

HERB CAEN RAN for the nearest pay phone to alert the *Chronicle*'s news desk, while the mayor called the San Francisco Police Department.

Charlene, it turned out, had been the one who'd brought the lights back on, flipping the switches in a fuse box between the Gold Room and the service kitchen, which someone had tampered with. She asked me to stand watch over the body of Terrence Hamilton Collier III, then dashed off to warn hotel security that a murderer might be loose in the house, and possibly still inside the Gold Room itself. She'd also had the presence of mind to order every door to the room closed and guarded, announcing from the stage that both guests and staff would have to remain inside until the police arrived.

To everyone's surprise, that took less than a minute. Even

before a siren could be heard, an inspector was kneeling over Collier's body, providing yet another shock for the city's assembled elite: He was a Negro.

"Inspector Hercules Platt," he announced matter-of-factly, lifting a flap of his jacket to display, on his belt, a gold badge in the shape of a seven-pointed star. "I'll be handling the investigation."

He rose stiffly to his feet, wincing as if his back was tight, and asked that we clear away from the body and return to our seats. Almost no one budged.

"No offense, officer," said Rosamund Kelly with a pat smile. "But I'm afraid we'll need a real detective, as soon as possible."

Hercules Platt was a solidly built man of medium height, pushing fifty, with weary brown eyes in a dark face that was heavily lined but otherwise gave away little. A neatly trimmed mustache adorned his upper lip beneath a broad, blunt nose. His suit and tie were inexpensive but clean and well pressed; his hat, speckled with old rain spots. Under his jacket, in a belt holster, he carried what looked like a snub-nosed .38, with a belt clip filled with extra rounds.

Without removing the hat, he touched the front brim. "No offense, ma'am, but here in San Francisco, an inspector *is* a detective."

"Oh, I see." Mrs. Kelly put a gloved hand to the big brooch at her throat, looking flummoxed. "I wasn't aware we had any Negro detectives."

"Just one," Hercules Platt said, his voice as neutral and unreadable as his face. Before she could say another word, he turned toward George Christopher and said evenly, "Mr. Mayor, it seems we have a homicide on our hands."

"Not just any homicide, Inspector."

"No," Platt said. "I suppose the name Collier makes it special."

"You recognized him, then?"

"I make a point of knowing who the important people are, Your Honor."

Platt's eyes shifted alertly, and he seemed to prick up his ears. A moment later, we heard what he'd heard first: the distant wail of a police siren.

Platt turned his attention back to the mayor. "Why don't you tell me what happened?"

"A district captain should be here shortly, Inspector."

"I'd appreciate any information you might offer." Platt spoke precisely, as if each word had a crucial function. "Even the slightest delay could prove helpful to the person who committed this crime. I know that none of us wants that on our conscience."

George Christopher pulled himself up, squaring his big shoulders, speaking crisply. "The lights went out a few minutes ago, about half past ten. We heard some commotion, then a heart-rending scream. When the lights came back up, Collier was dead. Miss Ashley was standing over him. That's really as much as I know."

Charlene came back into the room as Platt glanced over the crowd, asking for Miss Ashley. She stepped forward and identified herself. Platt removed his hat, revealing a healthy crop of black hair, straightened but still wavy, neatly trimmed and heavily pomaded.

"You knew the victim, Miss Ashley?"

"Mr. Collier and I came together." She spoke haltingly, looking pale and stricken. "We were dancing when—when the lights went out."

"What, exactly, did you see?"

The room became absolutely still, as if the crowd was holding its collective breath.

"When the lights first went out, Mr. Collier and I separated. He may have been searching his pockets for a lighter." Lenore Ashley looked down a moment, then up again, her eyes troubled. "A woman came toward us, very suddenly. I didn't see her clearly. Dark hair, I think. I'm sorry—everything happened so fast."

"I understand," Platt said. "Take your time."

"She was in a gown, though I can't be sure what color or style. From the sound of her footsteps, she must have been wearing heels. As she came at us, she turned toward Mr. Collier and raised her hand. I saw a sharp object."

"Which hand, Miss Ashley?"

"I believe it was her right hand. It's difficult to remember all these details."

"Gloves?"

"I think so, but I'm not sure."

"Please, Miss Ashley, continue."

"I saw her bring her hand down, toward Mr. Collier's upper body. He let out a groan, staggered a moment, then slumped to the floor. She slipped away, into the darkness. Off that way." Lenore Ashley pointed toward the door to the right of the stage—stage left from the position of the orchestra. "With so little light, it was almost like glimpsing a shadow." She began to tremble visibly. "Then—then I realized Mr. Collier wasn't moving. I looked closer, and I saw that he'd been stabbed."

"And at that point you screamed?"

Lenore Ashley nodded, then glanced toward Collier's body. His white hair remained unmussed, his big carnation intact, his eyes and mouth open. She put her hands to her face and her shoulders began to shake; we heard the sound of weeping.

"Miss Ashley, if I asked you to look at the women in this room, do you think you'd be able to tell me if any of them might be the person who stabbed Mr. Collier?"

Without removing her hands, she shook her head forcefully. "I wasn't able to see that clearly. It was all so confusing. I'm sorry." Her weeping grew louder, until she was convulsed with sobs. Instinctively, I stepped over and put an arm around her.

Platt said, "That's enough for now, Miss Ashley. We'll talk about this another time, when you're feeling up to it."

Lenore Ashley hardly glanced up, and I'm not sure she even knew that I was the one offering comfort. It was strange, holding her like that—almost like touching Diana again. There was a perverse thrill about it that both excited and shamed me; it left me feeling unsettled and weak. I caught the scent she was wearing—Chanel No. 5, the cologne Diana had been so fond of. It was all too much for me, too crazy, too improbable. I glanced to Joe DiMaggio for help; he nodded understandingly, stepped over, led Lenore Ashley away to sit at a nearby table with some society women, who immediately attended to her like a flock of mother birds.

MORE sirens were wailing now, blending into a chorus that quickly closed in on the hotel. The mayor glanced at the heavy Rolex on his hairy wrist, then at Hercules Platt.

"You got here damned quickly, Inspector. Unless I'm

mistaken, patrol gets the first call, then alerts the district captain if a homicide crew is needed."

"I was out front," Platt said, "dropping someone off."

The mayor raised his eyebrows. "You're friends with someone staying at the Fairmont?"

"My sister works the graveyard shift," Platt said. "House-keeping."

"Ah, that would explain it, then."

"The doorman grabbed me, said there'd been some trouble in the Gold Room. So I came straightaway."

Charlene stepped forward. "Regina Platt?"

"That's correct." Platt's voice registered surprise. "You know her?"

"Of course. Regina's been with us for years."

"Seventeen years, next month," Platt said. "You'd be Mrs. Statz. I've seen your picture in the society pages."

"My husband's away on business, which means I'm in charge. If you need anything—anything at all—I'm at your disposal." She leaned toward him, touching his cuff conspiratorially. "I should add, Inspector, that I'm something of a mystery buff. You might find me useful."

"Really."

"Oh, yes," Charlene said. "Miss Marple, Ellery Queen, Inspector Maigret, Lew Archer—I read them all. Although it would be nice if someone would write a hard-boiled female private eye. You know, a woman detective with balls." She shrugged hopefully. "Maybe someday."

"I believe there is something you can do, Mrs. Statz, since you're in charge."

"To help with the investigation?" Charlene sounded almost giddy. "Anything, Inspector."

"You might want to order more coffee brought in, because we're all going to be here for a while."

Chapter 6

ONE BY ONE, the sirens grew louder, then stopped. Moments later, muffled footsteps on thick carpeting could be heard from the Gold Room's reception area just off the Fairmont's main lobby. Moments after that, Inspector Hercules Platt was huddled near the double doors, dispensing assignments to patrolmen. Several of the uniformed officers rushed back out, presumably to search or secure the hotel. Three others entered the Gold Room to guard the various doors, while two stayed at the main entrance.

Platt returned to the dance floor, where most of us remained standing around its perimeter, in violation of his order to take our seats. Out on the floor, the corpse of Terrence Hamilton Collier III lay in stiffening repose, the color drained from his face. Rosamund Kelly suggested that

Platt cover the body, but he told her the coroner would first have to make his examination, a response that caused her neck and face to flush. Platt again instructed us to be seated until we could be questioned briefly by a uniformed officer when more arrived. When that caused a good deal of grumbling but little movement, he raised a finger that he pointed generally at the crowd.

"Anyone who attempts to leave this room before being excused," he said, "will automatically be considered a suspect."

"This is outrageous!" Rosamund Kelly stepped forward, red-faced, huffing her sizable chest.

"No, ma'am," Platt said, "this is police procedure."

"Surely you don't think someone in this room is responsible for this terrible crime?"

"I have no idea who's responsible." Platt offered the thinnest smile. "But I certainly intend to find out."

"Just so long as you keep in mind the good reputations of the people here." The crimson deepened in Mrs. Kelly's jowls. "Not to mention the reputation of the Catholic Youth League, which happens to be a favorite charity of the Archbishop."

"I'm sure that anything involving the Archbishop is quite above reproach," Platt said.

Mrs. Kelly raised her two chins, peering at him down the bridge of her nose. "I imagine *you're* a Baptist."

"Rosamund," Charlene said, taking Mrs. Kelly's elbow and turning her away, "why don't you have a seat and let the inspector do his work?"

She ordered more coffee from the kitchen, and most of the guests dispersed to their tables. A dozen uniformed policemen moved systematically among them, asking questions and jotting notes. The chief coroner arrived at eleven sharp, accompanied by a police photographer, and began a careful inspection of the body while the other fellow shot pictures. A few of us remained standing in an awkward cluster near the stage. Hercules Platt glanced our way, then turned to Charlene.

"By your estimate, Mrs. Statz, how many people in this room knew the victim personally?"

"Goodness," Charlene said, "I can't imagine anyone here who *didn't* know Terrence Collier."

"I didn't," I said.

Platt glanced over. "And who are you?"

"Philip Damon—the piano player."

Platt nodded toward the stage. "Then go sit at the piano."

I didn't like his dismissive tone, not a bit. But Charlene shrugged and raised her eyebrows. So I stepped back to the stage, where most of the band members sat on stools, smoking or fingering their instruments uneasily. That's when I realized Gloria Velez was not among them. I slid onto the piano bench and cocked an ear toward the continuing conversation.

"I knew the victim," a woman said, approaching Platt. She had a whiskey voice, on the haughty side. "I daresay I knew Terrence Hamilton Collier better than anyone in the known world."

Platt regarded her keenly. "How's that, ma'am?"

"We were married for thirty years, before the bastard dumped me."

She was a pint-sized woman in her sixties, trim and busty, dressed in a camellia pink evening gown and enough gold around her neck and wrists to fill a Tiffany window display. She was smoking a slender French cigarette through a long holder that matched her other gold accessories. Platt asked her name.

"Vivian Collier," she said, as if she might be royalty. "And I have no intention of remaining in this room one second longer. I've had enough coffee to wake the dead, if you'll pardon the expression. What I need, and intend to get my hands on, is an alcoholic beverage in the range of eighty proof."

"I'd also like to go, if it's all the same." A smiling young man—tall, tan, blond, square-jawed—stepped to Vivian Collier's side. "I'm Vivian's escort. Biff Elkins."

Elkins had the bland good looks of a Troy Donahue and the same sense of weightlessness, though his broad shoulders and tapered torso suggested more physical strength. He extended a well-manicured hand that Platt ignored.

"Escort," Platt said.

"Friends," Elkins said amiably, blinking his pretty blue eyes.

"You're both staying," Platt said, "along with everyone else."

"I don't think you understand." Vivian Collier's voice sharpened. "We have a party to go to, up in Pacific Heights. You do know Pacific Heights, Inspector?"

"We're expected," Elkins added, more diplomatically. He smiled genially, showing perfect teeth. "If we hurry, we can still make it."

"There's been a murder here," Platt said. "In case you hadn't noticed."

Vivian Collier pursed her lips smugly. "It's not as if we're common criminals and you don't know where to find us."

The patience was evaporating from Hercules Platt like steam. "Take a seat," he said, an edge creeping into his voice.

"Unless you'd prefer spending the night in jail."

Biff Elkins laughed good-naturedly. "I'm much too good-looking to go to jail, Inspector."

"He's bluffing." Vivian Collier turned on her heel, grabbing her purse from a nearby table.

"Try me," Hercules Platt said, his voice as hard as steel.

She pulled up, tension tightening her neck and shoulders, before she faced him in cold silence. Elkins placed a hand on her back; his touch seemed to have a calming effect, though her hazel eyes remained ablaze with indignation. Platt asked them if they'd both been in the room when the lights went out.

"Dancing," Vivian Collier said, tossing it at him like a crumb to a beggar. "Like my ex-husband, I favor a fox-trot."

"The orchestra had just launched into 'Just in Time,'" Biff Elkins put in. "If you're going to do the fox-trot, you can't ask for a better number. Do you fox-trot, Inspector?"

"If you don't mind," Platt said, "I'll ask the questions."

"Sorry," Elkins said, showing his fine teeth again.

"My former husband responded to that song like one of Pavlov's dogs." Vivian Collier glanced toward the body of her ex-husband. "The moment it began to play, he was up on his feet as if he was Fred Astaire. Of course, Terrence always had to be right in the middle of the floor, where everyone could see him."

"Who else would have known this, Mrs. Collier?"

"That Terrence loved the fox-trot?"

"And that song in particular."

Vivian Collier shrugged casually. "Most of the people in this room, I suppose. He was a regular at these functions. At one time, he and I did the fox-trot all over town, all the best clubs. As I recall, the last time we danced together was here at the Fairmont, in the Venetian Room." She shook her head, clucking. "The last great supper club in the city. What a shame. The world's going to hell in a handbasket, if you ask me."

"When would that have been, Mrs. Collier?"

"Four or five years ago, not long before Terrence and I began living apart. Same orchestra, in fact. Terrence always said that Mr. Damon played 'Just in Time' like nobody else."

"So you and Mr. Damon are acquainted?"

"No, but I wouldn't mind." Vivian Collier eyed me from a distance. "Such a strapping, handsome young man." Her eyes returned to Platt. "I met his father once, you know. Back in the thirties, when I was young and beautiful."

"I take it you didn't actually see the murder committed, Mrs. Collier."

"Unfortunately, I missed it."

"Anything else you can tell me that you think I should know?"

"Only that whoever killed Terrence should be given some kind of civic proclamation." She glanced toward the mayor. "George, would that be possible? I'd be happy to finance it."

"Have a seat," Platt said. "An officer will get some personal information from you. It won't be long. You, too, Elkins."

Vivian Collier stood her ground a moment, surveying Platt's off-the-rack suit, his dark face. "This isn't your world, sir. I'd suggest you learn some manners."

Platt held her gaze, but a vein in his neck pumped noticeably. She turned away as if in triumph, Biff Elkins following like a well-built pull-toy. Platt's chest filled as he took a slow, deep breath before facing his next guest.

*   *   *

"JAMES Brannigan," the man said in a rumbling, anxious voice. "People call me Big Jimmy."

He was a hefty, ruddy-faced man with thinning red hair who looked more like he belonged down on the piers unloading cargo than here with the cream of San Francisco's social crop. His hands were big and rough, his neck needed trimming, his tuxedo was a bit rumpled. Of all the people in the room, I thought—even Joe DiMaggio—this Brannigan fellow looked the least at ease.

"Not everybody calls me Big Jimmy," he went on. "Just people who know me pretty good."

"Would that include the deceased, Mr. Brannigan?"

Brannigan nodded earnestly. "Terry and I go back to college—Stanford. I played football, Terry chased girls. We been business partners since we graduated, over forty years." Brannigan gaped at the draped body, gnawing at a corner of his lower lip, while beads of perspiration formed on his furrowed brow. "Jesus, I can't believe he's dead. Not like this. This is awful."

"What business would that be, Mr. Brannigan?"

"You know, investments—real estate, venture capital, you name it. We been real lucky through the years, done real good for ourselves." Brannigan glanced around at the luxurious Gold Room, the finely dressed dinner guests. "Most of these people know me. You can ask just about any of 'em. I do a lot of philanthropy."

"Where, exactly, were you when the crime occurred?"

"Me? Where was I?"

"Yes, Mr. Brannigan. Where were you precisely, relative to the victim?"

"Out of the room, taking a whiz."

"Using the rest room," Platt translated.

"I don't know why they call it that. It's not like you go there to rest, is it?" Brannigan laughed until he realized Platt wasn't even smiling. "Anyway, I finished my business, but when I come back, the room was dark, pitch black. There was a bunch of screaming, and the lights came back on. Then I seen Terry there, on the floor."

"But you didn't actually witness the murder?"

"Me? Like I said, I was in the head. You can ask the attendant. I tipped him two bits. All he done was hand me a towel. Two bits, he oughta remember that."

"We will ask him, Mr. Brannigan. Why don't you take a seat for now? We'll be talking to you in a little while."

"Yeah, sure, whatever you wanna know. Just ask me anything you want, I got nothing to hide."

"No one's suggesting you have anything to hide, Mr. Brannigan."

"Listen," Brannigan said, "would it be OK if I left for just a minute to call home? Gwendolyn worries if I don't get in at a decent hour."

Platt glanced in the direction of Brannigan's gold wedding band. "Gwendolyn would be your wife?"

"Housekeeper." Brannigan stared at his shoes, chewing harder on the corner of his lip. "My wife's not well. She's being cared for."

Platt's voice softened. "Have a seat, Mr. Brannigan. We'll get to you shortly, so you can make your call."

There was a sudden pounding on a door at the back of the hotel. Platt nodded to an officer, who opened it. Herb Caen stuck his head inside. Platt motioned him in, displaying his badge.

"I'm one of the guests," Herb explained. "Ducked out for a moment after all the commotion."

"You're a columnist for the *Chron,*" Platt said wearily, "known as Mr. San Francisco and famous for gleaning colorful tidbits about city life."

"Caen and able," Herb said brightly.

"Where were you when the lights went out, Mr. Caen?"

"Out on the dance floor, trying to keep up with Mrs. Statz."

Platt glanced at Charlene.

"It's the truth, Inspector. Herb and I were dancing."

"Take a seat with the others," Platt told him, "and keep your notebook closed."

"Do I have time to grab a vodka rocks from the bar?"

Platt shot him a look. Herb shrugged and shuffled away to sit with his date, the Hitchcocks, and Kim Novak.

Platt swiveled to face Charlene. "I'll need a floor plan of the hotel. And we'll want to question every employee who had access to this room tonight. In fact, a complete list of names would help, with personal information, including Social Security numbers."

He studied the wood handle of the ice pick protruding from Collier's chest, then smiled grimly. "At least we don't have to search for a murder weapon, do we?"

CHARLENE left to get a copy of the Fairmont's floor plan and to put Platt's other requests into motion. When she returned, he was standing with his district captain a few feet from the stage, where I continued to perch on my piano bench, waiting to be interviewed. The captain was a few years older than Platt, taller, and white.

"I was the first inspector on the scene," Platt said. "First inspector on the scene gets the case. That's the way it's always worked."

"This is an unusual situation, Platt." The captain smiled benignly. "I'm sure you understand."

"I'm not sure I do," Platt said evenly. "Why don't you spell it out for me?"

The captain reddened and his nostrils flared, showing twin nests of white hair. "You're new at this, Inspector, barely a year up from patrol. I'll be taking this one."

"I was unofficially assisting on murder cases years before I got my promotion, Captain. I've taken every class in homicide investigation that's worth taking. When my chance came, I was as ready as any man in the department."

"All very commendable, Platt, but—"

"I'll make you a deal, Captain. I'll handle the investigation—the way it should be—and you can get your picture taken with the Mayor and the Chief at the press conferences."

"Now listen here, Platt—"

Charlene stepped closer, introducing herself to the captain, allowing her gloved hand to linger in his big paw.

"I believe we met last year," she said, "at the twenty-fifth birthday party for the Golden Gate Bridge." She reminded him that she'd organized the spectacular event, which had been attended by nearly a million people, including just about every cop on the payroll. "A woman doesn't forget such a handsome man in uniform, Captain."

The longer her hand remained in his, the more solicitous and flustered he became. She complimented him on the department's quick response and the efficient manner with which Inspector Platt had taken charge. Then she excused herself to Platt and took the captain aside, speaking with him privately in hushed tones. When she returned a minute later, the captain went in another direction.

"Always a problem," she said to Platt, "getting the brass out of your hair. Anyway, I don't think he'll be interfering with us again."

"Us?" Platt said.

Just then, James Brannigan approached, looking more burly and ill at ease than ever. He'd unfastened his tie and collar, showing more of his thick neck, which was chafed and red.

"Yes, Mr. Brannigan?"

"I don't know if it means nothing or not, but—"

"Please," Platt said, "anything might help."

"Just that I seen this woman when I was about to come back in. You know, coming back from relieving myself."

"A woman who'd been here in the room earlier?"

"Yeah, here in the room. Before all the trouble started. I seen her out in the hallway. She looked all tensed up, like she was agitated about something."

"Would you recognize her if you saw her again?"

"Sure. I even know who she is."

"By all means, Mr. Brannigan, tell us."

"She's that good-looking broad with the band," James Brannigan said. "You know, the singer."

Chapter 7

"I TOLD YOU," Gloria Velez said. "I stepped out for a cigarette."

It was well past midnight. Hercules Platt had found Gloria having a drink with Charlene, Herb Caen, and me in the Tonga Room downstairs, where we'd taken refuge after finally being released from the Gold Room. We'd chosen the Tonga over the hotel's other lounges, figuring our conversation there would be more private—camouflaged by the flowing waterfall in the lagoon behind the bar and the canned sound of wind, rain, and thunder coming from the recorded storm in the background. Across the room, beyond the frigate's bow where the Polynesian band had performed earlier, Vivian Collier and Biff Elkins were ensconced under a thatched roof, getting loaded on Mai Tais. All that was missing was Dorothy Lamour in a sarong.

Uniformed cops were everywhere, for general security inside the Fairmont and to keep out the reporters, who'd massed out front on Mason Street but made occasional forays into the hotel, looking for someone to interview. While tossing down his first vodka rocks, Herb had gleaned more details from Charlene and made another call to the city desk of the *Chronicle*, which would surely scoop its rival, the *Examiner*, in Monday's competing morning and afternoon editions. Herb had even rewritten his column over the phone, leading with *Bloodred at the Fairmont, and I'm not talking about all that plush carpeting and upholstery. Whatta night!*

Hercules Platt stood over our table, a pen poised above his open notebook, while he put his questions to Gloria Velez. His cheap suit was beginning to lose its crease, and dark stubble was cropping up along his chin and jawbone; if there was one aspect of him that remained intact, it was his carefully groomed hair, still glistening with pomade. He'd been off-duty when he'd dropped his sister at the hotel that night, and I had a feeling he wouldn't be getting much sleep for a while. Several other inspectors had shown up to assist in the investigation, all of them Caucasian, none of them seeming to be his partner, and most looking plainly unhappy that Platt was in charge.

"Where, exactly, did you take your smoking break, Miss Velez?"

"In that little lobby off the back of the house, between the Gold Room and the Venetian Room. At one point, I wandered over by the elevators to the tower."

"For what purpose? To ride up to the penthouse, take in the view?"

"Just meandering, that's all."

"I see—then you were restless. Upset about something?"

Platt's voice sounded nonchalant, almost naïve.

Gloria hesitated. "Not particularly." She glanced briefly in my direction; I picked up my Scotch, sipped at it, kept my eyes on the table.

"Roughly how long were you away from the Gold Room?"

"Long enough to smoke a king-size Chesterfield."

"Do the math for me, Miss Velez, if you don't mind."

"Five or six minutes I guess. Give or take half a minute." Her lips curled unpleasantly. "Close enough, Inspector?"

"Where did you stub your cigarette?"

"Where did I—?"

"We'd like to look for a king-size Chesterfield butt with your shade of lipstick on the filter."

"Chesterfields aren't filtered, Inspector."

Platt smiled briefly. "Just testing, Miss Velez."

"I believe I stubbed it in an ash container near the cloak room. You might check there."

"We will. And when you'd disposed of your cigarette, Miss Velez, then what?"

"I tried to get back into the Gold Room. A house dick outside the door stopped me. He told me there'd been trouble and that no one was allowed in except those who were inside when the lights went out. Until then, I hadn't been aware there was a problem."

"Did you speak to anyone while you were gone from the room?"

"I don't think so, no."

"Did anyone see you?"

"There were lots of guests coming and going, along with waiters and bellhops. Someone might remember seeing me. It was quite busy."

"Shelley Berman's appearing at the Venetian Room," Charlene said. "He always packs the house. And we had banquets in both the Crystal Room and the Fountain Room on the same floor. It was a zoo back there. The kitchens get a little crazy."

"So if someone wanted to slip in and out of the Gold Room in the rush of activity, they might do it without anyone taking notice?"

"If they knew their way around," Charlene said. "Which includes most of our registered guests and probably many of those attending the dinner dance."

"And exiting the hotel unseen—not a problem?"

"Possible," Charlene said, "if they didn't attract undue attention. The hotel has a number of exits and entrances. People come and go quite freely."

"Very insightful, Mrs. Statz. Thank you."

"You know," Charlene went on, before Platt could turn away, "I was recently reading a new Margaret Millar. She's married to Kenneth Millar, who writes as Ross MacDonald, though I've always suspected she helps him with his manuscripts. It happens with male authors far more often than you might think. Anyway, in the book, there was a woman suspect who made her escape from the crime scene by—"

"Thank you, Mrs. Statz," Platt said more firmly, turning back to Gloria. "Would it be fair to say that you know your way around this hotel, Miss Velez?"

"I've played the Fairmont a few times with the band. We all know our way around."

"And you have no way of corroborating your exact whereabouts at the time Mr. Collier was murdered?"

I looked up from my drink, feeling the alcohol, starting

to bristle. "That describes most of us, Platt. The room was pitch black, remember?"

"When I want to hear from you, Damon, I'll let you know."

I offered him a tiny salute. "Yes, sir!"

"Miss Velez?"

"I suppose not." Gloria's dark eyes were cool, dispassionate; not her usual look.

"Did you know Mr. Collier?"

"I'd never met him."

"But you'd seen him before?"

"Once or twice."

"When was that?"

An Oriental hostess in a red and gold cheongsam approached to check on our drinks. Platt waved her brusquely away, keeping his eyes on Gloria.

"When, Miss Velez?"

"A few years ago, on a couple of the dates we played here in town."

"You remember him, after all this time?"

"He's a striking man, outgoing, hard to miss. He liked to dance."

"The fox-trot?"

"That seemed to be the one he enjoyed the most."

"Did you notice anything different about him tonight? Anything I should know about?"

Again, the hesitation, the shifting eyes. "Not that I recall."

Platt was silent a moment, letting her squirm. Then he said, "You're staying here at the hotel?"

She nodded. "We start a three-week stand at the Venetian Room Wednesday night."

"Good, because we'll need to talk again." Platt straightened up, wincing with the effort, and closed his notebook. "You, too, Damon. We still have a few things to discuss— starting with whatever you can tell me about the late Mr. Collier."

"I told you before, Platt, I didn't know the man."

"But you didn't tell me you'd seen him on previous occasions, did you, dancing to your music?"

"You didn't ask me that, did you?"

"What else haven't you told me that I might have forgotten to ask about?"

"Why don't we discuss it tomorrow, Platt? You look beat."

"And you look a little drunk."

I raised my glass. "Care to join us? Charlene's buying."

"Thanks, but I'm on the wagon. Six years sober."

"No wonder you're so ornery."

"If your plans change, Damon, be sure to call me."

"I have no intention of leaving Frisco, Inspector." I drained my glass. "I love Baghdad by the Bay." I winked at Herb, who'd coined the term.

Platt distributed his business cards all around, picked up his hat, put it on, turned his back to us, and was gone.

"Phil," Herb said plaintively. "Please don't call it Frisco."

AFTER Gloria excused herself, the three of us pulled our chairs and our heads closer.

"He's very thorough, this Inspector Platt," Charlene said. "That was obvious when I took him on a tour of the first floor. Doesn't say much, doesn't smile much. But I get the impression he doesn't miss much, either."

"I don't like the guy," I said.

"He's a cop," Herb said. "Not Bert Parks."

"I think it's terrible that Terrence Collier met such a violent end," Charlene went on. "And I hate that it happened here, of all places. But, still, it's so exciting, don't you think?"

I swirled what little Scotch remained in my glass. "I think it's a dreadful nuisance, especially with Platt grilling Gloria the way he did. I wanted to haul off and pop him."

"Now that would make a nice item." Herb sat up, grinning under his twinkling eyes and sharp beak, reciting on the spot: *Nob foolishness! Philip Damon, pianist extraordinaire, suffered a nasty bout of machismo last night. Due to a sore hand from hitting one of San Francisco's finest, Damon's sold-out engagement at the Venetian Room has been postponed indefinitely. Half the women in town are said to be contemplating a leap from the Golden Gate.*

"Very funny." I slumped back in my chair, sulking. "I still don't like him."

AT Charlene's urging, we went over what the three of us had learned, separately or together, about the night's mysterious events. By the time we'd finished another round, Herb had jotted and numbered the most salient points in his reporter's notebook:

1) *Electricity to Gold Room shut off 10:30 P.M.—someone threw switch in fuse box off nearest service kitchen.*

2) *Murder weapon: common ice pick.*

3) *Collier craved attention; habit of doing fox-trot middle of dance floor, everybody watching.*

4) *Favorite tune: "Just in Time."*

5) *Plethora of folks aware of this—Vivian Collier, Biff Elkins, Jimmy Brannigan, Lenore Ashley, most of the band, et al.*

"There's one more thing," Charlene said. "I overheard Platt tell his district captain that the ice pick was lodged deep between Collier's upper ribs, all the way to the hilt."

"My God," Herb said, "do we need to hear this?"

"So what's the point?" I asked.

"No pun contended," Herb added.

"The point," Charlene said, "is that it took a strong person with a forceful hand to drive the weapon so deep. Or else a hand driven by extreme emotion."

"Whoever did it," I ventured, "certainly chose an unusual time and place. That's the part that's got me scratching my head."

"I say good riddance to the two-timing bastard." The diminutive Vivian Collier stood over us, a bit unsteady on her narrow heels. Biff Elkins was at her side, propping her up with a hand around her tiny waist. "Thank goodness I got my full settlement before someone did to the jerk what I should have done a long time ago." She turned to her handsome companion. "Biff, darling, remind me to send my attorney a dozen roses first thing in the morning."

"We should get going," Elkins told her. Then, to us: "I promised I'd take her to Finocchio's for the last show, to cheer her up after missing the party."

"Italian-Swish Colony," Herb said. "Been a while since I dropped in."

"I hear the new outfits are to die for." Vivian put a hand

to her mouth in mock horror. "Oh, dear, did I say that? I hope that won't end up in your column, Herb."

Herb was already writing it down, but paused to raise his glass. "Give my regards to Bawdway, Mrs. C."

We watched them weave out of the Tonga Room arm in arm, headed toward the underground garage, where they could hail a cab on Taylor Street without being besieged by the press out front. Somewhere above us, over the sound system, thunder rumbled, followed by drumming rain.

"Any old port in the storm," Herb said, "for a shipwrecked gigolo like Elkins."

Charlene shrugged. "What's the harm? Biff enjoys rich, older women who keep him in nice clothes. Vivian likes to be seen on the arm of a good-looking young man. Though I hear she throws a fit every time she catches him with a fellow."

"You're kidding." Herb swung his head for a last look at Elkins. "He looks as straight as Coit Tower."

"Switch-hitter," Charlene said. "Regular at the Black Cat, until the owner stopped paying bribes and the cops closed it down."

"Who's your source?" Herb asked, sounding envious.

"Valentino del Conte, my favorite waiter. You want dish, go see Val."

I stood, realizing I'd had one Scotch too many. "Maybe that's what I should do, over breakfast tomorrow. I have a few questions that need answering."

Charlene glanced my way. "Be careful what you wish for, baby." Her green eyes were bright, but I couldn't miss the serious tone of her voice.

"Pleasant dreams, everyone." I shook Herb's hand and

leaned down to peck Charlene on the cheek. "If that's possible after a night like this."

I lost my way in the labyrinth of carpeted corridors connecting the downstairs dining rooms and shops, unable to find the elevator that would take me up to bed.

Finally, I gave up and climbed a familiar curving stairwell to Laurel Court. As I was about to emerge, I caught a glimpse of Lenore Ashley hurrying across the lobby in the direction of the Gold Room. Seeing her in the hotel wasn't such a surprise; Charlene had told me that Terrence Collier kept a room for his paramour, as a convenient trysting place. She was still dressed in her blue satin gown but she'd removed her long gloves, revealing slender, pale arms and delicate hands. I could hear the rustle of the satin as she moved past.

I waited a moment, then stepped from the stairwell and followed, though I'm not sure why. Maybe just to keep her in sight a while longer, to imprint the lovely vision of her in my mind, should I never see her again. Maybe because my heart was still yearning so desperately for my late wife, and Lenore Ashley was surely the closest I'd ever come to getting her back.

Within seconds, she was across the lobby, deserted now except for vigilant cops and private security men. Just past the Grand Staircase, she pulled up in the reception area outside the main entrance to the Gold Room, where a uniformed officer stood guard. She said a few words to him, and he went inside.

Her back was to me as I moved slowly and quietly toward her, pressed close to the wall. A healthy Kentia palm stood between us, and I ducked behind its spreading fronds, feeling a little like Peter Lorre in a second-rate film noir. A moment later, Hercules Platt appeared, removing his hat.

"You needed a word with me, Miss Ashley?"

"I remembered something, after I went upstairs to rest. The woman who stabbed Mr. Collier—"

"Yes?"

"She said something, just before—" Lenore Ashley took a breath, regained her composure. "I was extremely upset earlier. I must have forgotten."

"What was it you heard?"

"Just before she stabbed Mr. Collier, she uttered four words—exactly four."

"That clearly?"

"The orchestra had stopped playing. The room was rather quiet. Even though she whispered, she spoke with such conviction, such—venom."

"What was it you heard, Miss Ashley? This could be very important."

Lenore Ashley hesitated, swallowing dryly before she finally spoke.

"She said, 'This is for Diana.' And then she killed him."

Chapter 8

"I'LL HAVE MY eggs over easy," I said, "a side of bacon—crisp—and two aspirin."

"Had a bit too much to drink last night, did we?" Valentino del Conte poured steaming coffee into my china cup from a sterling silver pot. His movements were studied and precise, every task performed with a flourish.

"I wish I could remember." I glanced at the *Chronicle*'s front-page banner headline: *High Society Murder on Posh Nob Hill.* "Or maybe I'd rather not."

"Have you had a chance to read the entire story, Mr. Damon?" Valentino sounded oddly solicitous. "That is, beyond the front page."

I sipped some coffee, shook my head. "Just seeing the headline is bothersome enough."

"I think they call it the jump." Valentino smiled awkwardly. "The inside page where the story continues." He fussed with the fresh-cut flowers on the table, his hands in perpetual motion. "I had a dear friend once who worked in newspapering. He ran off with his editor to a wonderful life in Rio de Janeiro. I visit them every few years, when I can afford to get away."

I picked the *Chronicle* up from the table. "Should I be looking at the inside pages, Valentino? Is that what you're trying to tell me?"

Valentino's expression turned sensitive, pained. "You may want to prepare yourself, Mr. Damon." He glanced unhappily at the newspaper. "After what you went through last night, you don't deserve this. Shame, shame on those nasty reporters, that's what I say."

"Valentino, what on earth are you talking about?"

He touched my shoulder delicately. "I'll get you that aspirin, Mr. Damon."

I watched him dash off, then opened the *Chronicle* with growing curiosity to the inside page where the article on the Collier murder continued.

There it was hitting me like a fist in the gut: a photograph of Diana. They'd dug up one of our wedding pictures, which had made the local society pages because Diana had grown up in nearby Hillsborough, a wealthy enclave to the south. This time, the photo was set inside the borders of a sidebar article recounting her unsolved murder, emphasizing the fact that we'd met in San Francisco. I skimmed the brief item. The connection to the Collier murder was tenuous, and, of course, I was the link. The headline summed it up: *Murder Makes an Encore in Bandleader's Cursed Life.*

Then came the opening lines:

The murder of Terrence Hamilton Collier III last night on a

*dance floor at the Fairmont Hotel was the second mysterious hom-
icide in two years linked to society bandleader Philip Damon, 32,
whose orchestra was playing when Collier met his violent end.*

*Police in New York are still investigating the unsolved murder
of Damon's wife, Diana, the former Diana Larocque of Hillsborough. Diana Damon was strangled two years ago in the couple's
Manhattan apartment while listening to a recording of "Blue
Moon," reportedly her favorite song. . . .*

I was staring at the photograph of Diana when Valentino
del Conte returned with a tin of aspirin on a small silver
tray. When I looked up, he hovered over me protectively,
tears brimming in his brown eyes.

"I had no idea your wife had been taken from us in this
way," he said. "Not until I saw the paper this morning. I
never knew her, but I'm sure she was a lovely person."

"I appreciate your concern, Valentino."

His glistening eyes suddenly sparked indignantly. "The
article on your wife's death was absolutely unnecessary, Mr.
Damon. As if you haven't had enough of a shock already,
witnessing that horrible murder last night."

"The lights were out, so I didn't exactly witness it. At
least I can be thankful for that." I studied the photo of Diana
again and the headline beneath it. "You're right, though,
Valentino. I could have done without this."

He blinked back his tears, stood up tall, lifted his chin.
"You take those aspirins, Mr. Damon. And we'll have a very
nice breakfast for you in just a minute or two, exactly the
way you like it. Then I want you to get out and stretch your
legs, take some air. There's nothing like a beautiful San
Francisco morning to lift one's spirits."

A few minutes later, he was back with my breakfast and
a pot to warm my coffee. By then, I'd read the entire article

in the *Chron*, as well as Herb Caen's three-dot column deeper inside.

Valentino opened and fluffed a linen napkin, and placed it across my lap. I thanked him with a smile.

"You've worked here for some time, haven't you, Valentino?"

"Nearly two years, Mr. Damon. Previously, I was with several of the other fine hotels in the city. Though I must say, there's none better than the Fairmont."

"You were familiar with Terrence Collier?"

"Oh, yes. Mr. Collier was quite the man about town, a real ladies' man. Especially after his divorce. Before that, he tended to be more discreet."

I sampled the bacon—crisp but not overdone, cooked to perfection.

"Poor Mrs. Collier," Valentino said. "The more the hubby dated other women, the deeper she dived into the bottle. Until finally she'd had enough—took him to divorce court and became a very rich woman. And I say, good for her!"

"I thought he dumped her."

"Oh, she likes to tell it that way—she loves to play the victim. But from what I hear, he tried desperately to maintain the marriage—except keeping his pants zipped, that is. The divorce cost him millions, you know. But money can't erase the bitterness of a jilted wife, can it?"

"And this woman Collier was with last night, Lenore Ashley—"

"The young lady he was dancing with when he was murdered." Valentino rolled his eyes. "Now that's what I call a truly bad date."

"What can you tell me about her?"

"I read a few lines about her in the *Chronicle*, of course."

Valentino glanced cautiously about. "Then there are some things that aren't suitable for the papers—not even our colorful *Chron*."

"Just between us, Valentino."

He leaned closer, lowering his voice. "Mr. Collier kept a regular suite on the third floor, if you know what I mean. She was to have anything she wanted from room service or the hotel shops. Nothing but the best for Miss Ashley."

"He must have been very taken with her."

"Lavished gifts on her," Valentino said. "Jewelry, furs, gowns, absolutely divine ensembles. I'm told that he personally picked out every item she wore, right down to her handbags and shoes. Even the way her hair was styled."

"How do you know all this?"

"The stylist and I frequent the same cocktail lounge down in Polk Gulch. You might say I'm well-connected within a certain social community here in The City." Valentino's eyes took on a wistful gaze. "I must admit, Mr. Collier had exquisite taste. Although I'm not sure Miss Ashley appreciated all those lovely outfits."

"What makes you say that?"

"A woman who loves a well-designed gown, fine fabric, an expert cut, shows it in the way she wears her things, the way she carries herself. She understands that in the right outfit, with the right hair and makeup, she's transformed." Valentino sighed deeply. "You could tell that Miss Ashley was rather blasé about it all. I think she wore all those gorgeous clothes just to please Mr. Collier. If you ask me, it was more a business relationship than a love affair. Though he was clearly smitten, judging by how much trouble he went to have her look a certain way."

"Like my late wife, you mean?"

Valentino cocked his head curiously. "I beg your pardon, Mr. Damon?"

I opened the *Chron* to the photograph of Diana. Del Conte took a closer look, put a slender hand to his cheek, and gasped in surprise.

"Goodness! There is a startling resemblance, isn't there? Oh, my, Mr. Damon, how troubling all this must be." His eyes widened with mortification. "And it's all my fault—I should never have called your attention to it in the first place."

"Not at all, Valentino. You've actually been very helpful."

"You're sure, Mr. Damon?"

"I wanted information, and I got it." I applied a quick smile. "Charlene was right, you're quite the waiter. I'll be sure to ask for you again."

"At your service," Valentino del Conte said, before making a small bow and then his exit.

Chapter 9

ornamental rule

AFTER BREAKFAST, I checked at the front desk to find a couple of dozen messages waiting for me.

Most were from friends in Hollywood or New York, responding to news of the murder in the morning papers or on the airwaves. With all the celebrity names involved, I thought, Hedda Hopper and Louella Parsons were surely having a field day. Jackie was out of the country, touring Morocco with her sister, Princess Lee Radziwill. Truman, however, had heard a radio report on the murder and fired off a telegram, asking me to keep him posted on developments should the crime turn out to be worthy of a fact-based novel, a literary concept with which he'd been toying. "I've already got my title," he messaged. "*In Cold Blood.* Now I just need the right crime."

One communication was local, by phone. It came from

Inspector Hercules Platt, requesting my presence at police headquarters that morning, no later than noon.

AT half past ten I dodged the horde of reporters out front by slipping out a side door that put me on California Street, where I hailed a cab and jumped in just as a pack of photographers came after me in a group sprint.

Minutes later, the cabbie dropped me at 850 Bryant Street, the new site of the Hall of Justice. It was an unimaginative gray block building, seven stories high—in operation for two years, according to a bronze dedication plaque out front. Across the street was a string of auto shops, bail bond joints, and counter-and-stool cafés advertising coffee for twenty cents a cup and fresh pie for four bits a slice. I entered with a stream of men and women of all ages and colors, crossing a gauche lobby of pink marble pillars and green terrazzo floors, wondering why so many people. Then I saw a directory listing what looked like every law enforcement agency in the city—police, courts, district attorneys, public defenders, probation, coroner—with the jail occupying the two top levels.

Homicide was on the fourth floor, next to Robbery. A corridor of pale green walls and darker green linoleum under sickly fluorescent light led me to the outer office. A pleasantly plump, middle-aged white woman behind a reception desk took my name, gave me a second look as if she recognized it, then went through a door behind her and came back with Hercules Platt. He'd shaved and put on a fresh suit and shirt, but the redness in his heavy-lidded eyes told me he hadn't slept, or at least not much or not well. That made two of us.

Platt thanked the woman before turning to me. "I appreciate you coming in, Damon, without making a fuss about it."

He led me into an office roughly the size of my suite at the Fairmont, infused with the musty smell of old paper. Two spartan interrogation rooms that looked straight out of *Dragnet* occupied space to the right. As we passed through the main office, I did a rough count of twenty desks, maybe twice as many file cabinets, and several Underwood typewriters that the twenty desks apparently shared. Dozens of Wanted posters were tacked to the walls, along with calendars going back quite a few years. Caucasian men in drab suits and ties occupied a few of the desks, on the phone or doing paperwork; one or two glanced up as we passed but otherwise seemed uninterested. A few unwashed windows along the far wall looked out on the dreary neighborhoods south of Market Street. Otherwise, the lighting was overhead and fluorescent.

"Coffee?" Platt asked.

I shook my head, and he poured a cup for himself from a pot that looked like it had been on the burner for a few hours. He took it without milk and made a sour face with the first sip.

"That stuff will kill you, Inspector."

"This job'll kill me first."

"Then why do it?"

"Because it pays six hundred bucks a month, which is a whole lot more than I was making when I was wearing a silver star instead of gold."

We reached an isolated corner farthest from the window, where a heavy wooden desk was lodged behind two ugly green file cabinets. On the desk, sitting atop a stack of file folders was a copy of *The Fire Next Time*, by James Baldwin, which was riding the current best-seller lists. Platt indicated a steel folding chair, brushing it clean before I sat, then took a wooden chair on wheels. He sat down gingerly.

"Back bothering you, Inspector?"

"I didn't get you down here to talk about my health, Damon." He sighed, and his voice lost some of its edge. "You're a material witness in a homicide case that's got a rich white man for a victim, national media attention, and the brass already squeezing my testicles. Frankly, I need all the cooperation I can get."

I glanced around. "What about your partner? I thought detectives always worked in pairs. Or is it different here in Frisco?"

"First, we don't call it Frisco. Second, it's Inspectors, not detectives. Third, we work in pairs, except in my case." Platt said it tersely enough to let me know the subject was closed. He put his coffee aside and leaned forward on his elbows. "I've been reading about you, Damon. *Who's Who* at age thirty-two. Not bad."

"My father was a well-known musician," I said. "My mother came from money. They both died when I was young. I was raised by Barclay Harrington when he was governor of New York, and his socialite wife, Isabel. I guess that kind of pedigree gets you into certain directories."

"I saw your father play once."

I cocked my head in surprise. "You heard Dad play?"

"He opened with Nocturne in E Flat. I remember that."

I was smiling now. "His theme song."

"It was back in the early forties, not long before I shipped out in the Army. My sister got me into the hotel where his band was performing." Platt paused briefly, his gaze even.

"I listened from the kitchen, with the rest of the Negroes."

"Just the same, I'm glad you got to hear him play."

"Personally, I lean more toward bebop."

"That's cool."

"Cool. Yes, I imagine you think it's cool." He opened a notebook on his desk. "Tell me about Gloria Velez."

"Divorced, no kids. Puerto Rican, out of New York. Parents are first generation on the mainland. Father's a butcher, mother's a seamstress. They saved their money, put her through the Berklee School of Music. She's quite talented."

"Rather good-looking, too."

"It doesn't hurt."

"How'd she end up in your band?"

"It's kind of a long story."

"Give me the short version."

"About ten years ago, Gloria was a chorus girl in *Gentlemen Prefer Blondes*. She met Marilyn during filming; they hit it off and remained friends."

"That would be Marilyn Monroe."

"I'm sorry, yes, Marilyn Monroe."

"You two were on a first-name basis?"

"We were acquainted."

"Go on," Platt said.

"Later, Marilyn introduced her to Joe DiMaggio. By then, Gloria was a singer, recently divorced, looking for a steady job. Joe pointed her in the direction of my band, where she's been the vocalist ever since."

"You and Mr. DiMaggio are also friends?"

"He and Dad were pals. We've stayed in touch."

"You have a lot of famous friends, don't you?"

"Do you hold that against me, Inspector?"

"Let's talk about what happened last night, in the Gold Room."

"All right."

"As the bandleader, you had the best vantage point from the stage. Something out there in the room must have caught your eye, something unusual."

"Not that comes to mind."

"Just another gig, another paycheck."

"That about sums it up."

"What about up on stage, with the band? Notice anything unusual there?"

"Not really."

"Come on, Damon. Something in that room must have seemed out of sorts."

"I don't know what you're getting at, Inspector."

Platt leaned back in the tilting chair, lacing his fingers behind his head. "I saw how Gloria Velez reacted last night when I asked her the same question. She hesitated, tensed up. Glanced over at you, as if she was looking for help."

"You were grilling her pretty hard."

"You dropped your eyes. Kept them there. I wasn't grilling you."

"You're pretty sharp, aren't you, Inspector?"

"You don't get to be the only Negro inspector in the San Francisco Police Department unless you're twice as smart as the white guy you're up against for the job."

"Maybe your back's sore from carrying that big chip on your shoulder." I stood to go. "I've got better things to do than sit here and listen to this."

"Sit down, Damon. We're not finished."

"I came in voluntarily. Give me a good reason I should stay."

"Maybe I pull in Gloria Velez and put her in one of those two rooms over there, show her what a real interrogation is."

I snorted a laugh. "Meaning what? That you'll rough her up?"

"I don't rough up ladies. But I can detain and question a suspect for a fair length of time. Have her thoroughly searched by a matron. Make life uncomfortable for her."

My throat suddenly felt dry, my stomach noxious. "You consider Gloria a suspect?"

"If not, then damn close."

I sat. "Gloria wouldn't hurt a fly."

"Dark-haired female, wearing a gown and high heels. No alibi for the time of the murder. Evasive during questioning."

"You're depending an awful lot on Lenore Ashley's account, aren't you, Inspector? How about Miss Ashley for a suspect?"

"You know something about Lenore Ashley that I don't?"

"I doubt it, considering how smart you are."

Platt found a key in his pocket, unlocked a desk drawer. He pulled out a small, sealed plastic bag, which he laid on the desk. Inside was the slip of pink notepaper with the request for "Just in Time" written in a graceful hand.

"You recognize that?" Platt asked.

"It was in the bowl on my piano, with quite a few other requests."

"You know who put it there?"

"I'm afraid not."

"Something interesting," Platt said. "We got handwriting samples from everyone who was in that room at the time of the murder—at least everyone we're aware of. Not one of those samples matches the handwriting on this slip of paper. The only sample we failed to get was from your friend, Miss Velez, since she ducked out of the room at some point and managed to avoid us afterward. That is, until I caught up with her in the Tonga Room."

"She told you, she went out for a smoke before the lights went out."

"That's what she tells me, yes. And maybe it's true. And maybe she doused the lights while she was out, then slipped back in with an ice pick in her hand. And then slipped out yet again in the commotion and confusion after ramming the ice pick in Collier's chest."

"Gloria wasn't wearing gloves. Check for prints."

"We did. The handle was clean."

"Then it couldn't have been Gloria."

"She might have slipped gloves on, or used a hanky or a tissue."

I took a closer look at the song request. "That's not Gloria's handwriting, Inspector. I know what her handwriting looks like."

"That's what you say."

"I'm sure if you asked her, she'd provide a sample for you."

"I did ask her. She said she's too upset to come in right now, too troubled to deal with any of this." Platt smiled thinly as I blanched. "You look surprised, Damon."

"That doesn't sound like Gloria. She's a pretty tough cookie."

"Tough enough to drive an ice pick into a man's heart?"

I swallowed hard as the phone rang on Platt's desk. He

took it on his right side, swiveled in his chair, showing me his back. Cradling the phone against his shoulder, he began jotting notes. For something to do, I reached for the James Baldwin book, upsetting the stack of file folders beneath it. As I caught them, the top file opened. It was marked *Collier, Preliminary Photos*. Inside was a set of black-and-white glossies of Terrence Hamilton Collier III, naked on a coroner's table. The first few photos showed the corpse on his back, with a puncture wound and ugly bruise just below the left nipple and dried blood matted in Collier's chest hair. The last few photos had been taken of the body facedown. Across Collier's pale upper back was a series of strange bruises unlike any I'd ever seen. There were five in all, an inch or two apart; each was dark and perfectly round, about two to three inches in diameter, forming a neat arc just below his shoulders.

I heard the phone being replaced in its cradle, but before I could put the file back, Platt snatched it from my hands and tossed it on his desk.

"I guess you finished your phone conversation," I said.

"I guess you have a problem keeping your nose where it belongs."

"You've aroused my curiosity, Inspector, with all your questions—and all your suspicions."

"You're good at this, aren't you, Damon? Maybe because you've faced this kind of questioning before."

He reached among the papers on his desk and produced a copy of that morning's *Chronicle*. It was open to the sidebar article about Diana's murder.

I looked him straight in the eye, my jaw clenched. "Diana's death has nothing to do with this."

"Really? Not even when Mr. Collier, our latest murder victim, was dancing with a woman who happens to be the spitting image of your late wife?"

"That came as a complete surprise to me."

"Then why didn't you mention it, when I asked a minute ago if you saw anything out of the ordinary last night?"

"It's an unsettling coincidence. That's all I can tell you."

"I imagine it's also a coincidence that whoever killed Collier invoked your wife's name just before doing the dirty deed. You know about that, don't you, Damon?"

"You saw me last night, listening in on your conversation with Miss Ashley?"

"You're several inches taller than that potted palm."

"If it's true—yes, that would be another coincidence."

Platt's face, like his voice, was implacable. "I don't believe in coincidence, Mr. Damon."

I was suddenly reeling, at a loss for words. Platt kept hammering at me. "That call I just took was from the New York Police Department. The homicide division is sending a copy of its most recent summary report on your wife's murder."

I became aware of how harshly I was breathing and of the feeling that the room was closing in around me while becoming uncomfortably warm.

"Does that trouble you, Mr. Damon?"

Finally, I spoke. "It's something I'd rather not dredge up." My voice was weak, small.

"No, I imagine not. But I'm afraid that's not possible any longer." Platt swung his chair and pointed to several calendars on the wall dating back to 1957 and filled with notations. "See those calendars, Damon? We use them to remind us that the statute of limitations is running out on certain cases."

He faced me again, his eyes keen.

"But there is no statute of limitations for murder. Murder cases don't conveniently go away."

CHAPTER

Chapter 10

B Y HALF PAST twelve, I was sitting in Trader Vic's with
Charlene and Herb at Herb's favorite corner table in
the Captain's Cabin, which afforded him a fine view of
the room.

"We're not going to talk about murder, motives, or hard-
nosed police inspectors," Charlene said, having heard about
my tough morning at the Hall of Justice. "We're in Vic's
now—a place where only pleasant things should be discussed."

"What we all need is a drink," Herb added. "It's past the
morning hour, and I have yet to sing my first martuni."

Our waiter arrived, and Herb ordered three-olive martinis
all around, mixed to his personal recipe: "Gin to the chin,
vermouth to the tooth." With that accomplished, his eyes
began to take on their usual twinkle, seeking out familiar

faces in the restaurant's recessed lighting. Lunch at Trader Vic's had been Charlene's idea, but Herb had been an easy invitee, since he invariably picked up an item or two at Vic's before returning to the *Chronicle* to polish his column for next day's publication. With its South Seas motif and exotic rum drinks, Trader Vic's had been San Francisco's most famous restaurant for more than two decades, its popularity dating from the 1939 Golden Gate International Exposition. Herb had named some of those potent drinks himself, including Missionary's Downfall and Sufferin' Bastard. He was also responsible for the caption scrawled beneath the two shrunken heads on display in the foyer: *My, that certainly WAS a dry martini!*

"God, I love this city," he said, after his first sip when the cocktails had been delivered. He looked around, then raised his glass to a fine-looking couple, trim and Coppertone tanned, in a distant booth. "Betty and Bud Dean, up from the Big Orange. Met 'em here in '52, on their honeymoon, when I was doing time at the *Examiner.* Cute kids. Told me a story about their Chevy convertible breaking down in Chico. Got a funny item out of it."

"We were talking about Inspector Platt," Charlene said.

"I thought we *weren't* talking about Platt," I said, "or anything else unpleasant."

Charlene patted my hand. "I wouldn't let him get to you. He's just doing his job." She sipped her martini, smacked her lips appreciatively. "On the other hand, I can have him taken off the case—one phone call to the mayor. I saved Platt's behind last night, but if he's going to be mean to you, I won't put up with it." She reached up, pinched my cheek. "Not my little Philly."

Herb leaned forward, lowering his voice. "So what's this

I hear from Tex about bruises on Collier's back?"

"I don't think you should know about that," I said. "I wasn't supposed to see those photographs."

He twisted his lips like a key in a lock. "I promise to sit on it until you tell me I can break it. Or at least until my tush gets sore."

Reluctantly, I described the five dark, circular bruises I'd seen across Collier's upper back, using the rim on my water glass to approximate their circumference.

"Probably some kinky new sexual practice," Herb said. "Definitely sounds like North Beach. Speaking of which, did I tell you about the discount massage parlor where it's strictly self-service?"

"You're way off track," Charlene said. "We should be thinking Chinatown, not North Beach."

"How did your noodle come up with that one?"

"Those bruises sound suspiciously like cupping. It's a Chinese healing technique. My cousin over in Mill Valley swears by it for back pain. She comes in once a month for a treatment in Chinatown."

"Marin County," Herb said, pinpointing Mill Valley, "where the nuts never fall far from the trees."

She showed him her tongue before continuing. "As I was saying, it's called cupping. The practitioner attaches heated suction cups to the flesh, which draw the bad blood and negative energy to the surface, cleansing the system. My cousin swears by it, along with acupuncture."

"This entire discussion," Herb said, "is starting to needle me."

"She tells me cupping can be quite painful." Charlene raised her eyebrows knowingly. "And that it leaves exactly the kind of bruises Philip saw in those morgue photos of Terrence Collier."

"Speaking of Collier," I said, "what more can you two tell me that I didn't read in the *Chron* this morning?"

"No serious enemies or scandals," Herb said, "other than his nasty divorce."

"Every great family has dark secrets," Charlene said. "Look at the Kennedys, for goodness' sake. Papa Joe's no saint." She leaned forward and we did the same, until our heads nearly touched. "I can tell you what *I've* heard about Terrence Collier. Since the divorce, which cost him half his fortune, he's been spending money like a spoiled wife on a shopping spree at Gump's."

"Heir today, gone tomorrow," Herb said.

"The grapevine has it that Big Jimmy Brannigan's been worried that Collier's been raiding their business accounts to pay for all the baubles he's so fond of, while keeping what's left of his personal fortune intact."

"Disgruntled business partner," I said. "Makes a plausible suspect."

"Only he wasn't wearing an evening gown," Herb reminded us, "and he has an alibi for the time of the murder. That puts the kibosh on that one."

"But he could still be in on it," Charlene said, "working with someone who was in the room."

I frowned. "Someone please explain that business partnership. Brannigan and Collier seem like Mutt and Jeff."

"No one's ever quite figured that out," Charlene said. "Brannigan's strictly blue-collar, rough around the edges. Went to Stanford on a football scholarship, got into Collier's exclusive fraternity because he could carry the ball into the end zone."

"Collier's old San Francisco money," Herb added, "strictly upper crust."

Charlene sipped at her martini, then picked up the story. "Collier and Brannigan become best friends—opposites attract, as they say. After college, they go into business together. From what I hear, Brannigan's the real backbone of the company—cautious with investments, Puritan work ethic. And Collier gives Brannigan entry into the upper social circles, which means a great deal to him. To stay on certain invitation lists, Jimmy's written some awfully big checks."

"With Collier dead," I asked, "doesn't Brannigan's social stock go down?"

"Not as much as if Collier were to spend them into bankruptcy. If you have enough money, a little dirt under your nails doesn't mean what it used to."

"Did Collier have heirs?"

Charlene shook her head. "Vivian Collier's as barren as the Gobi Desert, and Terrence refused to adopt. Another strain on their marriage, in addition to his philandering."

"Which means Brannigan may inherit the business outright," I said, "now that his partner's out of the picture."

Charlene clapped her hands. "Excellent, Philip! You know, Perry Mason solved a murder with exactly that motive. *The Case of the Lethal Ledger.*"

"Hardly novel," Herb said. "You two have got poor Brannigan convicted, and you haven't even looked at the best suspects yet."

"Like Vivian Collier," I put in.

"Too obvious," Herb said. "For years, she's been screeching publicly that she wanted the guy in the ground."

I suggested that it might be a clever cover, long in the planning.

"Yes!" Charlene's eyes shone with excitement. "And Biff Elkins must be in on it, providing the alibi. Vivian sneaks out, kills the lights, comes back in, finishes off her ex—and Biff swears they were together on the dance floor the whole time!"

Herb rolled his eyes. "Why don't we call Inspector Platt right now, let him know we've wrapped up the case?"

"Because," I said, "we haven't discussed the one person who was closest to Collier just before he was murdered."

"Let's order," Charlene said, putting her nose into her menu. "I'm dying for some Bongo Bongo soup."

"Lenore Ashley," I said.

"I'd also recommend the oysters Hambourg style." Charlene's eyes were moving faster than a game of dodge ball. "Although the last time we were here, the Indonesian rack of lamb with peanut butter sauce was really very good. How about you, Herb?"

"Butterfly steak, and the artichoke Tahitian."

"Charlene," I said.

"Order plenty, Philip. The portions tend to be small."

I removed the menu from her hands, laid it on the table, turned her chin until our eyes were aligned. "Lenore Ashley was the next item on the menu. Not the Bongo Bongo soup."

"I thought you wanted to avoid unpleasant subjects."

"It's a little late for that, don't you think?"

Charlene's smile became pained. "I'll tell you what. After lunch, you and I will do some snooping in Chinatown. Maybe we'll find the practitioner who treated Terrence Collier recently enough to leave those bruises."

"And we'll talk about Lenore Ashley at an appropriate time?"

"Yes, a more appropriate time." Charlene signaled for our waiter, broadening her smile. "I do so love a good mystery—and they're always so much more fun in San Francisco."

"I'll drink to that," Herb said, and ordered another round.

Chapter 11

◆——◆

ARMED WITH PHOTOS of Terrence Hamilton Collier III clipped from copies of the *Chronicle*, Charlene and I hopped into her new Ferrari GTO and headed for Chinatown.

We made our escape from the Fairmont through the underground garage around back, surprising the print reporters and TV news crews who now had every exit covered. It wasn't just local press any longer—journalists were in from New York and Chicago, and Huntley and Brinkley were planning a live interview with San Francisco Police Chief Thomas Cahill on the evening news. The media horde jumped aside as Charlene beeped her horn and made her tires squeal as we turned onto Taylor Street. Her Ferrari was a bright red hardtop, aerodynamically designed, possibly the only new GTO in the city at the moment. It was hard to miss, and when she saw reporters leaping into their own vehicles to chase after us, she punched the accelerator and left them in her dust.

THE western border of Chinatown lay a couple of steep blocks downhill from the Fairmont, but Charlene took a more circuitous route, entering from the south along Grant Avenue.

"The Chinese believe that south is the direction most favorable for entering a building or a city," she told me. "I always say, when in Chinatown, do as the Chinese do."

"Can't hurt," I said. "We could use a little luck right now."

As we crossed Bush Street from Union Square, we entered a world unto itself. The musky scent of burning incense filled the air, which pulsated with the thump of drums from a group of youngsters practicing a lion dance. The buildings were plain and functional, mostly brick Edwardian built after the great fire of 1906 but heavily decorated now with elaborate Chinese trimmings and pagoda motifs. Along the busy sidewalks of Grant Avenue, green dragons twisted around the tops of lampposts, gripping red lanterns in their fierce jaws. Shops overflowed with wind chimes, ceramic gods, bamboo flutes, painted fans, and jewelry of gold, jade, and amber. Restaurants were everywhere, their pagoda rooftops outlined in neon that by nightfall would set the streets ablaze with color.

"Chinatown," Charlene said, as we rolled slowly up Grant Avenue. "The only part of San Francisco that never seems to change."

She made a turn, then another, and we wound our way through narrower side streets, bustling with neighborhood residents picking through boxes of fruit stacked along the sidewalks. Dried ducks hung in shop windows above open wooden crates of dried mushrooms and fish, chicken feet and bok choy, or jars filled with herbs and teas sold in bulk. We turned a corner and for a moment caught the pleasant factory smell of fortune cookies baking.

"Diana loved this place," I said. "We must have eaten down here dozens of times."

"Diana loved all of San Francisco," Charlene said. "Every neighborhood, every nook and cranny."

"I should never have taken her to New York. If we'd just stayed—"

Charlene shot me a sharp glance. "Philip, *stop.*"

"Still, things would have been so different."

"You don't know that. You'll never know. So let it go."

Charlene found a parking spot on Waverly Place—the Street of Painted Balconies—between Tin How Temple and the Chinese Baptist Church. She must not have known this was Diana's favorite Chinatown street, with its dozens of iron balconies painted red, green, and yellow—red for happiness and vitality, green for longevity, yellow for wealth. Or maybe Charlene did know and had parked here deliberately; perhaps, like Jackie and Truman and the others back home, she was convinced I needed to immerse myself in the memory of Diana so deeply, so acutely, that I'd finally understand she was just that: a memory, someone forever gone. If that was Charlene's intent, Chinatown was ideal, this street especially. Each time we'd come here, Diana had insisted on climbing the three flights of stairs to the temple, where ceremonial lanterns hung from the ceiling, sticks of incense burned, and offerings were made to the deceased while the golden figure of Tin How, the ancient goddess of heaven and sea, looked on from her altar.

Not my kind of thing, really. But had I been on my own today, I believe I would have gone up and made an offering for Diana, if only to chase away the loneliness for a while.

FOR the next three hours, Charlene and I trudged up and down Chinatown's hills and side streets.

Most of our stops were at the shops of pharmacists, who prescribed treatments going back thousands of years, working from wooden drawers filled with roots, flowers, nuts, seeds, and barks. Few spoke English, or admitted to it; those who did, seemed reticent or distrustful. One or two knew of the murder of Terrence Hamilton Collier III from the newspapers or the evening news, although they seemed ignorant of just who he was. From three of the herbalists, we gleaned the addresses of several acupuncturists in Chinatown who also did cupping. Charlene felt we should make a purchase from each of those who helped us, as a sign of respect and gratitude, and we came away with ginseng root to boost our vitality, chrysanthemum leaves to improve our vision, and, for me, dried sea slugs to bolster my virility.

"Not that I have much use for it these days," I said, as we set out with a map of Chinatown to find the acupuncturists on our brief list.

One by one we made our stops. No one among those we spoke with knew or admitted to knowing Collier, or having treated him in the days leading up to his death. Their answers tended to be terse and veiled, their eyes carefully averted, which didn't surprise me. Through Charlene and Diana, I knew something of their history. Chinese immigrants had been brought to the region as cheap labor when it was needed during the late 1800s, then blamed for glutting the job market when the boom went bust. They'd concentrated in Chinatown, making it their refuge from the beatings and lynchings of white mobs. Today, absentee slumlords were the enemy: From street level, Chinatown was exotic and picturesque, but rising behind the decorative façades were thousands of tiny apartments crammed with immigrant families—often three generations—trying to get by on the minimum wage of $1.25 an hour, if they got even that; health conditions were terrible and safety code violations rampant, yet the city tended to keep a blind eye. Expecting the residents of Chinatown to be open and trusting would have been naïve, if not arrogant.

"We're down to a single name," Charlene said, looking at our list.

The name was George Chang. We found his office off a narrow side street and up a flight of creaky wooden stairs. A simple sign beside the door provided English translation beneath the Chinese: *George Chang, Acupuncture, Acupressure, Herbal Medicine.* He was out, so we left a photograph of Collier tucked into the door, with a note asking Chang to call me at the hotel.

"I'm not sure all this effort was worth it," I said, as we trudged back down the stairs. "I doubt we'll be hearing from Mr. Chang."

I hadn't done so much walking since my last fly-fishing excursion in August, and my long legs didn't have much tread left on them. Charlene, who'd worn sensible shoes, was accustomed to walking three miles each day for exercise, and hardly seemed fazed.

"Just one more stop, Philip, to reinvigorate your spirits."

"We've got ginseng for that."

"You'll like this better."

She treated me to an early dinner at Johnny Kan's, and we finished off a fine course of Peking duck sipping Almond Eyes and discussing the growing mess in Vietnam. But as we left Kan's, sated by the good food and alcohol, Southeast Asia seemed a million miles away. The sun was almost gone, and up and down Grant Avenue the neon dragons and pagodas were flickering on, along with the slashing characters of the Chinese alphabet.

In the shadows across the street, I glimpsed a solitary male figure among the neighborhood shopkeepers locking up for the night and the tourists looking for a last-minute bargain or a place to eat. He was well concealed by a dark topcoat and a hat with the brim pulled low, his face further obscured by dark glasses he had no use for at this hour. My first thought was Hercules Platt—the size and general shape were right—but the man's face, what I could see of it, was too pale to be Platt's. The stranger seemed to be watching us, but after a taxi passed slowly in between, he was no longer to be seen, and I forgot about him just as quickly.

CHARLENE and I drove out of Chinatown the way we'd come in, along Grant Avenue pointed south toward Union Square.

"They should have some kind of official entrance here," Charlene said, "something grand and beautifully Chinese, to welcome visitors. I'm going to bring it up with the Chinatown Merchants Association, first thing tomorrow."

Then, almost to herself: "Damn!"

She was peering peevishly into her rearview mirror, so I swung my head around. The news wolves had spotted her red Ferrari and were closing in from behind.

"They'll be all over the hotel," she said. "They've probably found their way inside by now. There will be no peace at the Fairmont for a day or two."

"Wonderful," I said wearily.

"I know what! We'll run up to the redwoods, lay low for the night. You can stay in the guest cottage." She shot through a yellow light, made a turn or two, got us over to Lombard Street. But traffic was thick at rush hour, and the wolves soon picked up the scent.

"I don't know," I said. "Platt told me to call him if I planned to leave town."

"You're not really leaving." Charlene made periodic checks of her rearview mirror as we drew closer to the northbound entrance to the Golden Gate Bridge. "It's just a little side trip. And you certainly didn't plan it, did you?"

"What about the hotel? You've got a murder investigation going on."

"We pay Karen Hori good money to manage the Fairmont, and Maggie Langley's handling the press like a pro. If we go back, we'll just stir things up."

I flashed a grin. "What the hell."

Charlene nudged me with her elbow. "That's the Philip Damon I'm more accustomed to."

We joined the rush of vehicles speeding across the vermilion-colored bridge, which spanned the mile-wide gap known as the Golden Gate that served as the entrance to San Francisco Bay. Directly ahead, the sunset was burnt orange, while the water spread out below us silvery blue. Across the long span, Highway 101 dumped most of the traffic in the woodsy communities of Marin County, then opened up into a stretch known as the Redwood Highway, heading through small towns and vineyards toward the coastal redwoods.

"Have we lost them?"

Charlene glanced again into her rearview mirror. "Honey, if we haven't, we're about to."

She pressed down on the accelerator, shifting with precision through the gearbox. The Ferarri took off like a rocket, quickly hitting a hundred miles per hour with the needle climbing. As the dusk deepened, she flicked on her headlights and the dashboard glowed like the instrument panel of an airplane—six dials, dominated by a big tachometer at the center. We cruised through the darkening green of the vineyards, their endless rows of grapevines so neat and regular and reassuring. Up ahead lay ageless forests, where the tallest trees in the world would hide and shelter us. Very softly, as she had so often when I was growing up, Charlene began singing "God Bless the Child," which had been my mother's favorite song.

The world seemed perfect just then. I leaned back in my deep leather seat, closed my eyes, lulled by the speed and power of the car and Charlene's comforting lullaby, happy to let her take me away, at least for a while.

Away from San Francisco, with its troubling questions, problematic past, and the meddlesome inspector named Hercules Platt.

Chapter 12

CHARLENE WAS UP at sunrise, hiking out for a look at the ocean, but she let me sleep in until after ten. When she finally woke me in the guest cottage, it was with a cup of fresh-brewed coffee and Mel Torme's "Blues in the Night" playing on the hi-fi.

We spent a glorious day tromping among the towering redwoods, fly-fishing along a creek that twisted through a glen not far from the house, and napping in the late afternoon. The cocktail hour found us on the veranda, our feet up on the railing and drinks in hand, as we listened to the peeps and titters of nuthatches and chickadees. The last of the sunlight filtered through the heavy canopy of branches, or found openings here and there to splash along the creek where the ferns stretched to meet the light. At sundown, we strolled through Charlene's favorite stand of mature redwoods, which she called Cathedral Grove. Lady ferns and sword ferns huddled along the trail, and redwood sorrel spread like a vast carpet of leafy green along the forest floor, where ancient redwoods lay uprooted and fallen, like giants sleeping peacefully amid the hushed beauty.

"I envy your life," I told her. "Not the money and the luxury, but the roots you've put down. The sense that you belong somewhere."

"Your time will come, Philip. You'll just have to work at it a bit more than the rest of us."

"You know how much I love New York. But a lonely apartment and life on the road just doesn't cut it."

Charlene slipped an arm around my shoulders. "You're still grieving, Philip, still feeling lost. Diana was your first real family. That makes it more difficult."

"I feel so unattached, like one of these fallen trees." I shrugged, confused. "Maybe I've always felt that way."

Charlene glanced up at the towering trees as we walked. "There's a lesson to be learned from these mighty redwoods. Their roots are shallow, and the trees go down rather easily, if the wind is strong enough. Yet even as they lie on the ground, they can put out new roots that sprout from the burls on their own bark. During the long, arid months of summer, they take their moisture from the coastal fogs that otherwise seem so cold and bleak. That's how these forests survive, how the trees go on." She took my hand, looking at me fondly. "You have the capacity to put down roots and rise again, Philip. Be patient. Trust time."

"Speaking of time," I said, and searched her eyes. She'd known me too long and too well not to understand why.

"Lenore Ashley, the unavoidable subject." As soon as Charlene said it, she found a handy diversion and pointed.

"Look, the old bridge. Still solid after all these years."

We'd reached a roadway near the southern border of the property and faced a venerable wooden bridge that carried the road across a shallow creek bed that was nearly dry in the deep autumn. It was constructed sturdily of redwood long gone gray from the elements. I strayed from Charlene's side to peer underneath, up into the darkness under the eaves and cross beams.

"I wouldn't go too far in," Charlene said.

I stepped in anyway, intrigued by how deep the rafters ran, forming recesses where the elements would never reach. Suddenly, a flurry of wings caused me to leap back. I fell flat on my behind as a swarm of bats fluttered past me and up toward the thickly needled branches of the trees.

"I warned you, kid." Charlene offered me a hand and I pulled myself up, feeling like an idiot. "I watched Diana do the same thing a few years ago," Charlene added. "She'd come up for the weekend while you were away with the band. We were out walking, just about this time. Then she spotted this old bridge and let her curiosity get the best of her."

"Doesn't sound like Diana." I brushed myself off, studying the old bridge again. "She had a strong aversion to creepy places."

"Maybe she learned her lesson here. Those nesting bats gave her quite a scare." Charlene paused, then added carefully: "Some places are better left alone, don't you think?"

"Nice try, Charlene. But I'm not buying the metaphor this time."

"You're certain you want to know about Lenore Ashley?"

"The whole story, beginning to end."

Charlene fixed her eyes on mine, took a deep breath, and

let me have it: "Before Diana met you, Philip, she and Terrence Collier were seriously involved."

WE walked on, while Charlene gave me a minute to absorb
the shock and regain my bearings.

"Collier was infatuated with Diana, totally smitten,"
Charlene said. "But he refused to divorce Vivian, so Diana
finally broke it off. Vivian learned of the affair anyway, and
used it as leverage when she sought a divorce."

"I knew Diana was no virgin when we married. I certainly
wasn't. Each of us had a past, I guess." I felt sick, but pushed
on with the toughest question. "Did she love him?"

"I think Diana loved the *idea* of Terrence Hamilton Collier III. She was fascinated by his wealth, his social standing,
the sense of history that came with his family name. But
did she love the man? Certainly not the way she felt about
you, Philip. After she met you, you became her life."

"But Collier's infatuation continued?"

"He became obsessed. There's a certain type who's utterly
insecure unless he's in control and everyone's aware of it.
That was Terrence Collier. His entire life, he knew nothing
but wealth and power. He was accustomed to getting what
he wanted."

"But he couldn't have Diana."

"She refused to become one of his prized possessions."

"Is it possible he—?" I broke off, unable to say the words.

"He may have wished Diana dead, out of rage or jealousy.
I told the detectives from New York what I knew of his
feelings. But Collier had an alibi, you see. Both Jimmy
Brannigan and his housekeeper vouched for Collier's
whereabouts that weekend."

"And Lenore Ashley?"

"Terrence apparently saw her in a play, at the ACT. About a year ago, quite by chance. Naturally, he was stunned by how much she looked like Diana. He introduced himself, began courting her, and set about perfecting the resemblance, starting with a change in her hair color."

"Turning Lenore Ashley into Diana's clone." I shuddered, thinking about it.

"When I introduced you to Diana back in '58, I saw no reason to bring up her past. I was so sure the two of you were right for each other, so happy for you both. It was her business to tell you, if she felt the need."

"I never suspected, not for a moment."

"Because she loved you, Philip, with every fiber of her body and soul."

"The way I loved her." I dropped my eyes as we walked. "The problem is, I still do. I'm as obsessed with her as Collier was. And now—"

Charlene stopped and faced me squarely. "Leave Lenore Ashley alone, Philip. No good could come of that."

Just then, we heard the cracking of a branch underfoot. We both scanned the deep shade of the forest.

"Probably a mule deer," Charlene said.

"Not unless it's the two-legged kind, wearing a hat."

I pointed toward a dense thicket of wild rhododendron not quite a hundred yards away. A male figure, barely visible in the fading light, crouched among the big plants. Charlene called out, but no answer came.

"I wonder how long we've been watched," I said.

Charlene squinted for a better look. "Or who the hell the intruder is."

"I believe it's a man. Possibly someone I saw on the street yesterday, in Chinatown."

Charlene called out again, warning that this was private property. The figure retreated a few steps, deeper into the leafy shadow. Charlene bent down, reached into one of her riding boots, withdrew the pearl-handled pistol she always carried with her, and fired two warning shots into the air.

The figure turned and fled, crashing through the woods and quickly disappearing, while the bats swarmed above us again, screeching.

"Whoever it was, he's gone," Charlene said.

We watched the bats circle in the dying light, then descend and disappear beneath the old bridge to settle again in its dark and secret recesses.

Chapter 13

LATE WEDNESDAY AFTERNOON, as I checked the sound system in the Venetian Room, Hercules Platt showed up. He didn't look happy.

"I missed you," Platt said, without a trace of humor in his deep voice.

"I wish I could say the same, Inspector."

"Would you like to tell me where you've been the past twenty-four hours?"

"Not particularly."

He mounted the stage as I tested the volume level of the monitors—the speakers that allowed the band members to hear each other as we played. He bent down, pulled the plug. The system went cold.

"Maybe your smart-ass routine plays well with the cocktail set, but I don't appreciate it. I've got a very tricky murder case on my hands, Damon."

I told him I'd made a brief getaway to the redwoods, for some needed peace and quiet.

"Now suppose you tell me about the affair your late wife had with Terrence Collier."

Our eyes locked while I digested his latest discovery. "I wasn't aware of Diana's relationship with Collier until yesterday."

"Why do I have trouble believing that?"

"It's the truth. Charlene told me. Ask her, if you feel so inclined."

"Mrs. Statz?"

"Yes." I turned to the Steinway, pulled out a clean handkerchief, buffed out a smudge on the shiny black surface.

"The same Mrs. Statz," Platt said, "who stamped her foot in the Gold Room and said she wanted to kill Collier, roughly half an hour before his death."

I stopped what I was doing, giving Platt my full my attention.

"One of the waiters overheard her say it," he explained, "as he was passing on his way from the kitchen."

"Figure of speech, Inspector. Nothing more."

"Maybe, maybe not."

"You can't seriously suspect Charlene."

"I look at all reasonable suspects until I rule them out."

"You're way off base, Platt." I turned back to the piano, plunking and testing keys.

"Then let's get back to your late wife's fling with Mr. Collier."

"She broke it off when Collier refused to divorce his wife.

Later, after Diana's death, he attempted to replace her with Lenore Ashley. Or so I've been told."

"Let's try another scenario. You learned of the affair long ago, but kept it to yourself. You were jealous of Collier, wanted to get back at him. You couldn't stand the idea that someone else had slept with your dear, departed wife."

I stopped fingering the keys to form a fist, feeling my jaw clench. "That's enough, Platt."

"When Collier brought Lenore Ashley to the dinner dance, that really set you off. So you hatched a plan to get him out on the dance floor, kill the lights, and put an ice pick in his heart. Or have someone do it for you."

"That ice pick—I guess I carried that conveniently in a pocket of my tux."

"No, you grabbed that down in the kitchen when no one was looking."

I laughed out loud. "Your imagination's working overtime, Inspector."

"Probably. But I can't discount the possibility, either. Because what I have is a very unusual murder and more suspects than the Mission District has murals."

"Maybe you ought to be looking harder at James Brannigan."

"I'm aware of Brannigan's business disagreements with Collier, if that's what you're driving at."

"Congratulations, Platt. You work fast."

"I also know that each man had an insurance policy on the other's life—double indemnity. The problem is, when the lights went out, Mr. Brannigan was in the men's room with his zipper down, like he says. The attendant confirmed it. He remembers Brannigan because he's such a cheap tipper."

"So maybe Brannigan had an accomplice."

"The same can be said for you, Damon. Motive, opportunity, plus you knew the layout of the hotel. Then there's that troubling reference to Diana by the killer just before the murder went down."

From across the room came the voice of Gloria Velez: "You're assuming that Lenore Ashley's telling the truth, which seems like a pretty big assumption."

We glanced toward the service doors to see Gloria standing among the tables, her dark eyes simmering with emotions I couldn't quite read.

"Miss Velez." Platt removed his hat. "Nice to see you again."

"Save it," Gloria said curtly, brushing past him. She stepped up on the stage, plugged the control board back in. Then she picked up the microphone, switched it on, and sang the refrain from "T'ain't Nobody's Business If I Do."

Platt studied her until she set the microphone aside. "As long as I have you both here, perhaps I could ask you a few questions."

I reminded him that we had a show to do in a few hours. "It's opening night. I don't want Gloria tired."

"Protecting her again, Damon?"

"Let him ask his damn questions." Gloria lit a Chesterfield, turned the piano bench to face Platt, sat down, and stared at him like she was looking right through him.

"I received the police report from New York on Diana's murder," Platt said. "After she was strangled, the rooms were thoroughly ransacked, yet nothing was taken. Not even her finest jewelry, or the cash in her purse. Strange, don't you think?"

I sat down next to Gloria. "Make your point, Inspector."

"Both of you were questioned by the police. You shared the same alibi. You were together, working an engagement in Atlantic City. At the time of Diana's murder, the two of you were even in the same room, practicing some new music. At least that's what you told the police." Platt opened his notebook, glanced at one of the pages. "Atlantic City is roughly two hundred miles from Manhattan. Either or both of you could have driven to New York, or taken the train, been welcomed into the apartment by Diana, killed her, and driven back to Atlantic City in time for your next date, without ever being missed. From what I understand, the other band members were off partying at the time. At your urging, Mr. Damon."

"We'd been working hard for a couple of months. We were at the seashore, and had a day off. I thought they should all get out, have a little fun."

"How convenient."

"Screw you and the horse you rode in on," Gloria said.

"You have quite a temper, don't you, Miss Velez?"

"I'm Puerto Rican, what can I say? A regular Latin spitfire, all hot blood and volcanic emotion." She stubbed her cigarette in an ashtray of heavy cut glass.

Platt glanced at the two of us sitting inches apart. "Perhaps you and Mr. Damon have a cozier relationship than just singer and bandleader."

Gloria, eyes blazing, grabbed the ashtray and raised her arm to throw. I seized her wrist and wrested the weapon from her tight grip, which took some effort.

"If nothing else," Platt said, "you seem inordinately strong for your size, Miss Velez."

"I think you've used up your time, Inspector." I picked

up my music folder, began arranging the sequence of tunes for the two sets we'd play that night.

"Your wife was mysteriously murdered, Mr. Damon. Now her former lover dies under equally baffling circumstances." Hercules Platt placed his notebook back in his pocket, preparing to go. "No matter which way I look, I always come back to Diana."

Chapter 14

B Y 9 P.M., the Venetian Room was packed and the band was in a groove, running through favorites by Gershwin, Porter, Kern, Berlin, and Rodgers.

As usual, we'd started out fairly fast to make our presence felt and get people out on the dance floor. In addition to my piano we had three saxophonists—two altos and a tenor— all able to double on clarinet; two trumpets, who could also play flugelhorn; and one man each on trombone and drums. As a precaution after the murder, hotel security had searched the instrument cases, with one house dick commenting wryly that the bass case was big enough to conceal a body. That did nothing to ease our nerves; everyone was keenly aware that a killer was on the loose, with easy access to the hotel. Two of the musicians claimed they were so shaken by the whole thing they wanted out, although it may have just been a ploy for more money. At any rate, I convinced them to stay by raising everyone's weekly salary from $350 to $500 through the three-week engagement. I was pulling down eight grand a week myself, so peeling off a little more dough for the band seemed the least I could do.

Still, we'd all taken the bandstand that night with a bad case of the jitters. The brass section—which we called the "Smirnoffs," for obvious reasons—had fortified itself extra heavily with vodka. My nervous drummer had smoked so much grass before show time that he forgot to slip on the golf gloves he always wore to protect his hands, and had blisters before the first break. Tuxedos were required, as always, but two of the guys were so distracted they'd forgotten their bow ties and one had worn brown shoes, so I put him in the back, where his feet were well concealed. As we moved through our sets, changing the tempo—fox-trots, slow two-beat songs, waltzes, some rumba and cha-cha, the Charleston and black bottom, and plenty of swing—I kept my eyes on the room, trying to gauge the sensibility and personality of the audience, and pace the sets accordingly. What people were wearing—particularly women's shoes—and how they danced were always important clues. The audience that night was classy, and we leaned heavily on Cole Porter and Noel Coward. As usual, I tried to communicate with each pretty woman in the room with my eyes, short of flirting so brazenly that I ticked off their dates.

The sumptuous Venetian Room contributed its own magic. From carpet to ceiling, the dominant colors were black, red, and gold, with subdued lighting about the room and a tall, five-point candelabra at each table for glowing effect. Theater seating behind balcony railings anchored each end of the rectangular room, where molded gilt arches framed hand-painted murals of Venice canal scenes. The band was set up on the main stage, facing the entrance across the dance floor and shallow seating area; I played from the thrust, a smaller platform that rolled out from under the main stage, putting the piano a little closer to the dance floor, along with Gloria's microphone for vocals. Gloria and I each had our own spotlight from the bank of lights positioned near the ceiling, just above the main doors. From my modest perch, I could look out across the room and see plenty of famous faces: Joe DiMaggio was with Charlene again, but Herb Caen was flying solo that night; I also spotted Shirley Temple Black, Billy Eckstine, Steve Allen with his wife, Jayne Meadows, and restaurateur Enrico Banducci. Sally Stanford, once America's most notorious madam, was holding court as if she were the Queen of England, wrapped in a lavish mink stole with a stem of pale yellow cymbidium orchids pinned to the left shoulder. Frank Sinatra caused the usual stir when he showed up with his regular retinue— Jilly Rizzo, Harry Kurnitz, a couple of other thuggish types—accompanied by a few flashy starlets who'd be replaced with new versions the next time around. During the break, Frank had me over to his table, where he sat with a cigarette in one hand and a drink in the other. We talked about music, the band business, and, of course, the press, one of his favorite subjects. His advice to me was typically terse: "They're vultures, kid, a bunch of losers, so piss on 'em."

He requested Billy Strayhorn's "Lush Life"—possibly because it had been Ava Gardner's favorite song—and it was the first number we performed following the break, with Gloria on vocals. Technically, she sounded as if she were singing with passion, but I could tell she was faking it; her heart just wasn't there. The same thing happened when she sang "I Left My Heart in San Francisco," the tune written in 1954 by two homesick San Franciscans, Douglass Cross and his lover, George Cory. Although Tony Bennett had a big hit with it in '62, Sinatra had recorded it before Tony but never released it. That wasn't widely known, and I had some fun letting the audience in on a trade secret, while Frank grinned and threw down more booze. I would have asked him up to sing—Billy Eckstine, too—but pros like Frank and Billy rarely, if ever, sit in with a band they haven't rehearsed with. That's a myth the movies created.

While Gloria was finishing the impromptu tribute with "One for My Baby," my eyes drifted to the south side of the room and the swinging doors to the service kitchen, where waiters scurried in and out. As one of the doors came open, I glimpsed Hercules Platt standing there, hat in hand. At first, I got the impression he was staring at me with those implacable eyes. But a minute or two later—as the band launched into a peppy version of "Perdido"—another waiter came through the door and I noticed Platt tapping his right foot to the beat, while his head bobbed in time ever so slightly.

So maybe, I thought, *Inspector Platt digs something besides bebop.*

Then the door swung closed. When it opened again, Hercules Platt was gone.

DESPITE Platt's distracting appearance, and the fact that my second trumpet player toppled over backward, dead drunk, toward the end of the show, the orchestra scored a wildly successful opening night. I secretly wished that it could go on forever, but by eleven o'clock, I knew it was time to play "Nocturne in E Flat," my father's theme song and the one I always closed with. With that accomplished, and people calling for their checks, I spent the next half-hour chatting with fans, signing autographs, and having my picture taken with two or three couples.

Charlene had a drink waiting for me when I sidled over to her table. She'd planned a party for me at her manse in Pacific Heights, and we'd just decided that I'd catch a ride with Herb when the concierge presented me with a folded, handwritten note: *I'd like to see you. I'll be at the City Lights bookstore in North Beach around midnight, if you're interested.*

I asked the others to go on without me, telling them I'd make a grand entrance later, when the party was in full swing. Charlene demanded to know the contents of the message.

"Don't worry," I said, "I'll make the scene."

"Sinatra's dropping around," she reminded me.

"Save me some Scotch." I pecked her on the cheek and dashed out.

OUT on Mason Street, at the Fairmont's main entrance, the newshounds had finally departed, but Hercules Platt had taken their place.

He sat across Mason in a black, unmarked '57 Ford, about as inconspicuous as the Embarcadero Freeway. I ignored him and asked the doorman to whistle me a cab, wondering if Platt would follow. If he did, I intended to stop the taxi, jump out, and give him a tongue-lashing he wouldn't forget, and damn the consequences.

But as my cab pulled away, his Ford stayed where it was,

and I was quickly rid of him. Minutes later I was entering bawdy, bustling North Beach, with all its bars, strip clubs, and fading bohemian hangouts.

In the back seat, I felt my heart pound as I again unfolded the note to read the message that ended with Lenore Ashley's signature.

Chapter 15

THE CITY LIGHTS Pocket Book Shop occupied the pie-shaped corner of an old two-story building on Columbus Avenue, just below Broadway. In the window was a handwritten sign: *Abandon All Despair Ye Who Enter Here.*

As I jumped from my taxi, several mellow bohemian types lingered on the sidewalk out front, along with a throng of drunk kids and gawking tourists bent on seeing a beatnik. The front desk sat just inside the door in a sliver of space the size of a large closet. Behind the cash register stood a thin young man with a scruffy beard, engrossed in a tattered paperback copy of Jack Kerouac's *Dharma Bums.* A creaky set of wooden stairs to my right led up; another wooden stairway straight ahead went down. That was it: a shabby cubicle for handling cash, with a musty room above and another below. I guess I'd expected more, after all the attention paid to the owner, Lawrence Ferlinghetti, during his 1957 obscenity trial for publishing Allen Ginsberg's *Howl*. The landmark decision established new protections of expression in America and put San Francisco's beat movement on the cultural map. And this modest little bookstore was its literary heart.

"I was looking for Lenore Ashley," I said, addressing the clerk.

He glanced up from his novel, barely interested, then surveyed my attire through his wire-rimmed spectacles: custom-tailored tux, pleated evening shirt from Brooks Brothers, bow tie, wine-colored carnation, patent leather Belgian shoes as shiny as a new dime.

I attempted a friendly smile. "Sorry, I didn't dress for the occasion."

"Magazines and comic books are in the loft." He indicated the stairway that led up, then shifted his eyes to the steps going down. "Ginsberg's reading in the basement. I don't know Lenore Ashley."

"I'll try downstairs," I said, but he'd already returned to his book.

I descended the unvarnished steps to cheers, hoots, and various other exhortations coming from below. Near the bottom, I stopped to take in the scene.

The basement, shaped at odd angles, consisted of concrete floor and rough pillars, walls and arched alcoves of raw brick, and crude wooden bookshelves. Allen Ginsberg stood center stage toward the back, instantly recognizable from magazine photographs—a rumpled, chubby figure with flowing dark beard and hair, and thick horn-rims framing mischievous dark eyes. Several dozen men and women had crowded into the basement around him, most under forty, many much younger than that. The attire was fairly predictable: turtlenecks, threadbare jackets, wash pants, sandals, work boots. The audience was rapt, passing around a gallon jug of Red Mountain wine while Ginsberg read *Howl* with unabashed zeal.

Then I spotted Lenore Ashley, and my pulse quickened the way it had when I'd first read her note inviting me here. She sat on the floor to Ginsberg's left, legs crossed, gazing upward and clapping her hands gleefully at one of his provocative phrases. Like many of the women in the room, her hair was brushed straight back, hanging past her shoulders. Gone were the fancy gown, high heels, and pearls, replaced by a plain dark dress and flat shoes. Yet her beauty was fully intact, her resemblance to Diana still striking. She might have been Diana if Diana and I had never met, and she'd stayed here in The City, and drifted into the bohemian culture of North Beach. And lived.

Lenore Ashley looked up and caught me staring. She smiled beatifically and beckoned me with an upraised hand. I glanced down at my tux, shrugging plaintively. She cocked her head, gave me a chiding look. I shook my head, refusing to budge. Finally, she stood, threaded her way through the others, joined me at the foot of the stairs.

"No one cares how you're dressed, Mr. Damon."

"I care."

"You'll have to get over that, won't you?" Her smile was gently teasing. "That is, if you want to be comfortable in the world."

"I am comfortable in the world. Quite comfortable."

"But the world's about to change, Mr. Damon." She gestured toward Ginsberg and the beats gathered around him like disciples. "In fact, it's well under way."

I smiled feebly, uneasy in the role of square. "I know I'd be more comfortable if you dropped the "mister," and we went with first names."

"Sure, we can do that."

Suddenly, a stocky, square-jawed man on Ginsberg's right—familiar-looking, though puffy-faced—was urging the poet on with drunken shouts of "Go, go, go!"

"Jack Kerouac," Lenore said. "He came west just for this event. It's an encore of Ginsberg's historic *Howl* reading at Gallery Six, eight years ago."

I raised my eyebrows. "Historic?"

"You wait and see." She pointed out other local writers in the crowd: Gary Snyder, Gregory Corso, Richard Brautigan, Michael McClure. I hadn't heard of a single one.

"I'm afraid my taste runs more toward Auden," I said. "Dylan Thomas and T. S. Eliot are about as adventurous as I get." Then: "You're not wearing cologne tonight."

"I don't care for cologne. I wore it only because Terrence Collier wanted me to."

She returned her attention to Ginsberg, mouthing the words to *Howl* as he read them aloud. I used the time to steal delicious glances—at the lovely slope of her neck, the small but perfect mouth, the incandescent blue of her eyes when they happened to flick my way. Stealing glances and feeling like a lucky thief, while wanting more.

Kerouac leaped up like a cheerleader, pumping a fist, shouting his encouragement as Ginsberg launched into the final lines of his lengthy poem. Then it was over. The crowd applauded wildly, pleading for more, as Ginsberg grinned like a Buddha and accepted a burning joint from an angelic-looking young man, who followed it with a kiss.

"Do you mind if we get out of here?" I said to Lenore Ashley. "Somewhere we can get a drink and talk?"

WE headed to Vesuvio Café, practically next door, but found it crammed with tourists and bohemian wanna-bes, and not an empty table in sight. Lenore grabbed my hand, dragging me back out, leaving the clamor behind.

"North Beach is ruined," she said. "Tour buses come through now, and the rents are ridiculous. Same thing's happening up on Russian Hill. Almost all the real beats have left."

"But you're still here," I said, as she pulled me between cars across Columbus Avenue.

"Not really. I just come back for the poetry readings. I found a little cottage in Haight-Ashbury. That's where a lot of us have resettled."

We ended up at the Tosca Café, a tiny place with Italian murals and opera on the jukebox. We took a cozy red vinyl booth and ordered two espressos, facing each other across the table.

"I expected this to be much more awkward."

She shrugged, smiling easily. "It doesn't have to be."

"I guess I'm wondering why you wanted to see me."

She looked down a moment, then back up, more somber. "I wanted to apologize, Philip. For any pain I may have inadvertently caused you."

"That's decent of you."

"I knew nothing about Diana until that story in the *Chronicle* on Monday. Seeing her photo was something of a shock. It was only yesterday that I learned of her relationship with Terrence and his fixation with her after she broke it off."

"Inspector Platt must have spoken with you."

She nodded. "It seems I was the only one in town who didn't know about it. In hindsight, it explains a good deal."

"Collier certainly molded you well."

"He was very specific in his instructions. I knew it was odd, but I just assumed he favored a certain type, a certain look and style in a woman."

"Forgive me, Lenore, but there's something I have to ask."

"Why would I willingly do someone's bidding like that? Submit so completely to him?"

"You read my mind."

She laughed, as if the question were naïve. "For the same reason so many people sacrifice their identities for the expectations of others—money and comfort. Isn't that what conventional jobs are all about—giving up our lives for a paycheck? Buying into consumer culture until our possessions own us, instead of the other way around? And marriage—all those dutiful women who grew up trained and conditioned to please men."

"Are you saying that Collier *paid* you?"

"Very well."

"I thought you beats were dead set against materialism."

She sipped her espresso thoughtfully. "I want to travel—and to write. The money and gifts I received from Terrence have bought me time to do both."

"You can't work, like everybody else?"

"Do you know what the pay's like out there, and what things cost these days? Tomatoes are up to a dime a pound. Bread's more than thirty cents a loaf. And wages for women are a crime. I'm not talking about *your* world, Philip. I'm talking about the real world."

"Cheap shot," I said.

"I'll bet your father left you a trust."

"If he did, it's buying that espresso you're sipping."

She reached suddenly for her handbag. "It's late. I should go."

I seized her wrist. "I didn't mean for it to go like this."

"But it did, didn't it, Philip? We're worlds apart, you and I."

"There's still something I need to know."

Our eyes connected, and her voice grew cold. "Yes, I slept with him. Yes, I played the role of Diana's surrogate in bed. Right down to his most exact stage directions. My background as an actress came in quite handy."

I let go of her wrist, sagging back against the vinyl, wordless.

"Looking back," she went on, her voice thawing, "I can see how utterly obsessed Terrence was with Diana. He couldn't let her go." Her eyes grew soft, sympathetic. "She must have been an extraordinary woman."

"She was." Suddenly, I wanted to hurt this imposter who had dared to take Diana's place. "It didn't bother you, turning yourself into a whore for him?"

Lenore didn't even flinch. "I've known plenty of wives who sleep with their husbands for financial security and like them less than I enjoyed the company of Terrence Collier."

"Still a tawdry business, though."

She slid from the booth and stood, unsmiling. "And how many women have you bought off, Philip, for the price of dinner and a movie?" Regret crossed her face like a sudden shadow. "I'm sorry. I came here to apologize, not to trade insults. It's a shame we had to meet under these conditions. Murder's not something I ever imagined I'd have to deal with."

I smiled ruefully. "What's that saying? Life is what happens when you're making other plans."

"You must have had quite a few plans yourself—you and Diana. The paper mentioned that she was pregnant."

"I'd rather not go there, if it's all the same."

"No, of course not." She reached out, brushed some loose strands of hair off my forehead. "Anyway, I'm glad we had a chance to talk."

I glanced at my wristwatch; it was twenty past one. "Look, I'm off to a party from here, over in Pacific Heights. Maybe you'd like to go."

"Thanks, but I'm not really in a party mood. It's been a rough few days."

"Sinatra's expected, if that makes a difference."

She smiled apologetically. "No offense, but Old Blue Eyes doesn't send me. Miles Davis, now that would be cool."

She started off, but I touched her arm. "When can I see you again?"

"I'm not sure that's a good idea."

"Please. Dinner, or just a cup of coffee. We'll go Dutch treat, if that makes you more comfortable."

"Why, Philip?"

"Because you fascinate me."

She studied me a moment, then tossed me half a hope. "If I change my mind, I'll contact you at the hotel."

LENORE stepped out into bustling North Beach, swept away by a tide of out-of-towners. Puccini's "E Lucivan le Stelle," from the last act of *Tosca*, began playing on the jukebox. Somewhere in the café a man with a fairly decent tenor tried singing along.

I ordered another espresso and carried it to the window, where I stared out across Columbus Avenue at City Lights, unable to get Lenore Ashley out of my mind. What struck me most about her was how nice she was. Maybe too nice.

When my coffee was gone, I caught a cab up to Charlene's manse in Pacific Heights, where I drank too much Scotch and laughed even when I didn't feel like it.

Sinatra never showed. I wasn't really surprised.

Chapter 16

THE NEXT MORNING, I ordered breakfast sent up to my suite along with my messages from the front desk. One was from George Chang, the acupuncturist.

I returned his call, and to my surprise he agreed to see me. Charlene—still exploring the idea of restoring the Fairmont—was reviewing blueprints and vintage hotel photographs with her architects, so I struck out alone for Chinatown.

"MR. Damon, welcome."

George Chang bowed slightly at the waist, pressing his hands together, just inside the half-open door of his upstairs quarters. He was a slim man, reaching not quite to my shoulders, with alabaster skin and a youthful, beardless face that made judging his age difficult. His attire consisted of a loose-fitting shirt of white cotton, similar pants tied by a cord at the waist, and sandals with thongs on his slender feet. He asked me to remove my shoes, and I obliged, carrying them as we stepped into a small anteroom.

"Frankly," I said, "I didn't expect to hear from you."

"But you have." His smile was unassuming. "Tea?"

"Thanks, I just had breakfast. Your English, by the way, is excellent."

"I'm an American, Mr. Damon. Born and raised here."

"Of course." I shrugged, abashed. "Forgive me."

Chang was looking at me without quite meeting my eyes. "You and your friend have been asking around Chinatown. You seem to have an interest in Mr. Collier."

"Word travels fast, I guess."

"We're a small community, rather insular."

"You've made me feel welcome, Chang. I'm grateful for that."

The easy smile again. "Perhaps each of us needs something from the other."

"Quite frankly, what I need is anything you can tell me about Terrence Collier, especially in the days before his death."

"Please, come inside." Chang parted beaded curtains, and we stepped through a doorway into a room whose spaciousness surprised me. It was musky with incense, illuminated by a large, paned window that looked down on the narrow side street I'd crossed only moments earlier. The furnishings and decoration were sparse and simple: on a low, round table, green bamboo shoots in rocks and water, contained in a small ceramic pot; a wood-block print on parchment, hanging on a wall, bearing the likeness of an ancient, bearded figure I believe was Confucius; two tiny, hyperactive birds singing in a cage that hung near the window; on a shelf, a colorful ceramic cat, a figure of good luck, with an upraised paw and Chinese characters on its belly. Against one wall was a writing desk; above the desk was a cabinet holding jars of herbs, leaves, and seeds as well as various instruments, including long, thin needles I took to be for acupuncture. A padded massage table, covered by a clean white sheet, anchored the center of the room.

"Do you live here as well," I asked, "or is this just a place to work?"

He dropped his eyes, as if embarrassed by my prying. "We have rooms in the back. My parents and I, and my four grandparents." He led me to the window, where he studied my face in the diffuse light coming from the overcast sky outside.

"What is it that troubles you so, Mr. Damon?"

"I have some questions, that's all."

"But these questions are connected to something that weighs heavily on you. I see the tension in your neck and shoulders, in the lines of your face. Not just tension but deep, personal pain."

I laughed. "Really, Chang, I'm fine."

"Mr. Collier was also troubled when he came to me. He worried about so many things he could not control. Always, he blamed his headaches and indigestion on too much stress. I told him there was no such thing as stress—only his internal reaction to potentially stressful situations. I explained to him that anxiety or the lack of it is entirely of our own making, and often quite unnecessary."

"Makes sense," I said. "Now, about Terrence Collier—"

"I told Mr. Collier that his emotions were out of balance,

that his life was without harmony. I explained that he needed to be in touch with his *chi*, his cosmic energy. Do you know anything of feng shui, Mr. Damon?"

I sighed, growing impatient. "Afraid I haven't heard of it."

"An ancient Chinese practice." Chang smiled placidly. "Perhaps one day Caucasians will discover it and find it useful."

"What, exactly, was it that worried Collier so?"

"If you don't mind, Mr. Damon, could you remove your jacket and shirt?"

"Remove my—?"

He nodded. "I would like to work on you as we talk, to unburden you of some of this tension you try so hard to conceal."

I hesitated, then realized that if I accommodated him, perhaps he'd be more forthcoming. He helped me slip off my jacket, then out of my shirt, which he hung neatly on a coat rack near his desk. He returned, gesturing toward the massage table.

"Face down, Mr. Damon, if you please."

I lay on the table, adjusting myself until I was comfortable. When I craned my head to look up, Chang stood with his eyes closed and his hands spread over me, as if praying.

"A deep breath, Mr. Damon. Let it out very slowly. Let everything go."

"Relax, you mean."

"A strange order to give someone, don't you think—'insisting' they relax. The idea is not more control, Mr. Damon, but the opposite. If one works properly from within, learning to let go, relaxation will come."

I closed my eyes, took a deep breath, exhaled slowly. His

soft hands moved like fluttering wings across my shoulders and along the contours of my back, caressing but never quite alighting. The sensation, I must admit, was exquisite.

"I prefer to work in quiet," Chang said, his voice low, "but Mr. Collier always came with his mind filled, and sometimes with his heart heavy. I let him chatter until he grew tired of talking and submitted to the stillness."

Chang paused momentarily until I felt his hands again, applying warm oil. During several minutes of silence, he gently kneaded my back and shoulders. When he resumed the conversation, he began to work more deeply, surprising me with his strength.

"The news of Mr. Collier's murder was most troubling. For someone to deliberately take another life—such a terrible thing. Yet I also realized as I read the newspaper that the investigation might very well lead the police in my direction."

"Because of the bruises on his back," I said.

"Yes, the bruises—from the cupping." Chang stopped massaging and padded across the room to the area around his desk and cabinet. "Eventually, the police will deduce that Mr. Collier was here, that it was I who left those strange bruises on him. They won't understand our customs and practices, and may suspect me in some way. I'd rather go to the police voluntarily than have them come here, into Chinatown."

"And what is it you want from me?"

"Information, Mr. Damon—about the murder, the investigation, whatever you might tell me." He paused, then added with significance: "The more one knows, the less one needs to say."

"And what is it that I get from you, Chang?"

He returned and stood over me. "In preparation for your visit, Mr. Damon, I took the trouble of heating several of these special suction cups. They'll be quite warm but they won't burn you. You'll feel some discomfort. If it's too much, please let me know."

I felt the first hot touch of metal, then sensed the cup drawing in and gripping my flesh like the hungry mouth of a voracious leech. It continued to suck my flesh more deeply; the pain grew intense, though bearable.

"Think of the pain," Chang said, "not as something to be feared or dreaded, but as another emotion. Just another negative feeling, Mr. Damon, a natural part of the life flow to be accepted and then set free. Let the cups draw your negative *chi* to the surface, so you can let it go."

I gritted my teeth. "I liked the massage better."

Chang laughed. "That was Mr. Collier's first reaction as well. But he came back, many times."

"You mentioned that he worried a lot."

"Why don't you tell me what you know of the murder, Mr. Damon? Perhaps it will help take your mind off your discomfort."

So I told him what I'd learned, including the mystifying link to Diana. As Chang predicted, the pain became not so much a physical experience as a mental one, and more tolerable. As I finished my story—explaining the strange connection between Collier, Diana, and Lenore Ashley—he began removing the cups one by one.

"Now it's your turn, Chang, if you don't mind."

He toweled the oil off my back and shoulders and asked me to turn over, face up. When I was resettled, looking up into his tranquil face, he placed his hands under my head, raising it slightly from the table.

"I call this the yoga head lift. Please, close your eyes. Now, allow your neck and shoulders to go lax, so that my hands are doing all the work and your muscles are at complete rest."

Suddenly, he let go of my head, which stayed rigidly where it was, inches off the table, my neck muscles taut.

"You must learn to trust, Mr. Damon—trust that I won't drop your head and hurt you. That's the purpose of the exercise. Again, the letting go."

I breathed deeply, exhaled, did my best to let my muscles become flaccid. Once more, he took my head in his hands and lifted. Very gently, he began to turn my head from side to side, increasing the arc of the rotation slightly each time, gently stretching the muscles. It occurred to me how vulnerable I was at this moment, how easily he could have snapped my neck. Yet his voice was as gentle and soothing as his hands, and I gave in to him, utterly passive.

"I first saw Mr. Collier six years ago," Chang said, "shortly after I was licensed to perform my therapies. As I said, he worried about so many things—his wife, his mistress, his finances, a collection of fine gems with which he seemed especially concerned. He mentioned these things as I gave him his weekly massage, or applied the cups, or the acupuncture needles. I sensed, after a time, that they were somehow all connected, although he never revealed quite enough for me to be sure."

Chang's hands grew still, and I opened my eyes. He appeared thoughtful, as if weighing a decision. A moment later, he resumed the gentle rotations. I shut my eyes again, happy to have my head literally in his hands. I'd never felt so relaxed, in such surrender; the effect was bliss.

"Then, one day, Mr. Collier spoke of the pearls."

Chang twisted my head far to the right and held it there, silent for a moment, as I became acutely aware of the rhythmic pattern of my breathing.

"I'm not entirely at ease speaking of this, Mr. Damon. Yet you've been generous with your information, and the pearls are all I have to offer you, figuratively speaking. They may have nothing at all to do with Mr. Collier's murder. Yet he was so enamored of the pearls, so desperate to possess them, they came to seem like a dark and destructive force in his life."

"How so?"

"They were all he talked about the past two years. Why he confided in me, I'm not sure. Perhaps because he'd come to trust me as you trust me now. Perhaps because I'm a Chinese in Chinatown, where we like to keep our secrets."

He rotated my head far to the other side and held it there, while my steady breathing continued to lull me like waves lapping endlessly along a shoreline.

"The story of the pearls," he went on, "has circulated around Chinatown for many years. At one time, they belonged to Helen Hop-Yik, who operates a popular restaurant here—the Pearl of China. Somehow, Mr. Collier acquired the pearls, then lost them, but how or to whom I'm not sure. I only know that getting them back became a quest that consumed him. I cannot tell you more than this, Mr. Damon, out of respect for Helen Hop-Yik. If she wishes to speak with you, that must be her decision."

Chang returned my head to its regular position, setting it gently on the table. He closed his eyes, spread his hands over me, and stood silent for a long moment. Then, softly, he said, "We are done now, Mr. Damon." I dressed and followed him back to the anteroom, where I slipped into

my shoes as he opened the door. "You'll show some bruising
for a few days, from the cupping. But like all painful things,
they, too, shall pass."

When I pulled out my wallet to pay, he raised a hand in
polite refusal.

"Your friendship and discretion," George Chang said,
"that will be enough."

Chapter 17

⟶

THE MASS FOR Terrence Hamilton Collier III was celebrated at 2 P.M. on Thursday in the Church of Sts. Peter
and Paul next to Washington Square Park.

Situated a few blocks from Fisherman's Wharf, the park
was considered by many to be the heart of North Beach, and
something of a melting pot: old Italians on benches, feeding
the pigeons; Asians going through the precise motions of
their tai chi chuan; hipsters lounging in the shade of trees,
smoking and reading poetry; Mexican families out with
their kids, eating, listening to music, and laughing as if
there was no mañana. If the breezes were blowing just right,
a visitor might catch a whiff of pesto and mozzarella or
homemade ravioli from Molinari's Deli across Columbus
Avenue. Herb Caen, of course, liked to remind everyone that
Washington Square Park contained a statue of Franklin but

not of Washington, that North Beach didn't have a beach, and that the park wasn't even square. "The only square I ever saw there was Richard Nixon," Herb told me once, "and I'm pretty sure even he was a little crooked. I never did buy that Checkers speech."

The Italian Cathedral—as Sts. Peter and Paul was better known—faced the park from the north, just across narrow Filbert Street. It was a fanciful Romanesque structure fit for a fairy tale, famous for its twin spires, abundant statuary, and forty-foot-high altar. Joe DiMaggio had married his first wife, Dorothy Arnold, at the popular church in 1939, although plenty of tour guides still got it wrong, telling visitors he'd gotten hitched to Marilyn there. I guess that was more romantic than City Hall.

The archbishop himself presided over the Mass for Collier, praising the deceased for his civic generosity and mentioning in particular the planned Catholic Youth League facility, which the archbishop said would stand as a monument to Collier's charitable nature.

Afterward, the body was transported for interment to Colma, a small town roughly ten miles south that some called "the city of the dead" because corpses there outnumbered the living a thousand to one.

CHARLENE and I rode down in her chauffeured Bentley, noshing on Beluga caviar and champagne.

Ahead of us was a slow procession of funeral cars, led by a police motorcycle squadron. It was a fine day, clear and surprisingly warm for late October, and the scenery was pleasant. Set in a bucolic valley protected by low green mountains and sun-baked hills, Colma seemed an ideal resting place for the dearly departed. By the time we reached the city limits, we were munching tea sandwiches and sampling homemade scones with Devonshire cream specially prepared by the pastry chef at the Fairmont.

"I know it's silly," Charlene said, as we passed a series of cemeteries and monument stores along Old Mission Road, "but this place always gives me the willies. I guess it's because of the way they handled so many of the bodies back in the forties."

She'd told me the story on our way down from The City: At the turn of the twentieth century, San Francisco had banned cemeteries as a "public nuisance" and detriment to public health and welfare. In truth, city planners and business leaders wanted the land for development. Eventually, they struck a deal with the churches—most important, with the Catholic archdiocese—to remove most of San Francisco's buried dead. Oakland got some of the bodies, but most went to Colma, where prescient priests had already opened a number of cemeteries in anticipation of San Francisco's urban sprawl. Among Catholics, Holy Cross was the biggest and most prestigious. In 1940, San Francisco pushed to have the last remaining bodies dug up, and they were shipped to Holy Cross and a dozen other Colma funeral parks by the tens of thousands. The process of mass disinterment was imprecise at best; the gravediggers left behind countless bodies or body parts, to be plowed under and forgotten beneath skyscrapers, apartment buildings, and parking lots.

"Of course," Charlene said, "the wealthiest got special attention. No lost limbs for the rich in the afterlife." She shuddered, thinking about it. "Pass me the champagne, will you, Philip? Perhaps some carbonation will lighten me up."

*   *   *

THE driver turned in at the big gates of Holy Cross and followed the line of mourners' vehicles climbing a gentle slope into a rising sea of grave sites. I'd been here once before, with Joe DiMaggio, to visit the hilltop mausoleum where his parents were interred. The staff at Holy Cross, noted for its graciousness and dedication, took great pride in its role as the caretaker of so many prominent souls: former governors, great bankers, captains of industry, legendary San Francisco figures like Big Jim Fair and the other Comstock Silver Kings. The church had also allotted space for the indigent, where, at some sites, several caskets were stacked one atop the other in a single grave. Parents and children of many poor families were interred together in a simple, single plot they'd reserved on a special payment plan that did not allow for any memorials.

"Holy Cross has everything from soup to nuts," Charlene said, as we passed a row of heavy stone Celtic crosses going green with moss on their shadowy side. "Although I notice by the names that the Irish and Italians seem to have their own neighborhoods."

"I guess some things never change."

Collier's final resting place was an opulent private mausoleum of marble and gold leaf, with a domed roof and sculpted angels spreading their wings above the arched entrance. Prior to the interment, a final committal service was held in a parklike setting on the adjacent grounds. A few dozen mourners gathered, most of them attired in black. I recognized James Brannigan among them, as well as Lenore Ashley, Mayor Christopher, and Rosamund Kelly, the florid-faced president of the Catholic Youth League, whom I hadn't seen since the night Collier made his transition.

Inspector Hercules Platt stood at some distance, off in the shade of a big pine, his hands clasped in front of him, looking pensive. From time to time, he pulled out a notebook to jot a few words, but otherwise maintained his stolid, vigilant stance. The press had been forbidden entry to the cemetery, but above us, two news helicopters hovered, shooting footage from the air.

Just as the brief service got under way, a turquoise Thunderbird convertible pulled up on the road nearby. Vivian Collier scrambled from the passenger side and staggered toward us as rapidly as her drunken condition allowed, while Biff Elkins set the brake and jumped out to give chase. He called after her as they ran, pleading with her to stop, but only succeeded in causing the head of every mourner to turn in his direction. As usual, the blond and blue-eyed Elkins looked trim and handsome, this time in a charcoal suit and gray tie, with tasteful silver accessories. Vivian Collier had decided to make a different fashion statement: a Chanel wool and gold lame pantsuit and matching gold boots, upon which she tottered toward us, her big gold bracelets jangling. In her right hand, she maintained a lethal grip on a bottle of Taittinger blanc de blancs brut champagne.

"I see Vivian's drinking what we're drinking," Charlene said.

A few mourners stepped forward, attempting to divert Mrs. Collier from the central circle, where a monsignor was committing the deceased back to God. She swung the champagne bottle in wide, threatening arcs that had them in quick retreat. Elkins caught up with her as she reached the coffin, beseeching her to come away with him, but to no avail.

"Shouldn't we christen the damn thing," she asked, indicating the coffin, "before we send the bastard to hell?"

"Mrs. Collier," the monsignor said, approaching her in his robes, reaching out with supplicating hands.

She raised the bottle ominously. "Back off, buster, or I'll knock that silly hat off your pious head."

The crowd gasped collectively, and two strong men were needed to assist Rosamund Kelly, who nearly fainted. Vivian turned and brought the bottle down across the brass coffin with a resounding thud. The heavy glass remained intact, while leaving a noticeable dent. Again, she swung and connected; again, the bottle failed to shatter. Once more, same thing, and she gave up.

"Screw it. I'd rather drink it than waste it on him, anyway." She guzzled from the bottle until it was half empty. Then she pulled a gold band from her ring finger, flung it at the coffin, watched it bounce off, and plopped down miserably on the fresh-cut lawn, dissolving into sobs. Elkins kneeled, removed the bottle from her grasp, helped her to her feet, and led her blubbering back to his car.

"If there's one thing I hate to see," Charlene whispered, "it's grass stains on a good Chanel."

The monsignor finished the service quickly, and then the mourners were heading back to their vehicles—relieved, I'm sure, to have the whole thing over. Brannigan bolted to his car, drawing down his head like a turtle retreating into its shell. Lenore Ashley paused a moment, allowing our eyes to connect briefly, but moved on without a word. Rosamund Kelly approached us, her face and double chins veiled, a hand to her big bosom.

"I've never been so mortified." Mrs. Kelly touched each of us briefly, as if we were family. "Vivian's little drama was particularly disgraceful in light of Mr. Collier's kindness to the Catholic Youth League."

"I take it you've heard from the estate attorney," Charlene said.

Mrs. Kelly nodded. "Mr. Collier left the League a very generous sum, enough to complete the new building. If I could, I'd nominate the man for sainthood."

Mrs. Kelly noticed Hercules Platt striding toward us across the lawn. "That detective," she said, glancing at him sideways. "Asking so many questions, and he still hasn't come up with a suspect in Mr. Collier's murder."

"It's only been a few days," Charlene said.

Rosamund Kelly lifted her veil while lowering her voice. "I realize we have to offer the Negroes more opportunity— no one's more open-minded than I am. But I'm sure they could have found someone more appropriate." She made a sour face. "He's so *dark*."

She offered us a quick good-bye and scurried off as if she had a snake at her heels. Platt greeted each of us perfunctorily as he came up, and removed his hat.

"You and I need to talk, Damon."

"Whatever you have to say, Inspector, you can say in front of Charlene."

Platt considered that a moment. "I got a call from a George Chang this morning, acupuncturist over in Chinatown. He explained that he'd treated Collier last week, leaving those strange bruises."

"I'm glad you cleared that up, Inspector."

"My problem, Damon, is that you got to him before we did."

"He told you I'd been to see him?"

"He didn't have to. One of the inspectors assigned to the case spotted you coming out of Chang's office this morning." Platt stepped closer, until our noses were inches apart. "This is my investigation, Damon. I don't need a loose cannon throwing a monkey wrench into the machinery."

"Nor any more mixed metaphors," I said.

Charlene leaned diplomatically into the conversation. "Actually, Inspector, snooping around Chinatown was my idea."

"Or two loose cannons," Platt said, while losing the tough guy tone.

"You got what you needed," I said. "Chang explained the bruises. So what's the harm?"

"For your information, we were already canvassing Chinatown. A Chinese patrolman tipped us off about the cupping the same day the coroner's photos came back. By the time we got to Chinatown, you'd already spooked half the community. No one wanted to talk to us."

Charlene clucked her tongue. "Oh, dear. Perhaps we did overstep our bounds."

"Look, Mrs. Statz, I'm grateful to you. To be honest, you're the only reason I'm still on this case. But I need you and Damon to stay out of my way."

"You have my word on that, Inspector." Charlene reached out with her right hand, brushed a piece of lint from his lapel, while her left hand stayed behind her. "Next time, if we have something useful, we'll be sure to call and let you know."

"I appreciate that, Mrs. Statz. Along with everything else."

Platt shot me a glance that was more baleful, placed his hat atop his head, and went on his way.

"The poor man's obviously under a lot of pressure," Charlene said. "It's clear that he needs our assistance more than ever."

"You just promised him we'd stay out of his way."

Charlene brought her left hand from behind her back, showed me her crossed fingers. "You'll see, Philip—Inspector Platt will come around and realize what valuable partners we can be." She clasped her hands with fervor. "This is *so* exciting! I feel like Harriet Vane, about to team up with Lord Peter Wimsey."

BEFORE leaving Holy Cross, Charlene asked her driver to take the Bentley up the hill so she could visit the Great Mausoleum, where Mr. and Mrs. DiMaggio were interred. As we climbed, I spotted a solitary figure standing with a bouquet of flowers on a slope above Collier's private mausoleum. He was dressed in a proper dark suit rather than a waiter's outfit, but I recognized him just the same.

"Isn't that Valentino del Conte?" I pointed along a row of crypts and monuments to the ridge where del Conte stood.

"I believe you're right," Charlene said. "He must have come to pay his respects."

"I never got the impression he had feelings for Collier. He seems to be keeping his distance."

"Valentino's a very private person." Charlene settled back in her seat. "He's probably waiting until the rest of us have gone."

We reached the hilltop mausoleum, a two-story structure of concrete block and marble pillars spread across eight acres, where all of the former archbishops of San Francisco were entombed in the rotunda. Charlene and I entered, climbed to the second level, and paid our respects to Joe's parents.

RIDING down the hill, I again saw Valentino del Conte, who continued to clutch his bouquet of flowers as he traversed a slope of grave sites with simple markers, moving in the direction of the poorer plots.

"How much do you know about del Conte," I asked, "other than his work as a waiter?"

Charlene stroked her chin, looking thoughtful. "Claims to have been quite a gymnast in high school, with aspirations as a performer. Said he ran off and joined the circus, learned the art of trapeze, worked for years in a group called The Flying Valentinos. Became enamored of the roar of the crowd, that kind of thing. Then age caught up with him, and he returned home to San Francisco and began waiting tables for a living."

"Colorful background."

"If any of it's true." Charlene winked. "He's something of a drama queen, that Valentino."

"But awfully useful for information on the confidential side."

The Bentley passed through the big gates and turned onto Old Mission Road in the direction of The City. "For someone who was so reluctant to get involved," Charlene said, "you're turning into quite the detective."

I stared out the window as we passed cemetery after cemetery, wondering how many of the buried had died violently, before their time. "If any of this is linked in any way to Diana's death, I intend to find out how."

"And if it's not?"

"I'd hoped for that—it would have been much more comfortable." My eyes came back around to find Charlene's. "But that no longer seems possible, does it? It's like Platt said, no matter where you look, it always comes back to Diana."

Chapter 18

——⌐

BACK AT THE Fairmont, I fell into a nap, slept off the afternoon's champagne, then called the Pearl of China and asked for the proprietor, Helen Hop-Yik.

A woman with a small voice and impenetrable Chinese accent took the phone. I explained who I was and asked if I might meet to talk with her about Terrence Hamilton Collier III. She apologized for her limited English, professed not to understand what I was saying, and politely ended the conversation.

THAT night we played our usual two shows in the Venetian Room.

Fewer celebrities were in attendance this time, although Phil Harris and Alice Faye made the first show with Danny

Kaye and his wife Sylvia, and Melvin Belli, the grandiose attorney, turned up at the second show. Gloria Velez seemed out of sorts—on edge, perhaps, from Platt's persistent probing—but she got through her vocals in reasonably good voice and the rest of the band did a more than competent job.

Following the final encore, Belli approached to introduce himself. The famed attorney Herb Caen had dubbed "Melvin Bellicose" was a broad-bellied, soft-shouldered man with a jovial, heavily jowled face. He was known for his sublime arrogance, sharp wit and dramatic courtroom tactics, but also for his enormous appetite for all things pleasurable, including and especially lovely women. Asian women, diminutive but striking, were among his favorite delicacies.

"Loved the show, Damon, damned fine work." He pushed his round horn-rims higher on his nose, closer to his mop of unruly white hair. "You don't hear much music like that anymore, I can tell you."

"Maybe that's why we always sell out the house, Mr. Belli. My guess is there will always be people who want to dance to these great old tunes."

"Right, right," Belli said, suddenly impatient. "Listen here, I was wondering if you had plans for the rest of the evening."

"The evening's pretty much gone. It's half past midnight."

"Not too late for a drink, is it?"

"Never too late for that."

"I was hoping you might join me for a nightcap." His eyes shifted to meet mine. "Down in Chinatown, at a place called the Pearl of China."

*   *   *

I rode with Belli in his gold Rolls Royce. He was voluble on topical subjects like Dr. King and the sit-ins in the South and the Rockefeller-Goldwater debates, but the name Helen Hop-Yik never came up.

At Belli's direction, his driver entered Chinatown from the south along Grant Avenue, as Charlene had done when we'd made our visit. It was a weeknight, and most of the shops and many of the restaurants were shuttered and dark, the streets largely deserted. Even the rickshaws for tourists were put away for the night. The air was cool and a fog was rolling in, creeping up the avenues and drifting around corners. In the mist, slender red pagodas glowed from atop the tall iron lampposts, in the grip of dragons' jaws.

The Pearl of China was located in the 900 block of Grant, situated in a four-story building that featured a pagoda rooftop façade at each level. Like most of the space-hungry businesses in Chinatown, the restaurant shared common walls with its neighbors and was built nearly flush to the sidewalk. A tall, vertical sign proclaimed the Pearl of China in both Chinese and English. Three steps led to the entrance, passing beneath an arch in the shape of a dragon with sharp claws and teeth, fierce eyes, and a flickering, forked tongue. All of it burned brightly in neon of red, green, and gold that was sputtering out for the night as Belli's big Rolls pulled up out front.

Belli trudged heavily up the steps, and I followed. Dragonlike dog figures guarded each side of the wide red door. The rotund attorney paused to observe them.

"Stone fou dogs," he told me. "That one's the female. See the pup under her paw? Symbolizes new life, rejuvenation. Very religious, the Chinese. Also very superstitious. I often wonder if they really aren't the same thing."

I glanced at the second stone dog. "And the other one?"

"The male. His job is to keep watch over a precious pearl that belongs to the village. If the pearl were to be lost, the village would suffer catastrophe. At least that's what the Chinese believe. I suppose, in a broader context, the pearl could symbolize any number of things. Honor, tradition— even a well-kept secret."

He pulled open the heavy door, and we went in.

INSIDE, Chinese men in colorful silk shirts and black pants were cleaning up or closing for the night; each one we encountered greeted Belli with a deference mixed with pleasure, as if he were a familiar and well-liked patriarch. We climbed stairs from the first level, which housed the bar, piano lounge, and a few booths for dining, passed through the main dining room on the second floor, and took more stairs to level three, which held offices and a small drawing room set up for tea.

Belli was huffing and puffing when we got there. "This is as far as we go, thank God. Living quarters are upstairs and off-limits." He winked lasciviously. "Although there was a time when I spent some long and wonderful nights up there, the kind a man remembers as he grows older and his capabilities begin to diminish." He indicated a heavy wooden chair of Oriental design that looked hand-carved. "Have a seat, Damon. What are you drinking?"

I asked for Dewars on the rocks, which Belli dismissed with a wave of his pudgy hand. "You want Glenlivet, straight up. Now, that's a real drink."

He picked up a phone, dialed a number, asked for the Scotch to be brought up, along with two glasses of absinthe. As he was hanging up, a tiny Chinese woman of perhaps fifty slipped into the room, as quietly as a cat. I was immediately on my feet, startled by her beauty. Slim yet modestly curvaceous, she was dressed in a Chinese gown of green silk trimmed in gold. Her face—pale, dark-eyed, with small, doll-like features—was exquisite.

"My dear." Belli accepted her delicate hand, which he kissed with great tenderness before turning in my direction. "Philip Damon, I'm pleased to introduce Helen Hop-Yik— *Princess* Helen Hop-Yik."

Helen Hop-Yik extended her hand, I shook it, and she asked me to sit in English that had improved noticeably since our brief phone conversation earlier in the day. She and Belli took chairs across a black table inlaid with polished brass.

She pressed her fingers together, dipping her head slightly. "Please forgive my rudeness when you called this afternoon, Mr. Damon. There are matters of grave consequence about which I must exercise extreme discretion."

"Terrence Collier, for example, and the pearls?"

She glanced at Belli, who was about to speak when a young Chinese man arrived with our drinks. He handed small, clear glasses containing a green liquid to Helen Hop-Yik and Belli, and a double shot glass filled with golden Scotch to me.

As he departed, Belli raised his glass to the light. "A beautiful color, don't you think? Baudelaire described absinthe as 'the green waters of summer.' Others called it the green fairy, for its seductive, mind-altering effect. No wonder it's been banned so widely. Anything so potent with pleasure always frightens the timid and wary."

"Yet you've acquired a glass," I said, "without much trouble."

Belli raised his bushy eyebrows. "By necessity, Chinatown has its own rules, its own way of doing things." He turned to the two of us, holding his glass aloft. "Here's to Mr. Damon's quest for the truth and the concern I'm sure he feels for the welfare of innocent parties."

We all touched glasses and sipped, each of us taking a moment to savor the fine liquor on our tongues. Then Belli asked me how much I knew about the pearls and their connection to Helen Hop-Yik.

"Not much. Nothing that makes any sense."

"And how much, if I may ask, have you passed on to the authorities?"

"Not a word."

Belli and Helen Hop-Yik exchanged glances.

"But if the pearls have anything to do with the murder of my wife, Diana——"

"The pearls in question are quite valuable," Belli said. "Priceless would be the more accurate term. I can assure you, there are those who would kill to get them——or find out where they are."

"Maybe the police should know that."

Belli finished his absinthe and set the small glass down. "Helen and I share a deep friendship. She's also my client. I've advised her not to see you, not to answer any of your questions. Unfortunately, she's of a different mind. She's a more compassionate creature than I."

She shifted to face me directly. "I was acquainted with your late wife, Mr. Damon. She came to dine here on a number of occasions."

"With Terrence Collier, I assume."

She dropped her eyes. "Yes, with the late Mr. Collier."

Belli peered at me through his thick lenses. "You know of their relationship, then."

"Only recently," I said.

"Mr. Belli has filled me in on certain details of your wife's death that I find troubling," Helen Hop-Yik said. "I'm especially concerned that the pearls might in some way be connected to her murder."

I sat forward in the chair. "Why would you think that?"

"Your wife must have meant a great deal to you, Mr. Damon, for you to go to such lengths seeking answers to your questions."

"She was everything to me."

"I also once lost everything, including all of those closest to me." The Princess spoke less with self-pity than with carefully modulated anger. "Millions are being slaughtered under Mao. The world will know that one day."

"Helen's descended from Chinese royalty," Belli explained. "Her family was deposed and detained during Mao Tse-tung's Great Revolution. She was forced to flee mainland China for her life. The rest of her family was not so lucky."

He went on to explain that the only possession of value she was able to take with her were six gems handed down from her ancestors. They were incredibly rare and precious pearls, he said, some twenty to thirty millimeters large, brilliant orange in color. They had come not from oysters, he explained, but from the *Melo melo,* a large snail of the South China Sea with its own lustrous orange shell.

"An otherworldly creature," Belli said, "limited in number, that produces pearls unlike any you've ever imagined."

Helen Hop-Yik picked up the story. "I smuggled the six pearls out, by carrying them where only a woman could hide them, a place so private no Chinese man, not even a Red Guard, would dare search. I came to America with nothing but my life, the clothes on my back, and the pearls." She reached into a pocket of her gown and brought out what looked like an oversized marble, luminous orange and slightly larger than a robin's egg. "I kept only one. The largest and most vivid in color. This I will never sell. It belongs here in Chinatown. The five others I sold seven years ago to Terrence Collier. With the money he gave me, I financed my business, my future."

At the time of the sale, she added, Collier already owned a quartet of the greatest gems in the world: the finest diamond, emerald, sapphire, and ruby. "He showed them to me right here in this room with inordinate pride. They were magnificent beyond description. He must have spent a great part of his fortune to acquire them."

"He'd heard about your pearls?"

She nodded. "He wanted them to complete his prized collection. Mr. Belli arranged a meeting between us. When I showed Mr. Collier the pearls, his eyes grew wide and he literally trembled, he wanted them so badly. With Mr. Belli's help, a sale was arranged. The sum was significant. I was most fortunate."

"How Collier came up with the cash so fast, I have no idea," Belli said. "I insisted that the transaction be sub-rosa, since the pearls were smuggled into this country illegally. No paper was exchanged, no record of any kind. It was strictly cash for the pearls, and that was the end of my client's contact with Mr. Collier."

Helen Hop-Yik slipped the magnificent pearl back into her pocket.

"I'm still not clear why you're being so open with me," I said.

"Believe me," Belli said, "I advised her otherwise."

"No one should have to dwell in sorrow for a lifetime, Mr. Damon. I've started a new life here. You must start over as well. If what I've revealed helps you accomplish that, then perhaps some good will come of all this."

"You're trusting that I'll be discreet."

She smiled demurely. "Should anyone come questioning me about the source of Mr. Collier's pearls, I'm afraid my English would suffer a sudden relapse."

"There are always translators."

"The pearls are part of Chinese lore. Maybe they existed. Maybe they are nothing more than one of our superstitious legends." Again the smile, broader this time. "We're such an inscrutable people, aren't we?" She stood, shaking my hand as I rose. "Good luck, Mr. Damon. May you find the answers you seek and the peace you deserve." With a fond glance at Belli, she departed as quietly as she'd come.

Belli walked me down to the first floor to see me out, letting me know that he intended to linger awhile with his former paramour. He offered his car and driver for the trip back to the Fairmont. I thanked him for his help and told him I'd catch a cab.

IT was after two as I stepped out to Grant Avenue, where most of the neon had gone dark and the fog had grown thick, wrapping itself around everything in Chinatown, masking its color, creating odd and eerie shapes. If there were any taxicabs here at this hour, I couldn't see them. I had no desire to test my legs on the steep climb up to Nob Hill, so I turned in the direction of North Beach and its late-night bars and strip joints, figuring I'd run into a cab down that way.

I hadn't covered a block when I heard heavy footsteps behind me. I stopped to look, but saw only a bank of mist and the fuzzy glow of lamplights that grew dimmer in the distance until the fog gobbled them up. I started walking again. The footsteps behind me quickened. So did mine.

I turned onto a side street, strode half the block, stopped, listened. The footsteps turned, coming after me. I broke into a trot, reached the end of the narrow street, rounded the corner, dashed down another street and across. I had no sense now of exactly where I was. Whoever was after me kept coming.

I started running, fueled by fear and adrenaline. When my long legs had put some distance between us, I ducked into the vestibule of a grocery store, pressing myself back into the shadows. Two dark eyes—inches from my face—gave me a bad start until I realized I was staring into the face of a trussed duck, dried and hanging alongside several others. Half a minute later, I heard rapid footsteps that diminished as they got closer to my hiding place. Moments after that, mingled with the slowing footfalls, came the rasp of someone badly out of breath. I held mine.

A figure in a dark topcoat passed, close enough for me to see a hand gripping a small, heavy gun. I couldn't make out the face, just a hat pulled low and a collar turned up, the features further obscured by fog and darkness.

I waited as the tense seconds passed, afraid to exhale, afraid to move. The footsteps and gasping grew fainter and then were gone. I stuck my head out, saw that I was alone, then ran the other direction, back the way I'd come. I sprinted through fog-shrouded streets, making turns on gut instinct, hoping they'd put more distance between me and whoever was after me. I was lost in fog now, plunging blindly on, fearful that at any moment I might turn a corner and run straight into the unknown.

Suddenly, I heard high-pitched laughter. Then I saw lights. After that, human shapes took form along a sidewalk.

As I got closer, I recognized the shapes as female—elaborate hair and makeup, extravagant gowns and high heels, breasts padded to extreme proportions. The sign on the nearby club spelled out Finnochio's in bright lights that burned through the mist, and a sandwich board at the top of the steps announced the evening lineup: Kitty Katz, Marilyn Monrovia, Sophie Loren, Miss Valentine, Barbra Strident. *Streisand's barely been discovered,* I thought, *and already the girl's being impersonated.* I'd ended up in North Beach, in front of one of the most famous drag clubs on earth, where the audience was usually more tourist than local, more hetero than homo. When the performers out front spotted me, they showered me with compliments, catcalls, and lurid proposals, and one or two blew kisses. I'd never been so happy to run into a bunch of irrepressible drag queens.

I flagged down a cruising cab, jumped in, made a hasty escape. It wasn't the gaggle of transvestites that worried me. It was the stranger with the heavy footsteps and the handgun, whose intentions struck me as considerably less proper.

Chapter 19

VIVIAN COLLIER CUT a haughty path toward our table at Alioto's on the pier, tapping her diamond-encrusted wristwatch while snapping at the maitre d' about having waited a full two minutes before being attended to.

"Vivian's the only person I know," Charlene said, "who's able to give narcissism a bad name."

We pushed back our chairs and stood, listening to the last of the tongue-lashing borne by the maitre d' in patient silence.

Charlene propped up a false smile. "Vivian, darling, so glad you could join us. We haven't lunched together since—well, never, actually. Take my seat, dear. The view's so much better."

Charlene offered her chair directly facing the window and moved around the table to sit next to me. She gave the waiter a prearranged signal, and he stepped forward to fill Vivian's wine glass with chilled pinot grigio.

"Drink up," Charlene said, as the waiter handed out the menus. "As they say, there's more where that came from."

We'd reserved a table overlooking the harbor, where fishermen were washing down their boats following the morning's catch. The Franciscan had a better view and Pompei's Grotto a reputation for the freshest crab and shrimp, but Alioto's had the distinction of being the first building on the wharf. It had risen from a simple fish stall in 1925 to its present two stories, operated by a Sicilian immigrant family that had become an important force in real estate and city politics. Charlene especially liked the place because after the premature death of Nunzio Alioto in 1933, his widow, Rose, had built the restaurant to its position of prominence. Without Rose, Charlene liked to remind us, the Aliotos might still be peddling steamed crab to sailors and tourists from Stall #8.

"Lunch is on me," Charlene said straightaway, for Vivian's benefit. "Not that you couldn't afford it with the settlement you got from the ex."

Vivian looked up slyly from her menu. "I did do rather well, didn't I?"

"You showed him, honey."

"Put him through the wringer!"

"Took him to the cleaners!"

"Ran him through the car wash!"

The two ladies laughed triumphantly, while Charlene picked up a menu and Vivian sloshed down more wine.

"Everything but the pearls, of course," Charlene said, keeping her eyes on the list of entrees. I'd filled her in on what I'd learned from Helen Hop-Yik—swearing her to secrecy—though I hadn't told her about being pursued through the foggy streets of Chinatown by the stranger in the dark coat.

Vivian sneaked an uneasy glance at me before settling her eyes on Charlene. "How did you know about the pearls?"

"Everyone knows about the pearls," Charlene said casually, without looking up. "I'm ordering the cioppino. It may just be shellfish stew to your average tourist, but it was Rose Alioto's specialty." She glanced up at us. "Did I ever tell you that Rose was the first woman to work on the wharf?"

"What do you mean, *everyone*?" Vivian demanded.

"I don't know anyone who doesn't know about the pearls," Charlene said. She reached over, patting Vivian's hand sympathetically. "We try not to speak of it in front of you, Viv. No sense in rubbing salt into the wound."

Vivian's eyes were as wide as healthy scallops. "People *talk* about it?"

"You can't blame them. The pearls are so rare, and no one seems to know how Terrence acquired them."

Vivian shot me another concerned glance, ducked her head, lowered her voice to a whisper. "*Philip* knows?"

"Philip? He was among the first to hear about them."

"Back in New York," I said. "Talk of the town."

Vivian slapped her menu down with alarm. "People are talking about the pearls coast to coast?"

"You know how good gossip travels," Charlene said.

Vivian grabbed the bottle of pinot grigio, poured herself another glass, gulped half of it down. "He had to have *everything*. He couldn't just look at something and appreciate it. He had to possess it, make it exclusively his."

"Including all those gems," I suggested. "The diamond, sapphire, emerald, and ruby."

"His damned quartet," Vivian said. "Then he got wind of the Chinese pearls, and a quartet wasn't enough. He had to have a quintet."

"I've known musicians who felt that way. It's ruined some fine groups."

"Exactly! The pearls proved to be his undoing. He got just what he deserved."

"But that's not the way we heard it at all," Charlene said, lying with shameless aplomb. "Everyone says Terrence kept the pearls for himself, safe from the divorce settlement. That he managed to dupe you, and cheat you out of his most prized asset."

"*That's* what people are saying?" Vivian looked mortified. "But that's all wrong—I got everything I wanted. Terrence was livid!"

The waiter appeared and took our orders: cioppino for Charlene, lobster thermador for Vivian—since Charlene was paying—and for me, fresh wavalone, a California mollusk with the flavor of abalone, exclusive to the wharf.

"But enough about those silly pearls," Charlene said, as the waiter gathered our menus and departed. "Have you tasted the scallopini bolognese at Oreste's? Between you and me, I think it's the best Italian restaurant in the city."

"Who cares about scallopini?" Vivian wailed. "People have the impression that prick got the best of me!"

"We've upset you." Charlene's face puckered into a frown. "It's all my fault."

"I suppose it's better that I know." Vivian fought back tears. "Still, it's an absolute disaster."

Charlene sat up resolutely. "Then we've got to do something." She handed Vivian a tissue. "We've got to right a terrible wrong."

Vivian dabbed at her eyes. "But *how?*"

"Tell us exactly what happened, dear. We'll get the word out, set the record straight."

"I'll certainly do my part," I said.

"You two would really do that for me?"

Charlene cocked her head, looking cherubic. "What are friends for, Viv?"

Vivian glanced my way. "Forgive me, Philip, for what I'm about to say."

"If it's the affair that concerns you, Vivian, I know all about it."

"Terrence and Diana?"

I nodded.

"Oh." Vivian looked deflated, but quickly perked up. "Well, then I can speak with complete candor."

"Please do," Charlene said, signaling the waiter for more wine.

As she began her story, Vivian judiciously watched the level rise in her wine glass. "Diana was quite taken with Terrence, at least in the beginning. I must admit, for all his faults, he had a certain way with women. And, of course, he was inordinately wealthy." The waiter stopped pouring an inch from the rim; Vivian tapped the glass with her spoon until he topped it off. "Diana was just out of college, barely more than a girl. At the same time, Terrence became utterly infatuated with her. Being the cad that he was, Terrence promised Diana he'd divorce me and make her an honorable woman. In truth, like so many two-timing lotharios, he never intended to divorce me at all. He had far too much to lose. You see, Terrence wanted to have it both ways—to keep Diana on a string, for himself, but also to placate me just enough to avoid a split and the loss of half our community property under California law. But Diana was more strong-willed than he'd bargained for. She threatened to leave him, and Terrence made the fateful decision to leave the pearls in her keeping."

I leaned across the table, stunned. "He gave Diana the pearls?"

"You hadn't heard that part?"

"No," Charlene answered for both of us, sounding equally surprised.

"They weren't intended as a gift." Vivian's words began to slur as her tongue loosened. "Terrence considered them a loan, a bauble she was allowed to admire for a time but never own. One of his typical stunts, a grand gesture to impress her, to keep her under his spell. The pearls were meant to remind her of his wealth, of all the beautiful things he could give her if she remained loyal. But Diana was too smart for that. She grew tired of his false promises and gave him an ultimatum. Terrence reacted angrily—even slapped her around once or twice."

I felt my guts churn. "The bastard," I said, through clenched teeth.

"So Diana broke off the affair. Terrence demanded the pearls back, but she refused to give them up. She told him they were the price he had to pay for the years he'd stolen from her and the violence he'd committed."

"Good for her," Charlene said.

Vivian beamed grandly. "And there wasn't a damn thing Terrence could do about it! Apparently, he'd obtained the pearls illegally, so he was never able to declare or insure them. In effect, the pearls didn't exist, so there was no crime to report. Even if Terrence had gone to the police, Diana need only swear she'd never seen them."

"But how did you learn all this?" Charlene asked.

"For years, I'd been building up an arsenal in preparation for a divorce." Vivian drained her glass and raised it for another refill. "I'd hired a private eye to keep Terrence under surveillance. I knew about the pearls, Diana, the other women Terrence had been with. We had photographs, dates, addresses, all of it. I'd made copies of all his business documents, including the cashier's checks he'd used to pay for his rare gems. He must have paid cash for the pearls, because there was no receipt. But I did find copies of his failed attempts to have them insured. Once, when Terrence was out of town on business with Jimmy Brannigan, I turned the house upside down and found the pearls, tucked away in the bottom of my husband's golf bag. I took photographs of them and had them officially appraised. This was just before Terrence left them in Diana's possession.

"When I filed for divorce in '59, Terrence told me Diana had the pearls but refused to return them. He begged me to understand, to let him off the hook financially. Naturally, I laughed in his face. He didn't dare bring Diana into it legally—there would have been a terrible scandal, and she knew too much about his wild spending habits. When he couldn't produce the pearls, the court assumed he was hiding some of his assets, as so many men do in these situations. The judge awarded me a very generous compensation. That's why I always tell my lady friends who are married to cads, which is most of them: Document, document, document!"

"By then," Charlene said, "Diana and Philip had married."

"Oh, yes! Terrence lost his marriage, half his fortune, his beautiful mistress, and his precious pearls. He was unspeakably miserable. It was fabulous!"

I gathered my courage and asked a question taking Vivian back two years.

"Is it possible your ex-husband was so upset with Diana and so covetous of the pearls that he'd commit murder to get them back?"

Vivian put her glass down, looking somber, if not quite sober. "The police from New York asked me the same question. But Terrence had an alibi, you see. He was with Jimmy Brannigan all that weekend in Jimmy's house out at Stinson Beach."

"Or so Brannigan claims."

"But it wasn't just Jimmy who swore Terrence was there. Jimmy's dowdy old housekeeper told the police the same thing."

"Gwendolyn Sparks," said Charlene, who never forgot a name. "I met her once, at that fund-raiser you had out at Jimmy's beach house. She didn't strike me as dowdy. I thought she was rather pleasant and on the attractive side."

"If you like your women large." Vivian rolled her eyes. "I suppose she has a certain charm—for someone who keeps house."

Our meals arrived not a moment too soon; the bottle of pinot grigio was empty, and Vivian was looking a bit green at the gills. I was still reeling from the news that the pearls had been in Diana's possession, and suggested that Vivian so inform Inspector Platt.

"But Philip, dear, Platt already knows all about the pearls. The whole thing was included in my confidential divorce settlement, which he got unsealed days ago as part of his investigation."

She lifted a morsel of lobster imperiously to her puckered lips.

"I don't care for Platt's uppity attitude," Vivian Collier said. "But he's rather smart, don't you think, for a colored man?"

Chapter 20

THAT NIGHT, WHILE nimble-footed couples swung along with the band to "Lullaby of Broadway," Lenore Ashley turned up at the Venetian Room.

It was toward the end of the second show, and a maitre d' escorted her to a table that had just become available, following the hasty departure of a couple engaged in a nasty argument. To say that I was pleased to see her would be a colossal understatement. She hadn't been out of my mind much, waking or sleeping, since our meeting over poetry and coffee in North Beach—though I must admit, my dreams were increasingly dark and troubled, even with Lenore Ashley in them.

As she crossed the room, she looked willowy and striking in an amethyst satin cocktail dress and three-inch heels, with a string of silver pearls at her throat; her golden hair was twisted into a bun in back, secured by a silver clasp. All that cool elegance brought to mind Grace Kelly, suggesting a complexity beneath the lovely surface that only deepened the beauty. As she took her seat, her eyes met mine with a directness that both baffled and excited me. I couldn't figure her out—much as I'd never quite figured out Diana—which made her all the more mysterious and tempting.

A group of foreign dignitaries was in attendance, and one sent over a request for Gloria Velez to sing "Blue Moon," unaware, obviously, that the song had been off my playlist since Diana's death. Gloria substituted "As Time Goes By"—the perennial audience favorite, due to the popularity of *Casablanca*—which she sang passably but halfheartedly, causing me some concern. When she finished, the orchestra took a short break.

I ordered a drink and joined Lenore at her table, where she sipped a champagne cocktail.

"I didn't expect to see you again so soon," I said. "If at all."

She twisted her string of pearls absentmindedly, as if it was a plaything. "I thought it would be interesting to hear your music again, in a different setting. How someone plays reveals so much, don't you think?"

"And what have you learned so far?"

"You like to keep things light, moving. You don't like to settle too long or delve too deep."

"Is that a problem between us?"

"If it is," she said, her eyes mischievous, "it's not insurmountable."

"So what are you doing later?"

"I thought I might catch some jazz. You game?"

"You seem determined to broaden my experience."

"It works both ways, doesn't it?"

"If both parties are willing."

She smiled, so warmly it melted away any reservations I had about her. "Is that a yes, Mr. Damon?"

"It's Philip, remember?"

AFTER the show, we were on the hunt for good jazz. It wasn't much of a challenge, because San Francisco was loaded with hot clubs—the Blackhawk, Sugar Hill, the Jazz Workshop, maybe a dozen more. Lenore Ashley thought we should try Jimbo's Bop City, which is where we ended up.

We arrived by cab just as a fascinating new rock group named Jefferson Airplane was finishing up. The group was opening for Dizzy Gillespie's band—one of those odd pairings that was happening more and more in The City, as the distinction between different styles and kinds of music blurred. The place was packed, so thick with smoke you could barely see the bottles behind the bar. Lots of white kids, of course, but also some interesting people you wouldn't run into at most clubs. The bright young comic Bill Cosby was there, fresh from opening for the Kingston Trio at the Hungry i. Cosby was bumping shoulders with another young comic, Woody Allen, who sometimes sat in on clarinet with Turk Murphy's local band. Herb Caen was down front, table-hopping and trolling for an item. Finally, he cornered a lanky young TV actor named Clint Eastwood, a true jazz buff and a pretty good pianist, who was just back from Europe after filming his first Italian western. Mose Allison, Gerry Mulligan, Nina Simone—they all dropped in that night after playing their own gigs at other clubs.

Before long, Diz took the stage with his sidemen, looking

colorful in his trademark beret, plaid jacket, flowered shirt, and a soul patch sprouting from just beneath his lower lip. When he played, his cheeks expanded like grapefruits about to burst. Dizzy was certainly the greatest trumpet player since Louis Armstrong, and he seemed incapable of playing anything that was less than astonishing; he'd even created a totally unique trumpet—the bell bent at a 45-degree angle pointing upward. He told me once that he thought he could project his sound over a larger area with his instrument angled that way. Others, though, figured it was just another gimmick to get attention—just typical Diz.

Lenore and I stayed at Jimbo's into the wee small hours, when things were really jumping and Dizzy was playing his head off. Suddenly, he called me up to sit in on piano. Until that moment, Lenore had no idea that Diz and I went back a few years, to some of the Big Apple's choicest jazz clubs that I used to haunt with pals during forays that lasted until the crack of dawn. While she looked on, astonished, I sat in with the band for the next half-hour, even playing a few solos that Diz seemed to dig. As always, when I was performing with a bunch of really good musicians—and when we were really cooking—my knees went weak and the group fused into one. Moments like that became a kind of out-of-body experience—we'd lose all sense of our selves and our surroundings, plunging deeper into the music and the collective interaction of the group. For me, it was the essence of the musical life, the reason I loved playing so much.

When we finally stopped, Diz anointed me with a big, wet kiss. I headed back toward the bar, where Lenore was applauding with the rest of the crowd while shaking her head in disbelief. She handed me a fresh drink as I squeezed in next to her. "That was really something," she said. "There's a lot more to you than I gave you credit for." Her eyes were curious, probing. "So how do you keep it all so well hidden?"

"Practice." Our eyes met and held, and I found the courage to reach over and take her hand in mine. To my happy surprise, she let it stay there.

FROM the stage, Dizzy announced that "a local cat" was going to blow with the band on alto sax, while Diz gave his lips a rest. Near the back of the room, a figure stepped from the smoky darkness, carrying a battered saxophone case in one hand and his hat in the other.

Hercules Platt.

While Diz joined us at the bar, the band started playing and Platt took up his instrument. Within seconds he'd melded with the group, playing far more skillfully than I would ever have expected. After a melancholy rendition of " 'Round Midnight," Thelonius Monk's great ballad, the musicians went into "Cherokee" at breakneck speed. Platt not only managed to keep up, his playing was close to superb. I introduced Diz to Lenore, bought him a drink, and asked him if he knew the sax player was a cop.

"Sure, I know he's fuzz," Diz said. "Got my horn snatched a few years ago when we was in town for a gig, down where we shouldn't have been, buying some tea. Platt was a uniform in those days, helped me get my horn back in time for my show. I offered the cat some bread but he turned me down. Very cool, Mr. Hercules Platt."

"But how did he end up sitting in with the guys?"

"Somebody tips me he's been blowing an ax since he was a kid back in Chicago. Now he sits in every time we come to town." We listened to Platt play for a minute or two. Diz laughed. "He's no Coleman Hawkins, but he ain't half bad, either."

"No, he's not." I listened to Platt run through his notes with finesse, improvising and finding the groove. "Not half bad at all."

I was in the restroom, standing at the long urinal, when Platt appeared beside me and unzipped. We stood relieving ourselves in silence for half a minute before I spoke.

"You're too much," I said, keeping my eyes on the wall in front of me. "You played really great."

"I get by."

"Must be tough to hang out in a club like this and not hit the sauce."

"Tougher home alone at night." He cut me a glance as he zipped up. "Not that it's any of your damn business."

We washed up at the sink, side by side.

"Maybe I should try a subject that *is* my business. From what I hear, you've figured out a few things about some pearls that once belonged to Terrence Collier."

"Far as I can tell, they still belong to the man, or at least to his estate. Seems they've gone missing."

"Given Diana's involvement, don't you think I have a right to be informed?"

"Sounds like you are informed, Damon."

"I had to find out the hard way, on my own."

Platt shut off the water, dried his hands on a roller linen towel. "It's not my responsibility to give you updates, Damon. If I'm not mistaken, it works the other way around. Anyway, I'm not convinced you didn't know about the pearls all along." Platt sniffed the air, then hollered at the door of a locked stall: "Whoever's smoking reefer in here, put it out until I leave." A toilet was hastily flushed.

"The New York police went through everything of Diana's after she was murdered. Even her safety deposit box. No pearls, Platt."

He faced the mirror, fussing with his hair. "Those pearls could have been tucked away in any number of places."

"Maybe Collier took the pearls that night, after killing Diana."

A black man wearing a felt fedora and gold chains entered the restroom and took a position at the urinal, his back to us. Platt lowered his voice. "The New York dicks investigated Collier's whereabouts that night. He and James Brannigan were holed up in Brannigan's weekend place at Stinson Beach, going over the books. Brannigan's housekeeper saw Collier within hours of Diana's death, when he asked her to make some sandwiches and coffee so they could work late."

"A woman named Gwendolyn Sparks. I heard."

"There's no way Collier could have gotten to New York and back and had his alibi stand up like that. Not even if he'd jumped in his private jet and broken the sound barrier. We checked with Collier's pilot. Neither Collier nor Brannigan booked a flight that weekend. And there's no record either one of them flew commercial."

"Maybe Brannigan's covering for Collier and paying off his housekeeper to do the same."

"Maybe." Platt went to work relooping and cinching his

necktie. "And maybe Gloria Velez is doing likewise for you."

I fought to keep the anger from my voice. "I'd never hurt Diana, not for anything."

"Let's try one possible scenario." Platt talked while cleaning up the knot. "You learned of your wife's affair with Collier, which set you in a rage. She swore it was long over, that there was nothing between them. Then you found out she still had the pearls—pearls *he'd* given her, which she'd been keeping secret from you. It flipped your switch, you lost control, she ended up dead."

"I already told you, Platt—I didn't find out about their affair until a few days ago."

Hercules Platt's eyes shifted until they found mine in the mirror.

"Then where are the pearls, Damon? Suppose you tell me that."

Chapter 21

TELLING HERCULES PLATT about the stranger who'd chased me through the streets of Chinatown would have been the prudent thing to do. But our conversation at Jimbo's Bop City so soured me on the man I wanted nothing to do with him, certainly not to confide in him just then. What I wanted and needed that night was some peace and comfort, the kind I hadn't known for a long time.

Lenore Ashley and I kissed for the first time in the back of a taxi, on our way to a party up on Russian Hill. Usually, I gravitated to a party like a bee to honey. But as we pulled up out front, I asked Lenore if we could skip it.

"You don't think you'd fit in with a bunch of poets drinking cheap wine?" she asked.

"It's not that. Half my pals in New York are writers."

"Why, then?"

"I'd rather be alone with you."

A moment later, we were cruising down a Russian Hill street so steep it took my breath away. In the backseat, in the shadows, I felt Lenore's hand on my leg, inching toward my thigh. I asked the driver to step on it.

IT was half past four when the cab dumped us just off Stanyan Street, which bordered the east end of Golden Gate Park. A thin fog was settling around the dilapidated Victorians packed tightly together in the run-down neighborhood known as Haight-Ashbury. The area had been a fancy resort that survived the 1906 fire and thrived, only to fall on hard times during the Great Depression. Now the beats were moving in, Lenore said, attracted by the low rents, the funky atmosphere, and the proximity to the long, rambling park with its open spaces, lovely gardens, and small lakes.

As the cab disappeared in the fog, we stumbled together, laughing and kissing, along a walkway of broken brick that led to a one-bedroom cottage well concealed from the street. Lenore let us in without a key, flipping on the light.

"So this is your pad," I said, looking around. "Not exactly the Fairmont, is it?"

"The Fairmont was a fantasy. This is the real thing. For me, anyway."

It was the kind of place landlords call "charming, with character" in their rental ads—buckling floors, drafty windows, peeling paint. The furnishings in the tiny living room were Early Salvation Army: for sitting, two mattresses on the floor, covered with old Army blankets and colorful big pillows pushed up against the walls; for a table, a hatch cover on concrete blocks; bricks supporting unfinished pine boards for book shelves; a moth-eaten Persian carpet covering half the floor; empty wine bottles stuffed with dry flowers. On one wall was a poster of Che Guevara, looking rebellious but properly photogenic in a beard and beret. The only nod to luxury in the room was a new Zenith high-fidelity stereo system, complete with four speakers and AM/FM radio. The price tag was still attached: $287.00.

"That was the first thing I acquired when Terrence asked me what I wanted." Lenore struck a match and began lighting candles. "I'd been looking at it for a while, but it was two dollars a week, which was beyond my budget. Naturally, he bought it for me with cash, right out of his pocket."

"Naturally," I said.

She put a finger to my lips. "Let's not judge, Philip. Let's forget everything outside this cottage for a while, and just enjoy each other."

She flipped off the lights, leaving us in the flickering glow of the candles, and we kissed again. I was torn between hunger and tenderness, wild for her but protective at the same time, still confused because Diana's ghost always hovered around her, sharing the same space. She may have sensed my unease, because she pulled away, asking if I ever smoked marijuana.

"Now and then."

"How about now?"

"Sure."

She found her stash and papers and started rolling a joint, while I looked around the house, flipping light switches on and off. A hallway led to a bathroom—rusting tub, no shower—and a bedroom at the end that featured a frayed poster from an old production of *Rhinoceros* at the ACT, with Lenore's name third in the billing. As I came back through, she asked me if I wanted a glass of wine, which was all she had.

"Not on top of all that Scotch, thanks." I stuck my head in the kitchen: rickety table, three chairs, an old gas stove, but no Frigidaire—just an old-fashioned ice box, the kind that needed to be replenished every week or two with a new block of ice. I switched off the light, went back to the living room, knelt down to look through her record collection.

"Collier couldn't afford an electric fridge?"

She smiled, twisting the end of the joint to finish it off. "That was next on my list."

I flipped through a stack of old 45s on a shelf until I realized what I was seeing: two or three dozen recordings of the same song, all by different artists—Sinatra, Sarah Vaughan, Billie Holiday, Nat King Cole, Betty Carter, Jo Stafford, Mabel Mercer, Kitty Kallen, Rosemary Clooney, Georgia Gibbs, all the greats. I felt a shiver run along my spine.

"You must have every version of 'Blue Moon' ever recorded."

Lenore looked over anxiously, her voice tight. "Terrence gave me those. He liked to play them when—when we were together."

"It was Diana's favorite song."

"I know. I read the article in the *Chron*." She came and stood over me, running her fingers through my hair. "I brought them over from the hotel a few days ago when I moved out." She knelt beside me, touched my face. "Come away from here, Philip. I didn't mean for you to see them."

"Why did you keep them?"

She looked at the old discs. "This may sound strange, but I feel as if I've come to know Diana—that part of her has become part of me." She pulled out one of the singles, a recording by Peggy Lee. "Maybe you'd like me to play it now, Philip. Is that what you want? To think of Diana when we're making love?"

"No." I shook my head. "I never want to hear that song again. It's you I want to be with."

She stretched out a hand. I accepted it, rising to join her, wanting to trust her, not sure why I didn't. She lit the joint, sucking on it until she had it burning, then passed it to me. After we'd exchanged a few tokes, pulling down and holding the smoke, she put an LP on the turntable. A moment later, I heard the sweet horn of Miles Davis as he played "So What," the first cut on side 1 of *Kind of Blue*. I began to relax as we finished the joint, feeling the high and grinning like a Cheshire cat, while all the tension melted away. She took my hand again, led me to a mattress, arranged some pillows, pulled me down beside her. I warned her about the bruises on my upper back, from the cupping George Chang had administered. She'd seen similar marks many times on Terrence Collier, she said, and the sight of them no longer bothered her. Then she drew me into what felt like a wonderful dream—the mellow jazz, the flickering light, the fine high, the rapturous sensation of smelling her, touching her, tasting her. The truth was, though, it was almost like being with Diana again, like making love to her one more time. Making love to Diana, making love to Lenore—it all blurred until it didn't matter anymore and the past dissolved into the present. It was like that tune by Frank Loesser and Jimmy McHugh, "Let's Get Lost," the dreamy way Chet Baker had recorded it back in '55.

Lenore Ashley and I got lost that night, lost in each other.

*   *   *

AFTERWARD, she got up and turned the record over, then lay down beside me again, her head on my bare chest, snuggling close. I don't think I'd ever felt so tranquil.

A vision came into my head of Lenore and me together, living in a house with a garden by the sea, raising a couple of kids, just the way Diana and I had planned to do. I didn't speak my vision aloud—it was too fanciful, too unrealistic— yet I didn't want to let go of it, either, it was so comforting. When Lenore fell asleep, I kissed her, covered her with a throw, took my clothes into the kitchen, and dressed quietly.

Dawn was insinuating itself through the fog outside, giving me just enough light from the kitchen window to see. I washed my face at the sink, dried myself with a paper towel from a roll on the kitchen table. Also on the table was a telephone; next to it, a notepad with a scribbled message, which I glanced at. There, in Lenore's handwriting, was Jimmy Brannigan's name, with a phone number beneath it. When I saw it, something inside me collapsed, leaving a void filled by confusion and suspicion. Almost as quickly came a troubling hunch. I peeked into the living room, saw that Lenore was still sleeping, then stepped back into the kitchen. I began opening drawers and cupboards and rummaging through them as quietly as possible. When I was done, I checked the area around the icebox until my search was complete. It struck me as odd that in a kitchen equipped only with a pre–Depression icebox there was no ice pick to be found.

I took a final look at Lenore Ashley asleep where we'd made love, where I'd found such pleasure and peace, and a lonely man's foolish vision of an impossible future.

As I left, I shut the door soundlessly, careful not to wake her.

STANYAN Street was deserted except for an old Dodge rattling by while the driver tossed copies of the morning *Chronicle* onto front steps littered with fallen leaves.

The Dodge rounded the corner onto Haight Street. I followed, turning up my collar against the damp, listening to the thud of newspapers grow fainter, moving in the direction of Haight and Ashbury, where I hoped to find a cab.

Chapter 22

IN THE MORNING, to buoy my flagging spirits, Charlene took me for breakfast to the Buena Vista Café on Beach Street.

She picked me up at ten in her 1959 Aston Martin coupe—cherry red hardtop, the DB 2/4 Mk III model—and got us down to Beach by way of crooked Lombard Street. We descended the snaking curves of the famously steep hill gazing across the bay at Alcatraz Island, while I filled her in on the events of the previous two nights. Later, over scrambled eggs and home fries, she chided me for getting involved with Lenore Ashley, scolded me for not telling Hercules Platt about the stranger who'd chased me through Chinatown, and suggested I was being too sensitive about Platt and the way he liked to ratchet up the pressure.

"I've seen detectives in the 87th Precinct do that," she

drawled. "They like to keep their suspects off balance, hoping the culprit will slip up."

"This isn't a mystery novel, Charlene. This is real life. And I'm fed up with Platt's insinuations and insults."

"I've discovered something that may bring Inspector Platt around to our side," she said. "He's coming to the hotel at four, when you'll see for yourself what I've dug up. In the meantime, we've got a few hours to kill."

By the time we'd finished our breakfast with a cup of the Buena Vista's bracing Irish coffee, I was feeling better, but only slightly.

"I won't have a Gloomy Gus on my hands," Charlene said. She suggested a visit to the Palace of Fine Arts in the Marina district, then a stop at the Garden Court for lunch. "You can't do better than lunch at the Palace. The grandest dining room and the best pastry chef in San Francisco."

I told her I wasn't really in the mood for nut cupcakes. She delivered a put-upon sigh. "What then, sweetie?"

"Stinson Beach," I said.

ACROSS the Golden Gate Bridge, Charlene left Highway 101 and picked up Highway 1 out to the coast, before turning the Aston Martin north up through the Muir Woods. As we cruised along, hugging the gray Pacific, I peppered her with questions about James Brannigan.

In short order, I learned that he and his wife, Elise, had raised six children, all grown, and now had a passel of grandchildren. Brannigan kept a house in the staid Parkside district, not far from the zoo, and one out here in Marin County at remote Stinson Beach. He was a workaholic, essentially running the business he'd shared with Terrence Collier; Collier had used some of his wealth to finance it at the outset, but Brannigan was the brains, a Stanford MBA who watched the investments like a hawk.

"Then he's not as simple as he appears," I said.

"Big Jimmy Brannigan? God, no. A bit rough around the edges, but when it comes to business, he's focused like Dr. Salk's microscope."

"And where does Brannigan's wife fit into all this?"

"Elise? In the loony bin, poor woman."

"I'd heard him mention that she wasn't well, but—"

"Institutionalized for years." Charlene slowed as a deer crossed the road into the woods. "From what I hear, she just couldn't take the pressure of the society life Jimmy wanted so badly. It's a lot of work, all those luncheons and benefits."

I laughed, scoffing.

"Honey," she drawled, "if I didn't come from such strong Texas stock, I would have flipped my wig years ago. The right hair, the right clothes, the right people, the right compliments, the right causes. Always flashing your ivories when you'd like to tell some of those dais divas to stuff it. Don't get me wrong, darlin', I'm proud of the money we raise and all the good work we do. And I've made some wonderful friends. But there are times when the egos and the preening can drive a sane person to the brink."

"Which is apparently what happened to Mrs. Brannigan."

"They married while they were still in college. She was pregnant when he got his diploma. From what I hear, she just wanted to stay at home and concentrate on her family. But Jimmy was a slave to his work, and obsessed with getting his name and picture on the society pages. Trying to raise six kids and play the society wife was too much for Elise. She finally snapped, and hasn't been seen for years."

"They never divorced?"

"Strict Catholics." Charlene pointed up the road. "That's the Brannigan place, with all that driftwood out front."

We pulled over alongside the road about a quarter of a mile south of the Brannigan house. It was an expansive but unpretentious Cape Cod, with an open view of the Pacific Ocean out front and the mountains of Mount Tamalpais State Park rising behind. The day had grown overcast and windy, and whitecaps laced the choppy gray water. The beach was largely flat, littered with driftwood and stones; along the water, a couple walked with a dog, but otherwise the shoreline was deserted.

"The water's cold here and the currents are strong," Charlene said. "And there are sharks out there. No facilities, either. You don't get the usual beach crowds at Stinson."

"Feels like Maine. Remote, windswept, beautiful in a bleak kind of way."

"I was out here once or twice at fund-raising functions. Diana came with me once, one Labor Day. Jimmy's housekeeper may remember me, if he still has her on. She was a real workhorse, that one. Kept the canapés coming, I can tell you."

I wasn't sure what I expected to find out this way, but I wanted to look around just the same. We hatched a plan, and minutes later we were crossing Brannigan's motor court, where a vintage Jaguar hardtop was parked.

"There's a fine old prewar relic," Charlene said, angling over to inspect the car. "A '39, if I'm not mistaken." She put her fingers to the long, narrow hood. "Still warm. Someone's home."

We mounted steps at the front of the two-story house and I rang the bell. A well-groomed woman about Charlene's age came to the door. She was of medium height but quite stout, with a pleasant face framed by soft curls tinted blond and small gold earrings for accent. She wore a long-sleeved floral print dress that looked like it might have come from a good department store. A frilly apron hugged her thick waist.

"Gwendolyn," Charlene said. "I'm Mrs. Statz, a friend of Mr. Brannigan's."

"Of course—so nice to see you again, Mrs. Statz." The housekeeper spoke in a voice more cultured than I expected. "We don't get many visitors out this way." She glanced apologetically at the oven mitts on her hands. "I saw you from the kitchen window—I've been baking all morning. I'm afraid Mr. Brannigan's out, visiting the grandchildren. I expect him back this evening."

"We were on our way to the Audubon preserve when my car stalled," Charlene said. "I was wondering if I might use the phone."

"Of course, Mrs. Statz. Please, come in."

Charlene introduced me. When Gwendolyn Sparks heard my name, her mild gray eyes widened with her smile. "Way back when, my beau and I listened to your father play. 'Loved Walked In,' that was our favorite. We danced to his music several times when he played the Waldorf Astoria in the late '30s. That vocalist of his, Lew Sherwood—I can hear him now, singing 'A Foggy Day.' That song always made me cry." She clasped her hands to her chest. "The slow tunes, that's what we really enjoyed. No one really dances cheek to cheek these days, do they?"

"They do when I play."

Gwendolyn Sparks positively beamed. "How I wish Bill could be here to meet you." Then, quickly, to both of us: "Bill was my fiancé."

"Did the two of you marry?" Charlene asked.

"Unfortunately, he was killed at Normandy."

"I'm sorry," Charlene said. "I lost a brother in the war."

"It's been almost twenty years," Gwendolyn said, "but it seems like only yesterday." She turned to me, lighting up again. "It's an honor to meet Archie Damon's boy. Though you're hardly a boy any longer, are you?" Then, to Charlene again: "You'd probably like to make that phone call, instead of listen to an old housekeeper chatter on."

She stepped back to let us in. Under the aroma of fresh-cut flowers, the odor of stale cigar smoke hung in the air.

"If I may," I said, "I'd like to use the toilet."

"Of course." Gwendolyn pointed me toward a hallway. "Just past the stairs, before you get to Mr. Brannigan's study."

"Is that where he and Mr. Collier did their work together?"

"Yes, that's the room." Gwendolyn seemed surprised by my question. "A terrible thing, what happened to Mr. Collier. I don't expect Mr. Brannigan will ever get over it."

She led Charlene away to a phone and I headed down the hall. I stopped at the bathroom, made sure I was unobserved, then moved quickly on to the next door, which I found unlocked.

JAMES Brannigan's study was filled with books and ledgers, a huge desk and several filing cabinets, and a sofa facing a coffee table stacked with copies of *Forbes* and the *Wall Street Journal.*

Behind the sofa, a large window framed by heavy curtains looked across the motor court and out to the road. One wall was filled with photographs of Jimmy Brannigan posed with noted political or social figures, smiling almost too grandly for the camera and pinching his cigar so tightly you could almost feel his anxiety. Another wall was covered with plaques and commendations attesting to his civic and philanthropic contributions. More photographs—Brannigan's children and grandchildren, I assumed—stood neatly arranged on a credenza. A woman I took to be his wife could be seen in some of the group family shots, looking drawn and a bit out of touch with the world; she was missing from the more recent photos, as the children grew older and the grandkids came into the pictures.

There was one other photograph in the room, a professional portrait, framed and sitting next to a humidor on the big desk. I picked it up and closely studied the round, pretty face of James Brannigan's housekeeper.

"Did you open the wrong door, Mr. Damon?"

I turned to find Gwendolyn Sparks standing in the doorway, still wearing her apron and oven mitts but looking less hospitable now.

"I suppose I did." I set the photograph back on the desk, glanced around. "This was the room where Brannigan and Collier were holed up two years ago, going over the books, on the night my wife was murdered?"

Gwendolyn nodded. "I tidy it up every day, just as I did that weekend."

"And you're positive Mr. Collier didn't slip out, long enough to jump a plane to New York and back."

Gwendolyn made the sign of the cross. "As God is my witness, Mr. Damon. He was right here that entire weekend."

I scrutinized her face and tone of voice for any hint of untruth, but found none; she seemed utterly sincere, her words above reproach. Then I studied the photograph on the desk again. "You've worked for Mr. Brannigan quite a few years, haven't you?"

"Sixteen, come February."

"It would be natural to develop a strong loyalty to an employer after all that time."

"Mr. Brannigan's a fine man. It's a privilege to work for him."

I glanced out the window at the Jaguar sitting on the brickwork.

"You're sure he's not here?"

"Actually, the car is mine."

"Yours? Really?"

Her voice grew resentful, almost chilly. "My fiancé arranged to have it sent over from Europe when he was on leave. It was to be our first automobile after we married."

"But he never came back."

"Only his dog tags, Mr. Damon."

"I'm surprised you never found another suitor. Such a personable and attractive woman as yourself."

"I was in my late thirties by then. The Depression had taken my best years, and the war got the rest. My prospects were hardly bright."

She pushed the door wider, stepping inside. "Mrs. Statz has made her phone call, Mr. Damon, and I have my baking to finish. Perhaps you should be going now."

*   *   *

FOR appearance's sake, Charlene got under the hood of the Aston Martin and detached one of the connections to the distributor. After that, we waited until a local garage mechanic showed up. He found the problem right off and was honest enough not to recommend a complete overhaul.

He wiped his hands on a rag, then closed the hood. "Just a loose distributor cable, ma'am."

"Silly me," Charlene said, and handed the mechanic a ten spot for his trouble.

She put the roadster into gear while he roared off in his tow truck. As we pulled away, I leaned over the seat for a last look at the Brannigan place. I could see a heavy figure framed in the window of his study, eyeing us as we headed south. It was Gwendolyn Sparks, right where she'd been since we'd left the house.

She remained watching until we were well down the road, then stretched her arms wide and pulled the curtains shut.

Chapter 23

AT MIDAFTERNOON, I poured a Scotch and called Gloria in her room, asking her to come down to the Tudor Suite. A few minutes later, she entered with her eyes on the glass in my hand.

"Kind of early to start drinking, isn't it, Philip?"

"Things have been piling up. I've got a lot on my mind."

"We've all got a lot on our minds, since last Sunday. Murder can do that."

"That's what I wanted to talk to you about."

She stopped in front of the fireplace, facing me with her arms folded across her chest. "So talk, Philip."

"I was hoping it might come from you." She stood silent and tough, waiting me out. Finally, I said, "Platt says you're not cooperating with him. Not even slightly."

"Screw Platt."

"That's not good enough, Gloria."

"I don't like him."

"Neither do I. But it's his investigation."

"Aren't we the good Boy Scout all of a sudden?"

"The sooner Platt can wrap it up, the sooner we can all get back to normal."

She laughed disparagingly. "Back to normal?" She began pacing the room. "How do you get back to normal, Philip, after someone you care about gets murdered? And then, two years later, you witness the murder of the man she was once involved with?"

"You didn't witness it, remember? You were out of the room. Or so you said."

Her dark eyes flashed. "What the hell does that mean?"

"It means I don't know who to trust anymore." I gulped some Scotch. "If I can't trust you——"

"I'm not involved in Collier's murder, Philip. Not even remotely."

"I wish I could believe that. I wish it was that easy."

"How long have we known each other, Philip? How long have I worked for you?"

"Five, six years."

"You saw how close Diana and I were, as improbable as our relationship was. Diana——upper-class, college-educated, sophisticated as hell. Me——Puerto Rican, working-class, out of Brooklyn."

"She never cared about that, Gloria."

"I know!" Her eyes welled up. "Don't you think I know?"

"Platt has questions to ask you."

"There's nothing I can tell him that would make a difference."

"But you're holding something back." Her eyes shifted,

the way they always seemed to when Platt put the hard questions to her. "Not just from Platt, but from me."

She turned again, showing me her back.

"You're wound up tighter than a tick, Gloria. I can hear it when you sing. You're doing your vocals on remote control, like you're somewhere else. Tell me I'm wrong, Gloria. Tell me I'm wrong, and then tell me why."

When she faced me, her eyes were moist, vulnerable. "You really don't know?"

"If I did, I wouldn't be asking."

She sighed and tilted her head up, her eyes roving the ceiling. "I wish we'd never made this trip, Phil. I wish we'd just stayed in New York and settled in again at the St. Regis for another long run at the Maisonette. There's too much of Diana in this city." Gloria swiped at a tear. "It's almost as if she's still alive—alive, yet beyond our reach."

"I know how much you cared for her. I know what her death meant to you."

Gloria smiled sadly. "Oh, Philip. You're so sweet. But you can be so naïve." She walked between the sofas and laid a hand on my shoulder. "There's so much you don't know, so damn much you have to learn. If you'd just settle for a while and look a little deeper. You surround yourself with people, Philip, but how well do you really know any of us?"

"I'm here now. I'm listening."

Her smile turned bitter. "I wish I could just blurt it out. But honesty comes with a price, doesn't it?"

She started for the door, leaving me more bewildered than ever.

"I know one thing," I said. "You've got to do something about the vocals. Something to break through whatever's got you locked up. You're just not yourself out there."

"I'll work on it," she said tersely, and opened the door.

"And one more favor. If you know something Platt should know, tell him. Unless you'd rather tell me first."

She made a halfhearted attempt to meet my eyes and then she was out the door, shutting it behind her, leaving me to finish my Scotch and pour another.

Chapter 24

B Y 4 P.M., Charlene and I were bent over her massive mahogany desk in her office at the Fairmont, sneezing from decades of accumulated dust. Spread out around us were crackling, yellowed blueprints and stacks of brittle black-and-white photographs—interiors and exteriors of the hotel dating back to 1907, the year it opened.

A secretary knocked on Charlene's open door, showing Hercules Platt inside for his scheduled appointment. His hat was already in his hand and the set of his mouth and jaw was severe.

"I'm afraid I have some unpleasant news. Vivian Collier's been murdered."

Charlene gasped and plopped down on the padded chair behind her desk. I took a seat on one of the sofas, seriously rattled. Platt continued standing while he talked.

"Biff Elkins discovered the body a few minutes past noon, up at her place in St. Francis Wood. He was supposed to pick her up for lunch. She didn't answer the bell, but he could hear her little dog barking up a storm. The dog didn't sound right, so Elkins used his key to get in. Found Mrs. Collier in her bedroom, face up on the bed. She'd been strangled."

Charlene and I locked eyes from across the room.

"Poor Vivian," Charlene said. "She had a sharp tongue and she could be a silly fool at times. But she wasn't a bad person. She didn't deserve this."

"The place had been ransacked," Platt went on, "but lots of valuables were untouched—jewelry, artwork, two silver settings, a wad of cash in her purse. It looks like whoever did it was after something in particular. No sign of breaking in, either. She may have known her assailant." Platt glanced my way. "Sound familiar?"

"Charlene and I have been together most of the day, since before ten this morning. In case you're ready to book me for this one."

"Relax, Damon, I'm just giving you the facts."

"Someone must have seen something," Charlene said.

"Her maid always has Saturday off. And Mrs. Collier's place is up a winding drive with heavy landscaping."

"Yes, I've been up that way. It's very private."

"Anyway, two other inspectors are on the case. They'll be handling it while the three of us compare notes. But if the murders of Terrence Collier and his ex aren't connected, I'll eat my badge."

"How about Biff Elkins for a suspect?" I asked.

"The man was an emotional wreck. He wouldn't let go

of that little dog—took it home with him, probably for keeps. I suppose he could be faking it, but my gut tells me otherwise." Platt stopped himself. "Why am I telling you two all this? These aren't things either of you need to know."

"They are if we're going to help you solve these reprehensible murders," Charlene said, reaching for a stack of photos on her desk.

"Please, let's not start that again."

"Elkins was Vivian Collier's alibi on the dance floor when her ex was murdered," I said. "Maybe he got scared she'd drink too much, start bragging about it, get him into trouble."

"Or maybe she'd promised him a payoff," Charlene said, "then reneged. He got angry, then he got even."

"We've considered all that, along with a few other possibilities." Platt glanced at the other sofa and said to Charlene, "You mind if I sit? My back's killing me."

"Please, Inspector. Aspirin?"

"I'll be all right once I get off my feet." Platt eased himself down, groaning.

"You should see a specialist," Charlene said.

"I've been to half the orthopedists in San Francisco. They all tell me I should take early retirement." Platt winced as he tried to work out the kinks. "Happened on the job, back in '58. I was working motorcycle patrol. Truck ran a red light, knocked me into the curb. Department offered me an early out with half pay, but I still had a kid in college and alimony every month. Besides, I'd always hoped to make Inspector." He smiled halfheartedly. "I got that much accomplished, anyway."

Charlene came around her desk with the photos, setting

them on the table in front of him. "Take a look at these. I found them in the hotel archives."

She handed him a black-and-white photo, the borders yellowing with age. Platt studied it, front and back, while I looked on. It was a wide shot of the Gold Room as it had looked in 1923, according to the date stamped on the back, along with other data printed in block handwriting. In the picture, the tables were filled with well-groomed young men nattily dressed in vested suits and broad ties, many with mustaches, and an equal number of young women attired in elaborate gowns. There were also some older men and women about the room, dressed just as fashionably.

"A Stanford University fraternity alumni dinner," Platt said, "according to the information on the back."

"Not just any fraternity—this one included Terrence Collier and his buddy, James Brannigan." Charlene pointed to two college boys with drinks in their hands, each with a young woman at his side, sitting at a table laden with flowers and food. "Right there. That's Collier, the handsome boy with the lean face and neat mustache. That's Brannigan next to him, with the ruddy face and those hulking football shoulders. The woman next to him is Elise, his future wife."

"How can you be sure?" Platt asked. "This was taken forty years ago."

Charlene handed him another photo. "I found this close-up of the four of them, with their names printed on the back. Both these photos were used last year in a Sunday magazine feature on the Fairmont that ran in the *Examiner*, along with some other historical shots. An editor was kind enough to call to make sure they had the date right for the caption—February 2, 1923."

She started going through the stack, showing Platt other

photos: Collier out on the dance floor, waltzing with his date. Collier and Brannigan with several fraternity brothers, arms around each other's shoulders, lifting their glasses in a jubilant toast. In each picture, Collier had a carefree grin on his face, while Brannigan's smile looked tense and forced.

"Interesting stuff," Platt said. "I'm just not sure what it means."

"Don't you think it's quite a coincidence?" Charlene asked. "Terrence Hamilton Collier III celebrates at a dinner dance in the Gold Room in 1923. Then, roughly forty years later, he's murdered in that very same spot."

Platt looked up somberly from the photos. "I don't believe in coincidence, Mrs. Statz."

"Exactly!" Charlene leaped to her feet. "So there must be some connection." She paced the room, glancing at each of us. "This is *so* exciting! I knew we'd make a good team."

"We're not a team." Platt grimaced as he rose slowly to his feet. "I appreciate your help, Mrs. Statz, I really do. But you could be in danger. You, too, Damon."

Charlene and I exchanged a troubled glance.

"What?" Platt said.

Charlene frowned. "You'd better tell him, Philip."

Platt fixed me with his unwavering eyes. "Damon?"

I told him about the scare I'd had in foggy Chinatown, running from a pursuer carrying a gun. Charlene mentioned that we'd also seen a stranger up in the redwoods who took off when she fired a shot in the air.

Platt reached for his hat but cast his eyes on me. "I want you to lay low, you understand?" He swung his eyes back to Charlene. "You, too, Mrs. Statz. My guess is that both these murders are somehow connected to those missing pearls. And anybody who knows anything about them could be at risk. Watch your backs, both of you."

"We certainly will, Inspector." Charlene sounded properly abashed, but kept one hand behind her back. "From now on, we'll leave the detecting to you."

Platt asked if he could take the photos with him to make copies, and Charlene said he could. He put his hat on, tipped it, and headed off.

"I think that went very well," Charlene said, when Platt was gone. "He seemed very impressed with my sleuthing skills. And I think the two of you may be starting to bond."

"When Honolulu freezes over."

Charlene glanced at her wristwatch. "Why don't we celebrate with an early dinner at Le Boeuf? I'm in the mood for a good steak."

I took a rain check, telling her I had an errand to run. A minute later, I was at the concierge desk, leafing through a local phone book. I turned to the D section and ran my finger down the page, stopping when I found the listing for Valentino del Conte.

Chapter 25

VALENTINO DEL CONTE lived in Polk Gulch, an area midway between Union Square and Japantown where a few watering holes were known to discreetly serve a homosexual clientele, though always at the risk of being closed down.

I'd read about the neighborhood after a "gayola" scandal had erupted in San Francisco a year or two earlier, when a group of bar owners had rebelled against paying any more bribes to the cops. They'd formed the Tavern Guild, hired an aggressive lawyer, and joined the nascent cause of homosexual rights. San Francisco had a long history of police crackdowns, dating back to the closing of its first known gay bar, the Dash, in 1906. Yet the city also had a reputation for tolerance—at least in some quarters—and queers from all over the country seemed determined to make it their mecca. Polk Gulch, a quaint district of small businesses along Polk Street and older apartment houses stacked up the hills, was one of the few neighborhoods in the city where they could socialize with a modicum of safety and hospitality.

Valentino del Conte lived in a ground floor unit of an Italianate Victorian that had been carved up into several apartments. It was located among less decorative buildings on Sutter Street just up from Polk. Dusk was falling as a taxi left me off out front. A strong wind had kicked up, chilling the air, and it felt like a storm coming on.

I climbed a few steps and rang the bell. While I waited, I noticed a Saks Fifth Avenue catalog stuffed in the mailbox, advertising the latest fashions for the ladies, and a copy of *Gentleman's Quarterly* with a handsome male model on the cover. Two names were neatly printed on the mailbox: *V. del Conte* and *D. del Conte*. A moment later, Valentino appeared at the door, dressed in a silk kimono and matching slippers. He appeared freshly shaved and slightly damp from a shower, his olive skin smooth and aglow with a vitality that belied his middle age. He opened the door just enough to peer out, but I could hear an Ethel Merman show tune blaring on a hi-fi behind him.

"Mr. Damon, what a surprise. Don't tell me you were in the neighborhood and decided to stop in."

"I had a few questions I hoped you might answer."

"I'm not averse to attractive gentleman callers during my off-hours." He gazed unapologetically into my eyes. "Unfortunately, I have a pressing engagement."

"Mrs. Statz and I saw you at Holy Cross Cemetery the other day. We weren't aware that you and Terrence Collier were friendly."

"What makes you think I was there for Mr. Collier?"

"I assumed—"

"Assumptions can be dangerous, Mr. Damon. Holy Cross is not reserved exclusively for the wealthy, you know."

"You have family there?"

"Our markers may be simple, and our plots among those of the less advantaged. But death is a great equalizer, don't you think?" Then: "I'd love to chat some other time, Mr. Damon, but I really must be going."

"Perhaps I've come at a bad time." I made a too obvious attempt to look past him, and he narrowed the door's gap. "You probably have company."

"I'm not without a social life, Mr. Damon. I have a special friend, who was by earlier. We had a nice lunch. But I can assure you, he's gone."

I glanced at the two names on the mailbox. "And your roommate? Someone in the family?"

"I'm quite alone at the moment."

"Then you do share the flat with someone."

"So many questions, Mr. Damon."

"I apologize for getting so personal."

"If you must know, my friend is more discreet than I, so we live apart. San Francisco may be more tolerant than most cities, but one still has to be cautious, if he's to keep his job and stay out of jail." He lifted his chin confidently, his eyes clear and direct. "Things will change, though. You'll see. It won't be long now."

"People keep telling me that."

"Numbers, that's all we need. Numbers and visibility, which translates into power."

"You're quite the political animal, Valentino."

"Like the Negroes, I came home from my wartime service

realizing America isn't quite as free as it likes to pretend. You might say the war opened our eyes, as well as giving us a dose of courage."

"And the circus," I reminded him. "That must have taken some bravery, up on the trapeze with the Flying Valentinos. Quite a career choice for a young man to make."

"I was always different, Mr. Damon, and quite aware of it from a young age. Fortunately, I had a dear older sister who loved me regardless, who made me feel good about myself just as I was." He crossed himself. "A saint on earth, my sister."

I glanced again at the second name on the mailbox, but Valentino made it clear that I'd worn out my welcome.

"Don't you have a show to do, Mr. Damon?" He again checked his watch. "A performer who's late, or unprepared, disrespects his audience, wouldn't you say?"

And with that, Valentino del Conte shut the door in my face.

Chapter 26

"**D**AMON, GET THE hell in here!"

I was striding down Sutter Street toward Polk when Hercules Platt hollered at me from his unmarked '57 Ford, which was parked pointing uphill. He leaned across the seat, pushing open the front passenger door. "I thought you promised to keep your nose clean."

"Mrs. Statz made that promise, Inspector." I slid in next to him, shutting the door. "Anyway, she had her fingers crossed."

"Damn you two!" Platt slammed his palms against the steering wheel. "I swear, the pair of you are going to drive me back to the bottle."

"The secret," I said, "is to stop drinking before you get to the bottom, and preferably closer to the top."

"Skip the sobriety tips." Platt kept his eyes on Valentino

del Conte's apartment. "And swear to me that you'll stop playing detective."

"I wish I could, Platt. Sniffing around after a cold-blooded killer isn't my idea of a swell time." He glanced over, drawn, perhaps, by the serious tone in my voice. "But I'm in too deep to turn back now."

He studied my face keenly, his eyes and voice softening. "I take it you're talking about the death of your wife."

I nodded. He let out a sigh, fixing his eyes on the del Conte pad again. "I suppose if I were in your shoes, I'd be doing the same damn thing."

Darkness was settling over the city, and litter danced up and down Sutter Street in the skittish wind. I was dressed in a rugby shirt and chinos but hadn't bothered to bring a jacket, and I'd started to shiver.

"Are we keeping the del Conte apartment under surveillance, Inspector?"

"Yeah, that's what we're doing."

"Any chance you could turn on the heater?"

He laughed. "You won't find a heater in any SFPD vehicle. No heater, no defroster, no radio, except for police calls. The Chief says we'd get too comfortable and start nodding off on the job."

"Sounds cheap."

"The Chief? Yeah, Cahill's tight with the purse strings. But he's starting to clean up the department, I'll give him that. Every rookie hears the same speech from Cahill, warning of the 'three Bs' that'll get him canned: booze, broads, and bribes. Wasn't always that way in San Francisco. There was a time when the three Bs were more like qualifications for the job."

"Can't be too bad, Platt. You've stuck with it, made Inspector. Who knows how high you'll go?"

Platt's laugh cut with a bitter edge. "I only made Inspector because they needed a black face to handle homicides in the Fillmore. There's basically one way a cop gets promoted in this city—by being Roman Catholic, with a good word from the Archbishop. If my name were Clancy or Rossi, and my skin were as white as yours, maybe I'd get welcomed into that secret society nobody in the department's supposed to talk about. Things might be different if we had Civil Service, but we don't."

"There's a secret society within the police department?"

"Going back to the last century. And believe me, they take care of their own." Platt shifted his eyes my way. "You're Irish, aren't you, Damon?"

"On my father's side. My mother was Jewish."

"And you were raised by the Harringtons of New York. They don't come much more WASP than that, do they? So where, exactly, do you belong?"

"Sometimes, I'm not sure."

Platt faced forward again, looking thoughtful. "I hear that. Still, you get to play your music for a living. I envy you that, son."

I glanced at my watch. "Speaking of music, Inspector, I've got a show at eight. I should probably get going."

"I saw you catch a cab outside the hotel." Platt talked through me like he needed the company. "I decided to follow you, see where you led me."

"I spotted del Conte at the cemetery Thursday. It aroused my curiosity."

"I saw him, too. Recognized him from his employee photo at the Fairmont."

"You went through all the employee files?"

"Top to bottom. After spotting him down at Holy Cross, I went back into his file again, took a close look at the signature on one of his time cards. To my eye, Del Conte's handwriting looks like a match for that note that was in the bowl on your piano last Sunday night."

"The one requesting that we play 'Just In Time.' "

"Yeah, that one."

"Valentino wasn't working that night. I remember Charlene telling me that. He only works days."

"Then maybe Mr. del Conte will have an alibi and I won't have to worry about him again. Alibis can clear up a lot of questions in a hurry, if they're airtight. Emphasis on the *if*."

A taxi pulled up in front of del Conte's place and the driver got out. Platt ducked low and told me to do the same. The cabbie trotted up the steps and rang the bell at del Conte's front door, where Platt kept his eyes fixed.

"There's something else I learned about Mr. del Conte. He's got a boyfriend who works in our Records Department. Clerk by the name of Lynn Osborn. He was over to see del Conte today, around lunchtime. Regular couple of lovebirds."

"You've been having them watched?"

"Off and on, when we can spare the manpower. I know where del Conte was when Vivian Collier was murdered this morning. Had breakfast with a few of his buddies over in North Beach, stopped by the cleaners to pick up some clothes, came back here, had lunch with his sweetie pie. So he's off the hook on the Collier woman. It's last Sunday night I want to talk to him about."

The door to del Conte's apartment opened and a dark-haired woman emerged with a wardrobe bag, which she handed to the cabbie. While he followed, she hurried down the steps in high heels. Her legs were slim and tapered, but otherwise she looked voluptuous, in the style of a Liz Taylor or Sophia Loren. She was bundled up against the cold in a vicuna-colored coatdress that was tie-belted and looked like it might be cashmere, with a matching pillbox hat and purse, further accessorized with beige gloves. The cabbie laid the wardrobe bag carefully in the trunk as she looked on, then scampered around to open a passenger door for her. Platt jotted down the taxi number as it pulled away.

"You don't see too many fashionable dames like that in this neighborhood," Platt said. "She looks more like Pacific Heights or Nob Hill."

"Valentino mentioned a sister."

We watched the taxi stop at the corner, then turn right on to Polk.

"You stay here." Platt opened his door, climbed from the car. "I have a few questions for Mr. del Conte."

BY the time I caught up with Platt, he was ringing the bell to Valentino del Conte's apartment, which occupied half the lower floor, its door facing the apartment just across the porch.

"I thought I told you to stay put," Platt said.

He rang the bell again, then pounded the meaty part of his fist on the frame of del Conte's door.

"He's got to be in there," I said.

"Not if he's got another way out." Platt peeked through the slats, then turned to a larger window with open curtains and peered in, while I took a position beside him.

Two matching porcelain table lamps were on in the living

room, casting just enough light to give us a decent look at the place. It appeared clean and tidy, though cluttered with antiques and large, dramatic prints from the Italian Renaissance, elaborately framed. Magazines were neatly displayed at each end of a coffee table—a copy of *Esquire* at one end, an issue of *Glamour* at the other.

Platt removed a slim flashlight from a jacket pocket and aimed the beam at the fireplace on the far side of the room. Lined up along the mantelpiece were family photos going back a century or more, by the looks of the sepia tones and daguerreotypes. The centerpiece was a formal portrait that must have dated to around 1920, judging by the clothes and hair: a mother and father standing above a little boy of perhaps ten and a girl several years older. She was striking, even at fourteen or fifteen, with dark, smoldering eyes and sensuous lips on the face of a budding young beauty. In the portrait, her little brother—if that's who the boy was—had the same eyes in a narrower face that was nearly as pretty. He was almost certainly Valentino del Conte, a good four decades back. In a series of individual portraits the young girl grew older through the decades, until she looked exactly like the dark-haired woman who'd emerged from the apartment minutes ago, disappearing in a taxi. At the end of the mantelpiece was the most recent photo, by the looks of it: a grinning Valentino del Conte with his arm around the shoulder of a shorter, pleasant-looking, bespectacled man, bald and pushing fifty.

"Lynn Osborn," Platt said, "the clerk in Records that I told you about."

"Quite the happy couple."

Platt returned to the window in the door and beamed his light through an opening in the blinds. Together, we could see across the entry and a hallway, and through the open door of a small bathroom. It appeared to be spotless, except for a pair of women's nylons draped over the shower rod; a man's razor and shaving brush had been rinsed and neatly laid out on a clean glass shelf above the sink, next to a fancy bowl of shaving soap.

"He's obviously the fastidious one," Platt said.

Before I could reply, Platt was gone, down the steps and moving around the east side of the house. He opened a gate and followed his flashlight along a narrow walkway that led to a small yard with a well-tended garden in the back. His light found a short stairway leading up to a door off a service porch at the rear of del Conte's apartment. Platt swung the light across the garden to the rear of the yard, where another gate provided a second exit. "Now we know how Mr. del Conte made his escape. He must have seen me coming and slipped out the back. Which leads me to believe he doesn't want to talk to me—and that maybe he's protecting his lady friend."

"Maybe we should break in and search the place. Cops do that kind of thing all the time, right?" Platt gave me one of his patented looks. "Sorry, partner."

Platt jabbed his finger at my chest. "Let's get something straight, Damon. I'm not your partner. Not now, not ever. Got it?"

He turned abruptly, striding back out the way we'd come, while I followed close at his heels. "It's because you're black, isn't it, Platt?" I saw the muscles of his neck go taut as he kept walking. "You made Inspector, but the department can't find a white cop with your rank who'll work with a Negro."

He continued moving, but fired back at me over his

shoulder: "When I got my gold shield, we had ten crews, two men in each. I was number twenty-one, the odd man out. So I work alone. They got no plans to bring anybody else up for a while."

"That's convenient."

Platt pulled up and faced me as we reached the street. "I don't need a partner, Damon. I do just fine on my own. I like it this way."

"Funny, I've never been much good with solitude myself."

The wind was coming harder, promising rain.

"If I'm not mistaken," Platt said, "you've got a show to do."

"Care to sit in with us? Come around with your horn. I'll leave a comp at the door."

"Not so long ago, Damon, you hated my guts. Why the sudden change of heart?"

"I don't see the point in butting heads if we're after the same thing." I let it sit there, sinking in. Then: "So, you coming around with your ax tonight?"

His voice was flat, his eyes steady. "I've got work."

"Just the same, the offer stands."

I turned away, heading down to Polk Street to catch a cab, while Hercules Platt stood alone, buffeted by the cold wind and pelted by the scattered raindrops.

Chapter 27

BY THE TIME I reached the hotel, I was more confused than ever about where to direct my suspicion or in whom to place my trust. It got worse after I jumped into a tux and dashed down to the Venetian Room, where I found Gloria Velez huddled with the other band members, talking in a whisper that abruptly ended as I mounted the stage.

I went over the program for the evening, then played an "A" on the piano and the band tuned up. From my bench I nodded to the maitre d', who prepared to open the doors at the front of the house and seat the early arrivals. It was then I realized how numbingly exhausted I was—no nap, too much alcohol, too many nights tossing and turning, and so much going on in my head I was starting to feel feverish.

Gloria stopped by the piano and straightened my bow tie, as she often did just before the music started. "You should do something about that hair, Philip." She attempted to fuss a few long strands into compliance. "It's all over the place."

"Frankly, that's not topping my list of priorities these days."

"If one of them is my singing," she said, "you can set your mind at ease. Before the night's over, I'll have that problem taken care of."

The room lights dimmed and the spotlight came on. My tenor sax man nodded the downbeat and my fingers responded from memory. We got through the first show in reasonably good form, although Gloria was still tentative and unfocused on her vocals. Charlene's hubby, Reinhold Statz, was back in town following his business trip abroad, and for the second show, she'd reserved a table near the dance floor. I pulled Gloria aside just before we took the stage to play and told her I wanted the show to be something special for Mr. and Mrs. Statz.

"One of their favorite tunes is 'Begin the Beguine.' Let's play that and some other Cole Porter numbers for them."

"I promise, Philip, I'll give them something special."

Just then, Charlene and Reinhold entered the room. Mr. Statz was a well-fed, roly-poly man, nearly half a foot shorter than Charlene, with a small mustache, an extravagant toupee, and bifocals he was always misplacing. He and Charlene shared a love of music, fine food, and good times matched only by their elegant taste and business acumen, all of which the Fairmont personified. She loved him madly, and accompanied him to their table, whispering in his ear and causing him to grin and laugh out loud. Joe DiMaggio and Herb Caen soon joined them, followed by the Cyril Magnins.

The lights changed and we opened with "Fascinating Rhythm," instead of our usual, because it was another favorite of Mr. Statz. He had Charlene up on her feet in a flash; seconds later, most of the other couples were following his lead, while Herb looked around for a pretty single lady he might squire to the dance floor. I kept the tempo extra fast and the energy high, and skipped vocals entirely, worried that Gloria might screw up a good show. No one among the diners seemed to mind dance after dance, and I decided to play it safe and keep it that way right through the end of the evening.

That plan abruptly changed, however, when Hercules Platt showed up.

HE arrived during the final break, carrying his battered saxophone case in one hand and his hat in the other, and offering me nothing more than a perfunctory nod. Before I called him up, I played a few more swing tunes, figuring he'd rather sit in on slower, bluesier numbers. I asked Herb Caen to join us as well, on drums; I'd heard him once years ago, sitting in with Steve Allen at Mai Tai Sing's Rickshaw Lounge; for an amateur, Herb played more than passably, in direct relationship to the amount of vodka he'd consumed, which that night was plenty. Platt blew his horn on three or four numbers, all standards that he seemed to know without looking at the sheet music, and every bit as well as my regular alto sax man, a young guy with longish hair who was happy to step outside in privacy for a few tokes on his funny-looking cigarette.

As we finished up the set, Gloria emerged from the backstage shadows, crossing down to the thrust where I sat at the Steinway.

"I'm starting to feel like a piece of furniture, Philip. It's time for me to sing."

"You sure you're up to it?"

Her dark eyes were intense, her face somber. "I've never been more sure."

She nodded toward the other musicians and took her microphone into the spotlight. A moment later—without waiting for my selection or cue—the orchestra broke into "Blue Moon."

At first, I was furious, close to exploding. I signaled the band to stop, but the guys looked away and just kept on playing, something they'd never done in all the years most of us had been together. Platt played fills on his sax where I might have contributed piano fills; I hated to admit it, but the band sounded pretty damned good without me. As I listened, I sensed something different in Gloria's voice— nuance, depth, complexity of feeling I'd never heard before. Reluctantly, I picked up the beat and joined in, but it was Gloria's voice and persona that carried the song; she'd become one with the music and the lyrics, a perfect marriage of singer and material in one transcendent moment. The musicians were drawn in almost hypnotically, merging effortlessly with her; the audience was riveted. Across the empty dance floor, I saw tears streaming down Charlene's face. Then I realized I was weeping as well, in a way I hadn't allowed myself since Diana had been taken from us.

> *Blue moon, you saw me standing alone,*
> *Without a dream in my heart,*
> *Without a love of my own.*

If we'd been recording that night, Gloria Velez would have waxed a "Blue Moon" for the ages. It was haunted, infused with both pain and hope, and as soulfully sung as the best of the great renditions. A second of silence followed the final note before the hushed crowd burst into unbridled applause, rising to its feet in ovation.

Gloria ran from the room in tears, straight through the nearest doors at the front of the house.

As the room slowly cleared, Herb stopped at the piano, looking wistful and a little drunk.

"It doesn't get any better than this, Phil." He looked around at the sumptuous colors and elegant table settings, the dim lighting and plush carpet—the room where Ella Fitzgerald had been queen and Tony Bennett king. "Problem is, it feels like an era ending. How many more nights do we get like this? Why did Elvis have to pick up that damned guitar?"

"Blame it on Chuck Berry, I guess." I closed the keyboard cover on the Steinway, put my music back into the folder. "Even Presley recorded 'Blue Moon,' back in '56. Of course, that was the same year he released 'Hound Dog,' so there you are." I clapped Herb on one of his slumping shoulders as we stepped down from the thrust. "Don't worry about rock 'n' roll, Herb. Give it another year or two, and it'll go the way of 3-D movies."

The room was empty now except for busboys and waiters picking up and a small group gathered at Charlene's table— Charlene, Joe DiMaggio, and Hercules Platt, talking low with their heads together. I was desperate to put my own head on a pillow and close my eyes, but Herb dragged me over for "just one drink," asking a waiter to bring a coffee for Platt and Manhattans for everyone else. Charlene looked up as we approached, explaining that Reinhold was off to bed with jet lag. But her smile was uneasy and her eyes told me she had something else on her mind.

"Why don't you sit down, Philip?"

I sat. So did Herb. Platt quickly took charge. "Mr. DiMaggio has been kind enough to volunteer some information. It involves Gloria Velez. And, in a sense, your late wife."

"I thought we went over all this before."

"This is a new twist, something you might not be aware of."

I glanced across the table, where Joe cast his distressed eyes at his big hands, which were folded tightly in front of him.

"What, Joe?"

He finally looked up, his long face etched with chagrin. "This is awkward, Phil. We've known each other a long time, since you were in knee pants. You know I'm not the type to get into the business of other folks."

"Sure, Joe, I know that."

"But with all that's happened, I—"

"It's all right, Joe. Spit it out."

"You know how much Gloria cared for Diana."

"Sure. They were like sisters."

Joe looked toward Charlene for help. "Phil," she said, "Gloria didn't just love Diana. Gloria was in love with Diana."

The waiter set a bar napkin in front of Charlene, placed a Manhattan on the napkin, then repeated it all around, except for Platt, who got coffee. Charlene signed the check while Herb dug into his pocket and tipped the waiter. I sat there numbly, trying to recover from what I'd just heard.

Finally, as the waiter departed, I managed to sputter something silly: "But Gloria was married once."

Charlene shrugged. "So's Cole Porter."

"Anything goes," Herb added.

"I'm not sure I'm ready for this," I said.

Joe smiled painfully. "I'm with you, Phil."

Platt sipped his coffee, then set the cup back in the saucer. "It seems Gloria's feelings go back to when you and Diana first met."

I leaned forward on my elbows. "You're sure about this?"

"What may be more significant," Platt went on, "is that Miss Velez also knew about Terrence Collier and the pearls. Diana confided in her, swearing her to secrecy."

"Then why didn't she tell the police this when Diana was murdered?"

"That's one of the more troubling questions," Charlene said.

"It's possible she didn't connect the pearls to Diana's death," Platt said. "We still don't know for sure that there's a direct link. And she may not have wanted to get involved, for fear of exposing too much about herself—her feelings for Diana, and the rest of it."

"That kind of thing can ruin a career," Charlene reminded us. "After all, it's why the movie studios arrange so many marriages. And why Liberace has that convenient fiancée no one's ever seen. It must be the longest courtship in history!"

"Given the feelings of Miss Velez for Diana," Platt said, "it's possible she might have wanted to even the score in some dramatic fashion, assuming she suspected Terrence Collier in your wife's death."

My head was going a thousand directions at once. "How do you know all this?"

All eyes turned back to Joe. He sighed painfully before he spoke.

"Gloria confided everything to Marilyn a few years ago. After the tragedy involving Diana, Marilyn called me about it. I didn't come forward until now because I wanted to keep Marilyn out of it." He clenched his jaw in a rare display of anger. "You know how the press was after her death, scavenging after every sordid morsel, feasting on the body. I couldn't bear having her name dragged through the mud again." Joe reached across the table, laid his hand over mine. "I'm sorry to put all this on you, Phil. As if you didn't have enough on your mind already."

I sat back in my chair, sipping my Manhattan and wishing it were Scotch. "It certainly explains a few things. About the way Gloria's been acting, anyway. I'm not sure what else it means, though." Then, directly to Joe: "Did Diana know? About the way Gloria felt?"

Joe nodded. "Marilyn told me that Diana was very openminded, that she cared for Gloria a great deal, but in a platonic way." He glanced around the table with an embarrassed smile. "To be honest, I'm not too knowledgeable about these things."

Charlene touched his sleeve. "You should read *The Price of Salt*, Joe. It's a crime novel by Patricia Highsmith, framed as a lesbian coming-of-age story. Came out in '53, under the pseudonym Claire Morgan. Bittersweet, but you'll learn a lot."

"If it's all the same," Joe said, "I'll stick to *Baseball Digest*."

"All this must have been awfully hard on Gloria," I said. "In her own way, she loved Diana as much as I did." I shook my head. "How could I never see it?"

Hercules Platt sipped his coffee thoughtfully. "There's a lot we never see, often when it's right in front of us."

BEFORE we broke up for the night, Platt asked that each of us maintain absolute discretion about what we'd heard and seen regarding the murder of Terrence Hamilton Collier III and of Vivian Collier as well. "I'm breaking some rules, confiding in the four of you like this."

Charlene rested her chin on her folded hands, her Manhattan untouched. "Why have you been so open with us, Inspector? Most of the detectives I'm familiar with are never so trusting. Sam Spade, Philip Marlowe, Mike Shayne—they tend to play it close to the vest."

"The simple truth is that I need you," Platt said. "I'm faced with a murder in a room filled with several hundred men and women." He showed us a rare smile. "That's a lot of suspects." Just as quickly, the smile was gone. "Caucasian suspects."

"Not all," I said. "There were several—"

"The only exceptions," Platt continued, "were a handful of celebrities—performers or sports figures allowed into your world because of their talent for entertaining. Lacking the ability to sing or hit home runs, it's not a world to which I've been welcome or privy. As you surely know, there are people in this town who are outraged that I'm assigned to this case, people who would rejoice if I fail. The pressure mounts every day to have me replaced. I need some insiders as sources, even if it means breaching the usual confidentiality." He glanced around the table. "You're those insiders."

Charlene's lilting voice took off like a bird. "This is *so* exciting." She laughed nervously. "It's also a great relief to know I'm no longer considered a suspect."

"Believe me, Mrs. Statz, you were never thought of seriously as a suspect."

"Inspector, don't you think it's time you call me Charlene?"

Platt smiled awkwardly. "Charlene, then."

Herb pulled out his reporter's notebook, flipping it open. "So who *is* left? I've been trying to keep a scorecard, but this town's got more murder suspects than pigeons." He reeled off a few names: Gloria Velez, Lenore Ashley, James Brannigan, Biff Elkins, Vivian Collier. "Oops," Herb said, crossing off the last name. "She's been eliminated, so to speak."

"I can think of one or two more possibilities," I said, but Platt's shifting eyes silenced me.

"We shouldn't discount a team of two suspects working together," Charlene added. "One providing an alibi for the other, that kind of thing. It's proved to be true in a number of Georges Simenon's books."

I pushed my chair back and stood, glancing at DiMaggio.

"Personally," I said, "I think Joe did it."

Everyone laughed, though a bit uneasily. I mentioned how badly I needed some shut-eye, thanked everyone for coming to the show, and wished them sweet dreams.

HERCULES Platt walked with me as far as the top of the Laurel Court stairway. I asked if he wanted to drive down in the morning to Colma, where I planned to visit the del Conte family plot at Holy Cross Cemetery.

"I was planning on going down myself," he said. "Given the way bodies are piling up, it's probably safer if I go down with you. In the meantime, if I were you, I'd stay in my room with the door locked. I've told Reinhold Statz the same thing. He's hired a bodyguard for the wife. She worries me, but not as much as you."

"Duly noted, Inspector."

"In case you're interested, I traced that taxi we saw leaving del Conte's apartment earlier this evening."

"I'm interested."

"The driver dropped the woman down at Enrico's, on Broadway at Kearny. The cabbie waited for a minute or two, hoping to pick up a quick fare. He says she sat at a table by the sidewalk, just out of the weather. Had a coffee alone, looking out at the rain. He took off a moment later, so he didn't see her leave, or if anyone joined her." Platt glanced at my disheveled head. "One more thing, Damon—you really should do something about that hair, a guy in the spotlight like you."

He put on his hat and headed down the stairs.

"Platt, thanks for sitting in with the band. Your playing was first-rate."

He tipped his hat and was gone.

I was crossing the lobby in the direction of the elevators when I saw Gloria Velez hunkered down on a couch in a distant alcove, partially camouflaged by a potted palm. She was speaking quietly but urgently with someone who sat next to her, just out of my view. I circled widely around the lobby's central grouping of sofas and settees until I had a clear view of Gloria and her confidante. When they looked up and saw me, it was like a pair of deer caught in the headlights—two females with wide, startled eyes.

Not until that moment was I aware of Gloria's cozy relationship with Lenore Ashley.

Chapter 28

UP IN MY suite, I flung off my jacket and poured a deep Dewars straight, listening to a hard wind drive the rain like pellets against the cold windows.

Charlene had sent someone ahead to light the fire, and I sat in front of it, watching the flames waggle like loose tongues, while I slowly got drunk. After catching Gloria Velez huddled with Lenore Ashley—and all that had gone before—it was no longer possible to put a single name to my emotions. I felt angry, suspicious, betrayed. Mostly, I was wrung out and confused, desperate for answers.

There was a knock at the door. I waited, and it came again, more urgently. I got to my feet, recalling Platt's warning, and used the peephole before touching the lock. Lenore Ashley stood in the foyer. She was wearing a gray wool suit with dark blue trim, and a handbag and high heels in the same azure tone, like a model come to life from a fashion spread in *Vogue*. The muscles were tight along the fine lines of her neck and jaw, suggesting anxiety. Yet she also looked as attractive and alluring as ever. I closed the peephole, unlocked the door, pulled it open.

"I saw you in the lobby, Philip. I thought I should come up and explain."

"I believe you both saw me—you and Gloria."

She moved quickly into the room, turning, gripping her handbag so tightly her knuckles were white.

"How are you, Philip?"

"Having a grand old time, trying to figure out who my friends are."

"You didn't call. I thought that after the other night—"

"After the other night, what? That everything was going to be hunky-dory between us?"

"What is it, Philip? You seem on edge."

I laughed. "Yes, that's what I am. On edge." I picked up my glass, drained the Scotch. "On edge enough to put my fist through the nearest wall."

"I'm not sure I understand."

"Let's start with your connection to Jimmy Brannigan, shall we?"

She shot me a curious look. "There's no connection, except for Terrence Collier. They were business partners. You know that."

"I guess that slip of paper by your phone with his name and number on it must have blown in the window on a strong breeze."

"You saw that?"

"Yes, Lenore, I saw it. On your kitchen table, the night we made love. If that's what we were doing."

"There's a simple explanation, Philip."

"I'll bet."

"Brannigan keeps calling me. I've asked him to stop. He thinks you have the pearls, or know where they are."

"You know about the pearls, too?"

"Terrence told me. One night when he was going on about his divorce, his dwindling wealth."

"And Brannigan?"

"He figured you'd be attracted to me, because—well, we know why, don't we?" She turned away again, toward the fireplace. "Brannigan wants to use me to get to you. He offered me money to see what I could find out."

"My goodness. Why on earth would someone think that Lenore Ashley could be bought like that?"

"I turned him down flat. I told him to leave me alone."

"Then why did you write down his phone number?"

"Reflex, I suppose. Are you going to crucify me for writing down someone's name and phone number?"

"Why is Brannigan so crazy to get his hands on the pearls?"

"He claims Terrence acquired the pearls with money diverted from their business. Apparently, Terrence was bleeding the company for years, making all kinds of outlandish purchases. Now that he's gone, and Brannigan faces heavy taxes as the surviving partner, the business is on the brink of going under. He discovered the missing funds years ago, but now he's desperate." She faced me again, laughing archly. "A good example of what can happen when you allow yourself to be seduced by money."

"You're not exactly in a position to preach, are you?"

"I came hoping to ease your mind, Philip. I can see that was a mistake."

She started out past me, but I grabbed her. "You'll go when I say so."

She glared at my hand on her arm. "I'm capable of anger, Philip." When she raised her eyes to mine, they looked dangerous. "Don't underestimate me."

"Is that what Terrence Collier did, Lenore? Last Sunday, on the dance floor—was that his punishment for the way he'd used and degraded you?"

"You're coming unhinged, Philip."

She tried to pull away. I tightened my grip on her arm.

"Am I, Lenore? Suppose you explain the missing ice pick."

"What?"

"Your cottage is equipped with an icebox. Shouldn't it have a tool around for chipping ice?"

"I swear, Philip, you're going mad."

"I searched your kitchen, Lenore. No ice pick. Is it possible you left it in Terrence Collier's chest, driven all the way to the hilt?"

She glanced again at my hand. When she looked up, her eyes and voice had softened. She seemed close to tears. "Could you please take your hand off me?"

I let go. She rubbed her arm but didn't step away.

"A neighbor borrowed that ice pick, Philip. He was having a party. He forgot to return it. If you'd like, I'll arrange for you to speak with him."

If she was lying, I couldn't see it. Then again, I couldn't ignore her training as an actress, either. I turned, faced the dying embers in the fireplace. "And your little confab with Gloria down in the lobby a few minutes ago? I guess you have a story to cover that, too."

Behind me, I heard her purse being unclasped, then listened as she rummaged in it. A second later, I sensed her approach. It occurred to me that she might have an ice pick in her possession at this moment, drawn from her handbag, or some other instrument just as lethal. She laid a hand gently on my shoulder. In her other hand was a tissue that she used to dab her eyes.

"Gloria and I are worried about you, Philip. We care about you. Both of us."

"That's touching."

She tossed her handbag on one of the couches, turned me so our mouths were inches apart. "It happens to be the truth."

"That's all you two were talking about—my state of mind?"

"That's all." She found my eyes with hers. "You need to rest, Philip. You need to stop worrying so much." She reached up, tugged on my bow tie, opened the knot, slipped it from my collar. One by one, from the top, she unfastened the studs, then reached inside my shirt. Her hands felt electric as she touched me. "Everything will work out in the end, if you'll just let it."

The danger was still there, crackling between us, infusing the air with an erotic charge. I took her face in my hands and kissed her hard on the mouth. I didn't stop kissing her until the phone rang a minute or two later. My hands were on her body by then, and answering the phone hardly seemed important. Finally, on the fifth ring, I gave in, picked up the receiver, and spoke my name.

I heard a muffled voice at the other end. It suggested that if I wanted to find out the truth about Diana's murder, I should go straightaway to Lands End.

"Who is this?" I demanded.

Silence.

"Why do I have to come now?"

Because it will be your only chance to find out who murdered Diana and why, the voice said.

"Why should I trust you?"

Because you have no other choice, the voice explained.

"How will I recognize you?"

Just come to the trail at the edge of the cypress trees, the voice said. *Come alone and tell no one,* the voice added, *or I'll take the truth about your wife's murder to my grave.*

There was a click, and the line went dead.

I went directly to the bedroom, got out of my fancy clothes, slipped on a wool turtleneck, pulled on a pair of corduroy pants.

Lenore stood in the doorway. "Who was that?"

"Where's Lands End?"

"Out by the old Sutro Baths and the Cliff House. Due west, where the city ends at the bluffs above the ocean. The baths have been converted to a skating rink."

"Sure, now I remember it. Diana and I had always intended to get out there." I sat on the bed, pulling on sneakers. "How do I get there?"

"Philip, what's going on? Who was that on the phone?"

"Dammit, Lenore, how do I get there?"

"Geary Boulevard, all the way out."

I started out past her, and she followed with alarm. "Philip, it's almost three in the morning. There's a storm out."

I stopped at the door and kissed her on the lips.

"Philip, don't do this. It's too risky."

"It's all I have, Lenore."

"You're going to trust someone who calls anonymously like this?"

"That's the problem. I don't know whom to trust anymore. Even Diana kept secrets from me. I'm no longer sure I even know who my wife really was."

I unlocked and opened the door. Lenore reached for me, but I pulled away.

"I'm begging you, Philip, don't go. Stay here, with me." She took a step forward, reaching for my face, pleading with her eyes.

"Keep the sheets warm," I said, and was gone.

Chapter 29

RAIN BEAT AGAINST the taxi as it descended a steep road to drop me off at Lands End. I stepped out into a merciless wind. Somewhere below me in the darkness and the storm came the roar of waves crashing on rocks.

The driver told me I was nuts to be left off in this desolate spot at such a late hour in such inclement weather. I couldn't deny it. But neither could I turn my back on this opportunity, because it might not come again. I thanked the cabbie for the ride, tipped him a fin, and told him to take off.

Come alone, the voice had ordered me. *Tell no one.* I'd told Lenore, and maybe that was a mistake. Now I was alone. And now, maybe, I'd finally learn the truth.

* * *

THE taxi headed back up the hill toward the city. I charged north, leaning into the keening wind, putting up a hand to shield my face against the worst of the weather. I crossed a roughly surfaced parking lot toward a hulking black landscape slanting eerily east, away from the ocean—a dense forest of windswept cypress trees. I reached the edge, standing on a trail going soft and muddy, staring into near blackness.

I put my hands to my mouth and shouted: "Hello!" I repeated the cry several times, so loudly the word tore at my throat. I was struck suddenly by the reality of what I was doing—the sheer recklessness of it. Though I'd missed combat during the Korean War, I'd been through boot camp, done my share of marching and jousting, even performed reasonably well in hand-to-hand combat training. I could stand up for myself in most situations. But this was something altogether different. Fear seized me like a sudden sickness coming on. I turned to holler after the taxi, but all I saw were two tiny red blurs disappearing in sheets of rain.

"Damon!"

The voice came from behind me, deep and rumbling, male. I turned and saw a dark figure standing up the trail. He stepped from the dense growth, protected from the storm in a dark hat and topcoat—the same figure who'd chased me through the foggy streets of Chinatown, gun in hand. Again, stark fear swept over me. I turned, prepared to flee.

"Damon! I know who murdered Diana!"

His words stopped me in my tracks. As I faced him again, he swiveled and dashed off, quickly swallowed up by the trees. Decades of relentless wind had shaped them into a community of battered souls, bowed but desperate to stay rooted, to hold on to life. I thought of Charlene's redwoods up in Cathedral Grove, standing tall and proud until they were blown down, when bending with the gale force might have saved them—if bending had been an option.

I'd bend if I had to, I thought; I'd follow this man through thick and thin and fall to my knees and beg for the truth, if it would help. I might even give him my life for it, if that's what he had to have. Just to know. Just to find some closure, some peace.

I chased after him. The winding trail took me deeper and deeper into the forest, intersecting other paths that disappeared up or down. I found myself in groves so thick with cypress that the lower limbs were dead and brittle from lack of light, while the uppermost branches formed a heavy canopy through which the night sky could not be seen. Each time I became disoriented and lost, stopping for a moment, the stranger appeared, beckoning with an upraised hand. Each time I called out or chased on, he disappeared once more.

I came upon a posted sign: *Caution—Extremely Dangerous—People Have Been Swept From the Rocks and Drowned.* But I could see no rocks, no ocean. Only the trees, the maddening forest, the drenching rain, as I climbed.

Off to my left, I heard someone crashing through the naked lower branches that formed a dark tapestry all around me. I followed the sound, able to glimpse the elusive figure from time to time, until he was gone again and I found myself alone, floundering blindly on in my wet clothes, crashing through stiff limbs that stabbed and tore at my hands and face, drawing blood.

Then, suddenly, I broke free of the forest, my eyes wide as I cried out. I pulled up, trying desperately to keep my footing as I stared down at the storm-tossed sea and rocky shore a hundred feet below. Another few steps and I would have plummeted from the edge. So the stranger had led me here, I thought, to the brink of my death. It would have been so easy for him to step from the darkness behind me and give me a shove, to send me into my fatal plunge. Yet he'd spared me. Some game was being played—some diabolical game in which truth was being dangled as the prize. *I've come this far,* I thought. *I'll play the game, gambling with my life, if that's what it takes.*

"Where are you?"

"Here," came the voice.

The stocky figure—crouched perhaps a hundred feet away—turned and disappeared again into the thicket of cypress. I followed obediently, back through the forest as the trees reached and grabbed for me while I pushed them away with my bleeding hands. We were angling down now, toward the sound of pounding surf, although the figure had once more disappeared. Suddenly, I emerged again and found myself staggering through a patch of wild hollyhocks as the sound of crashing waves grew louder. I spotted the figure below on a clearly marked trail—lumbering heavily toward the sound of the ocean, his pace slowing nearly to a stumble. In my eagerness, I slipped on the slick wild verbena that covered the slope, tumbling and scrambling and falling until I landed at the bottom in a painful heap. I got to my feet, bruised and aching, and picked up the path of the fleeing man around the slope and ever closer to the sea.

Immediately to my left and below me was a sight too startling to miss, even under the circumstances: an immense structure of concrete and wood, rising several stories high, covered with arched glass. The famous Sutro Baths, I realized, one of the few San Francisco landmarks Diana and I had never visited together, an engineering and artistic marvel dating back to the nineteenth century. Now it was just a signpost on my terrifying journey to an unknown destination, an unknown fate.

"This way, Damon!"

I turned and saw my tormentor at a distance, off to my right. He stood atop a low bluff at trail's end, veiled by rain. I trotted toward him, slowing as the trail ascended. He retreated, all the way to the edge of the paved bluff and a low wall that separated him from the craggy rocks and cascading surf below. The wind lifted his hat and carried it away from his head as easily as an autumn leaf. Then I was up on the bluff, advancing, seeing him more clearly. Finally, I was close enough to recognize his ruddy face and see a small, heavy gun in his right hand. Except for Army training—serious but make-believe—I'd never faced the muzzle of a gun before. It caused my guts to roil, my heart to race impossibly fast. I tried mightily to muster some aplomb. My voice trembled just the same.

"Out sightseeing, Brannigan?"

"I don't like doing this, Damon. I want you to know that."

"Why don't we both go back to The City, then? Pretend this never happened. You can call me up the way civilized people do, invite me out for a drink, like the gentleman I know you to be." I laughed, trying to fool him, but my voice caught and the laughter cracked. "Preferably, someplace nice and dry."

"I can't expose myself that way. I'm sure you can appreciate that." He ran his free hand through his wet hair and over his bald spot. "God, what a mess."

Thunder cracked, and a moment later a flash of lightning briefly illuminated the scene. I moved a step closer, saw the stricken look in Brannigan's eyes, saw how anxious and miserable and out of his element he was.

"I'd feel more comfortable if you'd put the gun away."

"I wish I could. Honest to God, I do."

"What is it you want from me, Brannigan?"

"I think you know."

"I don't have the pearls. If I did, I swear, I'd give them up. Then you could tell me who killed my wife, and why. And we'd call the whole thing even."

"It's true, then?" His eyes were all pain and regret, his face twisted with confusion. "You really don't have them?"

"You could have asked, long before this."

His laughter sounded pitiful. "And you could have lied just as easy."

"And now? Would I die just to keep them for myself? It makes no sense."

He kept his gun on me and turned as I moved slowly to his right, so that his back was to the trail with the massive outline of the Sutro Baths behind him. I reached the wall and looked over, measuring the drop. It looked like several stories, but fear may have gotten the better of my imagination. At the bottom were massive outcroppings of barnacle-covered rock, awash in heavy surf. Not a gentle landing.

"You look worn out, Brannigan, not exactly in your right mind. You could call this off and I wouldn't hold it against you."

"I've got to find those pearls. So much depends on it. You wouldn't understand."

"Try me."

"My whole life, Damon. My wealth, my social standing. The respect of my six kids. The legacy I leave them."

"You don't strike me as a homicidal maniac, Brannigan."

"I didn't hurt your wife, Damon. Or any of the others." He sounded anguished. "It wasn't until tonight that I considered—"

"Murder?" He nodded, ashamed. My smile was grim. "I suppose I should feel privileged, then. I'll be your first."

"Don't talk like that!"

"Perhaps, before you finish me off, you'd like to tell me who killed Diana. Maybe you're just decent enough to do that for me." I took a step toward him. "It was Terrence Collier, wasn't it?"

"Stay back." Brannigan thrust the gun forward.

"Was your housekeeper lying to protect him, at your bidding? Is that why Gwendolyn Sparks backed up his alibi when she spoke with the New York police?"

"Leave Gwendolyn out of this!" He raised the gun until it was aimed unsteadily in the general vicinity of my eyes. I saw his finger close on the trigger while his hand shook uncontrollably. Behind him, the Sutro Baths loomed grotesquely, framing him as another lightning bolt fired up the sky.

"Tell me, Brannigan. At least give me that much."

As the light flickered across his face, I realized that he was blubbering like a baby.

"When you pull that trigger, Brannigan, are you going to watch the slug blow my face away?"

"Shut up!"

"Maybe you'd rather put the bullet in my heart. Not so messy that way."

"Shut up! Shut up!"

"After you kill me, Brannigan, explain to me how you'll look your grandchildren in the eye, knowing what you've done."

I saw his eyes falter.

"Please," he begged. "If you know where the pearls are—"

"I swear, Brannigan. I haven't a clue."

He sagged; the resolve seemed to go out of him and he eased his finger off the trigger. I swallowed hard, believing I just might have a chance at surviving.

Thunder rumbled again. There was a sudden commotion to my left, and then Lenore Ashley was rushing in our direction, bathed eerily in stormy light as the sky flashed. With both hands, she held aloft a rock the size of a football, which she brought down with a horrible thud on the side of Brannigan's skull. The force of it sent him into the wall and toppling over, leaving behind only his gun, which clattered to the pavement without discharging.

I leaned over, looking down. Brannigan sprawled on his back, one of his legs twisted under him, cradled in the crook of a mossy rock that protected him from the waves' full force. Lenore grabbed me, asked if I was OK, although she was shaking as badly as I was. I told her to get to a phone and call for an ambulance and the police, getting word to Hercules Platt if possible. She didn't want to leave me there, but I insisted, so she went.

As she ran, I called after her, asking her to have the police send a priest.

CROSSING the rocks was a challenge, but by timing my movements between the incoming waves and crawling like a crab, I managed to work my way out to Brannigan in a matter of minutes. I found him alive and conscious, though not by much.

I held him in my arms and encouraged him to talk, hoping he might stay conscious and tell me what I needed to know. Blood trickled from a wound in his head and he was unable to move, save for his eyes and mouth; by the look of him, he hadn't long to live, and I think he knew it. In a hoarse whisper, he swore he'd never intended to kill me, that he'd only meant to scare me so badly I'd tell him where to find the missing pearls. He apologized for what he'd put me through, insisting that he was basically a good man who'd gotten into a bad situation that had spiraled out of control. He whispered that Terrence Collier had both enriched and ruined his life, that all of his misery and success stemmed from their unlikely friendship formed in college.

"I made a deal with the devil." Brannigan began to weep, rambling, barely coherent. "Now I'm paying for my sins." Through his tears, he lamented his wife's mental state, taking the blame for trying so hard to be something he wasn't, and for the legacy of shame he'd leave his children. "If only I'd never met Terrence Collier. If only we'd never gone that day to Strawberry Hill."

I told him a priest was coming, which seemed to ease his anxiety. He grew calm, asked me to tell each of his children how much he loved them. Then he settled heavily into my arms with his eyes open, no longer struggling for breath.

"Gwendolyn Sparks has been covering for Terrence Collier," I said, trying to shake some life back into him. "That's it, isn't it, Brannigan?" He remained still as I screamed to be heard above the surf that pounded furiously around us. "Tell me, please! Tell me who murdered Diana!"

But there was no point in pleading with him any longer.

I hung my head in despair, hearing the faint wail of sirens that gradually grew louder.

HERCULES Platt was not among the officers who arrived, so I assumed the department didn't want him there.

Brannigan had apparently been telling the truth when he'd claimed he'd only wanted to scare me. The gun he'd dropped had no bullets. Lenore Ashley took the news hard, since she'd been the one responsible for his death.

As I held her there on the bluff after the rain had stopped, the two of us wrapped in blankets provided by the cops, I assured her she'd had no choice, that she'd done the right thing, that I would have done the same if our roles had been reversed. Yet a troubling question kept after me as the pale moon broke through the clouds: Had Lenore killed James Brannigan to save my life—or to prevent him from telling me something she didn't want me to know?

In my head, I began to hear the haunting refrain of "Riptide," recorded by the Archie Damon Orchestra back in 1934, three years after I'd been born. It was a Gus Kahn-Walter Donaldson tune, the title song from an M-G-M picture about someone in too deep, pulled emotionally in different directions, caught in a dangerous undertow.

I drew Lenore Ashley closer, hearing the tune but also the ocean behind us, rising up to pound relentlessly against Lands End, while its dark currents ran just beneath the surface, unseen.

Chapter 30

I T WAS DAWN when Lenore Ashley and I stumbled up to my suite at the Fairmont.

She got me out of my clothes and into the shower, soaped me down, cleansed my cuts and abrasions, kissed my bruises, rinsed me off, toweled me dry. When I was finally in bed, she slipped in beside me, naked and warm. The last thing I remember as she caressed me was touching her marvelous body while exhaustion dragged me away from her, toward sleep.

I woke a few hours later to the sound of church bells chiming across the city. Beside me, the bed was empty. The next thing I heard was the voice of Hercules Platt.

"You've been having quite a nightmare." He sat nearby in an upholstered chair, dressed in a well-pressed suit a cut above his usual in quality; as always, the short weave of his dark hair was pomaded carefully into place. In his lap, one hand clutched the brim of his hat, while the other gripped a leather-bound Bible, frayed at the edges.

I raised myself up, wincing, as pain wracked my body. "How long have you been sitting here?"

"Miss Ashley called me a couple of hours ago, told me what had happened out at Lands End. She said you were sleeping fitfully, and felt someone should be here when you woke up. I wouldn't do much moving around, Damon— you're going to be sore for a while."

"I suppose I deserve it."

"You deserve a lot worse. I thought I told you to lock yourself in, stay out of trouble."

"I believe I'll start listening to you, Inspector." Then: "I'm sorry the department kept you out of the loop last night. It wasn't fair."

Platt smiled thinly. "So who said life's fair?"

"The press must be in a frenzy."

"That's why Miss Ashley cleared out early this morning. She was worried that if reporters found out you two were shacking up, they'd make a scandal out of it. With Brannigan dead, they've got plenty to work with as it is."

James Brannigan dead—I'd almost forgotten. "What's the body count now, Inspector?"

"Including your wife, two years ago? Three unsolved murders—Diana, Terrence Collier, Vivian Collier—and now Brannigan on a justifiable homicide." Platt regarded me keenly. "That couldn't have been easy, seeing him die like that."

"Harder on Lenore, I'd think."

"Still, you were there when he bought the farm."

"So what do you think—is Brannigan good for the murders? After all, he threatened me, made it clear how badly he wanted the pearls. And he had motive in the other deaths."

"What do you think, Damon?"

"That's the first time you've asked me that, Inspector."

We looked up as Charlene appeared in the doorway. She was dressed in a gray wool suit with fur-trimmed collar, looking like she was on her way to brunch at the Sir Francis Drake.

"I see our young adventurer is alive and well."

I shifted in the bed, groaning. "Alive, anyway."

Platt reached into his coat pocket. "I've got a little present for you. Think of it as a get-well gift." He tossed me a small can, bright orange, not much deeper than a tin of chewing tobacco. On the lid were the faces of a handsome, well-groomed black couple, framed by a copyrighted brand name: Murray's Superior Hair Dressing Pomade. "Been using it for years," Platt said. "You might want to give it a try. Soften it with hot tap water before applying. It's industrial strength."

Charlene held up a paperback book. "Look! Hercules brought me a gift as well. A mystery novel, by someone named Chester Himes. Looks very promising."

"The tone may be a little darker than you're used to," Platt said, getting to his feet.

"The darker, the better," Charlene said.

Platt smiled to himself, took hold of my stubbly chin, turned my head from side to side. "You won't be so pretty for a while, Damon. But you'll heal up soon enough." He put on his hat. "Now, if you folks will excuse me, I'm due to pick up my sister for the second service at First Baptist. And, please, no more escapades."

"What about our trip down to Colma?"

"Just get some rest," Platt said. "We'll worry about cemeteries later."

WHILE Charlene kept the reporters at bay, I slept through Sunday afternoon, waking just before five as dusk began to fall.

Moments after I opened my eyes, Charlene was playing one of Dad's old records—"Too Marvelous for Words," with Jerry Cooper vocalizing—on a hi-fi she'd ordered in to cheer me up. I rose from the bed stiffly, showered, and put on fresh clothes while Charlene had dinner sent up.

The Brannigan incident had hit the news wires, and we ate together in the sitting room surrounded by flowers and telegrams sent by well-wishers. Truman Capote called from New York, thoroughly in his cups but sounding sincere as he inquired after my welfare. Attached to one of the bouquets, I found a card from Jackie K. in Washington, designed to buoy my spirits, but ending apologetically: *Perhaps sending you to San Francisco was not such a good idea after all.* Joe Kraft, George Plimpton, Anita Loos, Bobby Short, at least a dozen others—they'd all sent something to cheer me up.

Charlene squeezed my hand. "You're lucky to have so many good friends, Philip."

HERB Caen dropped around with a bottle of champagne as we finished our meal. We opened it and pushed back one of the sofas, and I watched as Herb and Charlene danced nimbly to "Pennies from Heaven." Herb was a great twirler, even with a moderate beat, and he had Charlene spinning again and again. Another of Dad's recordings from the early thirties dropped to the turntable—"I'm Going Shopping with You." Each time the refrain came up, repeating the title, Herb and Charlene sang along together, laughing afterward like it was a secret joke between them.

Finally, she said to me, "Baby, to understand, you'd have had to suffer through the Great Depression."

I left them to their hoofing while I shaved and got into my tux. When I applied some of the Murray's Pomade that Platt had given me, I found my hair falling into line like a squad of obedient cadets, wondering why it had taken me so long to discover the stuff. Except for some cuts and bruises, I thought, I was practically back to my old self.

Then I caught my eyes in the mirror, and the reflection held me for a moment. It was strange, dressing for another show, grooming my hair, hearing the bouncy lyrics of "It's Delovely" coming from the other room, on the same day a man had died in my arms after baring his life's regrets. Not the kind of thing one shakes off easily, if at all.

I wasn't my old self, I realized. I hadn't been my old self since losing Diana, and I'd never be my old self again. It just doesn't work that way, not for any of us, no matter how hard we work to put on a good show.

THE Venetian Room was empty as I seated myself at the Steinway; it would be another half-hour before the waiters would begin setting up for the night.

For the next thirty minutes, I let my fingers fly, feeling Dad inside me, knowing he was part of me every time I sat down to play or selected a new piece of music or attempted a difficult chord change and pulled it off. I ran through some of his favorite numbers—"La Cumparsita," "Let's Fall in Love," "Moon over Miami," maybe half a dozen others.

My mother, whom I'd never known, was more elusive. But Dad was right there with me when I played, in a way he'd never been when he was alive, in a way that always reminded me where I'd come from and left me feeling less alone.

Chapter 31

LATE THE NEXT morning, Hercules Platt dropped around and offered to buy me breakfast before we drove down to the City of the Dead.

He took me to Moar's Cafeteria on Powell Street near Market, close to the cable car turntable. We found a table on the left railing of the balcony, which allowed us a view of the mosaic murals created for the cafeteria by Beniamino Bufano. Bufano was a San Francisco institution, a genuine eccentric Herb Caen affectionately called Benny Bufoono; his famous sculptures and murals, reflecting his deep commitment to peace, were all over town. Interracial peace was his special passion and the theme that dominated his murals at Moar's. Platt mentioned that he often came here to eat just so he could spend time gazing at them.

"Helps keep my anger in check." He spread a thick linen

napkin across his lap. "In my case, no small accomplishment."

"It's hard to believe," I said, studying Bufano's work, "but even today I play hotels that don't allow Negroes to stay there."

"You should stop," Platt said matter-of-factly, and asked me to pass the salt.

AFTER breakfast, Platt ran a couple of business errands, and it was close to noon when we finally got out of the city. His Ford blew a radiator hose on the way down to Colma, and we lost another hour at a filling station before we got back on the road. Platt was hungry by then and insisted we stop in Daly City to pick up some fried chicken at Estrada's Spanish Kitchen, famous regionally for its golden bird. It was nearly two when we pulled through the big gates at Holy Cross Cemetery.

Platt went into the main office, where he received a map marked with the location of the del Conte family plot. He steered the Ford up the hill while I followed the map, directing him to make several turns that took us to the southern side, near the top. The exposure was greatest here, the trees sparse, the lawn thin and parched. There were no private mausoleums or monuments out this way, just flat stone markers embedded in the ground, with engraved inscriptions simple enough to fit within their narrow borders.

When we'd found the general area circled on the map, we got out and began a search for the del Conte plot, which was marked with four Xs. We found it in the third row up from the road, baking in the late October sun—three inscribed markers in succession, with a fourth spot kept in reservation, presumably for Valentino, the surviving son. I expected to find one or both of del Conte's parents occupying the first two gravesites, but it turned out differently.

According to the inscription on the first marker, the site belonged to Valentino del Conte's sibling: *Diana del Conte, Beloved Daughter and Sister, March 15, 1906–February 2, 1923.*

Platt and I did a double take on the first name.

"You still don't believe in coincidence, Inspector?"

Platt shook his head in wonderment. "Two Dianas, unrelated and separated in death by thirty-eight years." He pulled out his notebook, riffled its pages until he found the notes he'd taken during his recent visit to Charlene's office at the Fairmont. "Diana del Conte died the same day those photographs were taken in the Gold Room forty years ago. The ones that caught James Brannigan and Terrence Collier having such a swell time with their fraternity pals."

"The photos the *Examiner* used in its spread on the Fairmont within the past year." I glanced again at the dates atop Diana del Conte's grave. "She never made it to her eighteenth birthday."

We stood there studying the inscription for a while, saying nothing. My mind was racing, and I imagine Platt's had shifted gears as well.

"What now, Platt?"

He turned and strode back to his car, like a bloodhound on the scent, while I trotted to keep up. "First," he said, "I have a serious conversation with Mr. del Conte. With any luck, we find out how his beloved sister met her untimely end back in 1923."

*   *   *

THE lunch shift was over when we reached the Fairmont, but several waiters were still in the Squire Room, taking their meals. Valentino del Conte, however, was not among them. When Platt inquired after him, the dining room manager told us that del Conte had given his notice more than two weeks ago, and had worked his final shift the previous Friday.

"Did he say what his plans were?" Platt asked.

"No, sir. Just picked up his final paycheck this morning and said good-bye. Waiters come and go all the time. It's not unusual."

TWENTY minutes later, through the thick of afternoon traffic, we reached Polk Gulch, where Platt pounded on del Conte's front door. The blinds were drawn tight so we couldn't see in. Platt rang the bell long and hard, waited half a minute, then turned abruptly to cross Sutter Street back to his car, while I chased after him.

"I don't have enough to take him into custody, anyway," Platt said. "Just a bunch of odd circumstances and pesky questions."

One of them, I suggested, was whether del Conte had known Terrence Hamilton Collier III would be attending a benefit in the Gold Room two Sundays back.

"Seems likely," Platt said. "The Catholic Youth League was a major beneficiary of Collier's tax-deductible donations and the dinner dance was well advertised." Platt slid behind the wheel while I leaped in beside him. "I need to make a phone call to the Hall of Justice. You got change?"

I dug into my pocket while he pulled away from the curb.

By the time he turned onto Polk Street, I'd found a quarter, three dimes, and a nickel.

"Just the dimes, thanks." Platt parked in a red zone, took the change he needed, hopped out, and spent the next twenty minutes at a pay phone, quizzing a clerk in the records section of the Coroner's Office.

When he climbed back in the car, he said tersely, "At least we know one thing. Diana del Conte didn't die from natural causes."

"WE keep the old homicide case files down here."

It was half past four when Platt led me into a storage room in the basement of the Hall of Justice. He flicked on a bank of overhead fluorescent lights, illuminating rows of metal shelves crammed with hundreds of cardboard boxes tied with string. Most of the boxes bore the brand names of popular whiskeys, but they'd also been hand-marked with numbers and letters.

"There's more than half a century of records in this room," Platt said, "dating from the 1906 earthquake and fire. Throw in a couple of floods down here in the decades since, along with general neglect, and you've got quite a mess."

We heard a *cheep* and the scrabble of rats' feet somewhere in the dank space. Platt moved about the room, straightening tottering stacks, nudging errant boxes into place, inspecting the numbers inked on the upper edges. "The first two numbers signify the year. The letters indicate the alphabetical range of the case files in a particular box."

"So we'd be looking for 23 and D."

"That's the plan." He looked around at the disarray. "If there was a system in place, it went out the window eons ago. Let's get to work."

For more than two hours we searched for the box marked with a 23 and D. We finally found it deep in a corner where it didn't logically belong, buried under several boxes dating back to 1910. Together, we carried the box into better light. Platt blew away a layer of dust, untied the string, opened the box, and began flipping through a series of case files that started with the last name D'Agostino. A few of the files were slight, a single manila envelope holding several sheets of paper. But most were much thicker, including bulging accordion files bound together with string, with enough photos, notes, and data to flesh out an Irwin Shaw novel.

"Here it is." Platt read the slug on the sealed envelope in his hands: *del Conte, Diana, Case # 23-014.* "She was the fourteenth homicide in 1923. Makes sense, that early in the year. Some of those would have been accidental and vehicular."

He opened the envelope, pulled out a manila file, and unfolded it atop a stack of boxes. Inside were handwritten notes and typed reports that together didn't add up to a quarter inch of paper, and a set of photos that caused me to turn my head away in respect to Valentino del Conte's sister, who lay cold and naked on a coroner's slab. "I've seen thicker case files on fistfights," Platt said. He pulled the final report, put on his reading glasses, and took his time scanning each line. After that, he glanced through the other papers, then slapped the file shut.

"This is bullshit." Speaking briskly, he gave me the summary of what he'd just read: On February 2, 1923, in the late afternoon, a patrolman named Charles O'Flanagan had found Diana del Conte's body in an alley near lower Pacific Avenue and Broadway, not far from the Hippodrome. That was the heart of the saloon and strip club district, Platt said,

that had once been known as the Barbary Coast—a onetime
hotbed of prostitution and public sexual acts, including bes-
tiality on stage, that had finally been tamed by morality laws
passed in the early 1900s. The victim—not quite eighteen—
had been beaten and strangled; her body had borne evidence
of recent sexual intercourse, possibly forced. No witnesses
to the crime ever came forward and none were located, according to the final report, and material evidence was virtually nonexistent. The victim's parents had insisted their
daughter was a devout Catholic and a good student with a
part-time job at Woolworth's. The two inspectors assigned
to the case, however, had concluded that Diana del Conte
was a whore who'd had the misfortune of picking up a violent client. They'd moved on to other investigations, leaving the murder unsolved.

"There are a few things that bother me," Platt said. "First,
the other cases in this box—and I looked over a few—all
seem to be closed. Homicide doesn't ordinarily file open
murder cases down here, even the old ones, because no statute of limitations applies. Second, it's hard to believe that
not one citizen saw or heard anything at that time of the
day, that close to a busy street like Broadway. Third, I see
a brief coroner's note that there was a copious quantity of
blood on the victim's undergarments. Now why would a
young lady bleed like that during intercourse, unless she
was a virgin? And what the hell would an innocent girl be
doing in that section of town back then? The worst days of
the Barbary Coast ended back in 1914, with the Red Light
Abatement Act. But it just wasn't the kind of place a decent
young lady ventured in 1923."

Platt opened the file again, pulled out a set of photos.
"And look at the pictures of the crime scene. The surface in

this alley is gravel. Look at the wide tracks leading from the middle of the alley to the body, as if it's been dragged a short distance." Platt put the photos back in the file, which he slipped into its envelope. "I don't think Diana del Conte was killed down in the Barbary. I think somebody dumped her body there, hoping it would look like a murder involving a chippie or a whore."

Platt closed the box, keeping the case file out, and retied the box with string. "No arrests, no real investigation. Yet the case file ends up down here, tucked away deep in the basement. Kind of makes you wonder why."

He headed for the door and hit the light switch as I caught up. "There's one more problem with this case file." Platt closed the door behind us and strode back toward the elevator. "The date on the patrolman's report that's included in the file—February 5, 1923. Why would a patrolman wait three days to write up his report on a homicide?"

Before I could offer an opinion, Platt was inside the elevator, punching the button for the fourth floor. "Unless maybe somebody asked him to rewrite the original, fix it up a little." I jumped in after him, just as the doors closed. "We keep the original of every patrolman's homicide report in Records. The Records Department is where Lynn Osborn works."

"Valentino del Conte's boyfriend."

"Lucky Strikes," Platt said.

THE elevator doors opened on the fourth floor facing an open counter and a sign above it signifying it as the Records Department. A peroxide blonde in a tight sweater, wearing bright red lipstick and chewing gum, looked up as Platt came through.

"Evening, Inspector," she said, but her eyes were on me.

Platt tipped his hat. "You're working late. It's almost eight."

"We're all working late these days," she said, snapping her gum. "What with these high-priority murder cases and all." As Platt came around the counter with me in tow, she looked me over the way a housewife might size up a porterhouse steak at the butcher shop.

"He's with me," Platt said. "Protective custody."

"Be careful with him," the blonde said, and gave me a wink.

I followed Platt around the counter and into the records room, which was filled with row after row of filing cabinets and desks. Several men and women were preparing to go home for the night or were on their way out. It took Platt a few minutes, but he eventually found the file cabinet he was looking for; he kneeled, pulled open a deep drawer, riffled through the manila folders inside, looking frustrated. He started over again, from the front. Finally, he shut the drawer and got to his feet, cursing and clutching his stiff back.

"Either Charles O'Flanagan forgot to file his report forty years ago, or it's conveniently missing."

I followed him to the front counter, where the gum-chewing blonde was powdering her nose like Lana Turner in a bad B movie. Platt asked her where he could find a clerk named Lynn Osborn. She told him Osborn had given notice three weeks ago, and a small farewell lunch had taken place the previous Friday.

She looked up from her compact mirror. "I think he's planning a vacation. I saw him studying travel brochures and airline fares. South America, I think it was. Is there something I can help you with, Inspector?" Her eyes—long lashes, heavy mascara—slid in my direction again. "You and your nice-looking friend?"

Platt asked her if she'd ever heard of a patrolman named Charles O'Flanagan. She said she hadn't, which put Platt on the move again, striding down the green linoleum toward the homicide office. "Lynn Osborn quits his job in Records about the time Mr. del Conte gives notice at the Fairmont. It seems our two lovebirds may be planning to fly the coop together. Who knows, Osborn may already be gone. You know what else I think?"

"That Osborn removed that patrolman's report at del Conte's request, so he could do his own digging into his sister's death."

"I wouldn't be surprised if del Conte's parents never told him about his sister's death when he was a little boy. He was the sensitive type, they wanted to protect him. As he grew older, he started to get curious. Maybe the parents finally spilled the beans. Valentino meets this Osborn character, who works in police records. They get close, and del Conte asks Osborn to pull the file."

"But wouldn't Valentino have seen exactly what you saw down in the basement? The same report, giving the same account of his sister's death?"

"It's the date on the report that mystifies me," Platt said. "It shouldn't take three days for a patrolman to write down what he saw when he stumbled on a crime scene, before it was turned over to a homicide crew."

Platt pushed open the door to the homicide office. The same middle-aged woman I'd seen on my first visit was behind the counter, catching up on her filing. As we entered, Platt got right to the point.

"Esther, you've worked in the department a long time, right?"

"Almost thirty years, Inspector."

"You remember a patrolman named Charles O'Flanagan?"

"Oh, yes, I remember everyone who was with us for any length of time. Charlie retired as a sergeant, back in the late forties, when he made his 25/50."

"You know what happened to him?"

"I believe he owns a building over in the Castro." She put a finger to her chin, thinking hard. "Yes, that's right, he has a building with a bar on the first floor. O'Flanagan's he calls it. Some of the men like to drink down there after work. Usually on Fridays."

She laughed and gave us a self-deprecating look. "O'Flanagan's—now you'd think I'd remember that right off, wouldn't you?"

It was after eight when Platt pulled out of the underground police garage, flicking on his headlights.

He turned right on Bryant Street in the direction of the Castro. As he maneuvered through traffic, he asked me if I knew what Herb Caen was up to this evening.

"Dancing at El Matador with Charlene and her hubby and some visiting dignitaries," I said. "The mayor and his wife are joining them." I glanced at my watch. "They're probably ordering cocktails right about now. Why?"

"We may need some help from your friend Mr. Caen."

I settled back with my hands behind my head and a smug

look on my face. "Thank goodness the Venetian Room's dark Mondays and I've got the night off. Otherwise, Inspector, I'd have to leave you on your own."

Hercules Platt gave me one of his looks and tramped on the gas pedal.

Chapter 32

T HE CASTRO WAS a working-class neighborhood, primarily Irish-American, nestled between Noe Valley and the lower Haight, just west of the Mission district.

Its distinguishing feature was the Castro Theater, a flamboyant movie palace located on Castro Street just below Market. The historic building dated to the early twenties and featured an ornamental Spanish façade accented with colorful Art Deco neon that had been added in 1937. The last time I'd been there—with Charlene, back in '55—*The Seven-Year Itch* had been playing to a sold-out house. This evening, as Hercules Platt drove past, the marquee advertised *Gidget Goes to Rome*, without a single customer in line at the box office.

We found O'Flanagan's at the bottom of the hill, around the corner on 18th Street, between a dime store and a small grocery. Platt parked and we crossed through traffic to the bar, a drab place with a neon Pabst Blue Ribbon sign in the single window. We pushed through a set of heavy black curtains to the smell of beer, sawdust, and stale urine.

Behind the bar, a dumpy, round-shouldered man with red hair going gray filled the two-ounce glass of an old-timer hunched on a stool. In the back, two men in Transit uniforms shot pool. Four more men were seated in a booth to our right, working through a pitcher of draft while comparing the assets of Jayne Mansfield and Mamie van Doren. A couple of dozen bottles stood at attention along the wall behind the bar, where a long, gold-framed mirror gave the place its only touch of class. Overhead, a black-and-white TV set was tuned to *The Patty Duke Show*.

The bartender looked up as we entered and did a double take when he saw Platt. Platt took a stool midway down the bar and I sat beside him. The bartender moved toward us slowly, limping on a gimpy leg and puffing a cigarette lodged at the corner of his mouth. He stood in front of us but said nothing, keeping his rheumy eyes on Platt.

"My friend will have a beer," Platt said, "and I'll have a Tab."

"We don't serve Tab."

"Then I'll have a Coke."

"Don't serve Coke, neither."

"How do you make a rum and Coke?"

"Don't."

"My buddy O'Flanagan told me you did."

The bartender scoffed. "Charlie O'Flanagan?"

"The same," Platt said.

"You're no friend of Charlie O'Flanagan's."

"And how would you know that?"

"Because I'm Charlie O'Flanagan."

"Then I should introduce myself." Platt buzzed his gold badge. "Hercules Platt, Homicide." He smiled tightly. "The pleasure's all mine."

Recognition dawned in O'Flanagan's sickly eyes. "I heard about you, Platt. They brung you up from patrol to work the Fillmore. Last time I looked, the Fillmore's a couple miles north. You got no business here."

"You don't serve police officers in this establishment?"

"I serve plenty of officers, present and retired."

"Maybe you serve the two inspectors assigned to the Diana del Conte murder case back in '23, when you were working patrol. If they're still breathing, that is."

O'Flanagan's jaw went slack, revealing tobacco-stained teeth. "Like I said, I serve a lot of cops. But I don't know nothing about a Diana whatever you said her name was. So why don't you and your friend go drink somewheres else?"

Platt got off his stool, walked to the end of the bar and around it, and pulled the plug on the TV set, sending *Patty Duke* into oblivion. O'Flanagan hollered and limped in Platt's direction while Platt picked up the old-timer's glass and dumped what was left of it into the sink. By the time O'Flanagan got there, Platt was showing his badge at the pool table and removing the sticks from the hands of the surprised players. Then he crossed to the booth and told the beer drinkers to drain their glasses fast and get lost.

"Everybody out," Platt shouted. "Now."

As the bar cleared, O'Flanagan humped on his bad leg back to the cash register, where he faced the mirror while reaching under the counter. By the time he came up with his pistol, he saw Platt reflected in the glass, his snub-nosed .38 aimed across the bar at the back of O'Flanagan's head.

"This doesn't have to be so complicated," Platt said. "I just have a few questions, then we'll be on our way."

O'Flanagan hesitated a moment, then put the pistol back and turned to face Platt again. His rage had reddened his face and twisted his mouth into an ugly shape. Platt slipped his gun back into the holster at his belt, then looked O'Flanagan directly in the eye. "Diana del Conte. Seventeen years old. You found her body in an alley near lower Columbus and Broadway forty years ago. Strangled, beaten, probably raped. Tell me about it."

"Means nothing to me." O'Flanagan's eyes flew around like a pair of uncaged canaries in a houseful of cats. "That's all I got to say on that."

"Your report's in a case file, O'Flanagan, identifying you as the first officer at the scene. Does that refresh your memory?"

"There was a time when the department didn't have no coloreds on the payroll, especially coloreds that didn't know their place."

Platt reached across the bar with both hands and grabbed O'Flanagan by his shirt front. He dragged him halfway across the bar until they were eyeball to eyeball. The rage in the old man's face was gone now, replaced by unvarnished fear.

"Times are changing, Charlie."

"It was forty years ago, for Chrissake." O'Flanagan swallowed hard as the color drained from his face. "Why do you want to bother about a whore who's been gone that long?"

"I'll ask the questions, you provide the answers. And if you answer real good, you might come out of this relatively intact."

"You got nothing on me, Platt. Anything I might have

done as a cop, the clock ticked away on years ago. It's called statute of limitations. Maybe you oughta look it up."

"Obstruction of justice, maybe. But not accessory after the fact."

The word *accessory* seemed to dash O'Flanagan's bravado; he began deflating like a punctured tire. Platt let go of him, dropping him back to the floor, but kept talking.

"This story's about to break wide open, O'Flanagan. You can be a hero by stepping forward with vital information in the cause of justice and maybe wiggle your way out of trouble. Or you can be a chump and spend your last miserable years behind bars. At this point, it's really up to you."

"You don't seem to understand how the department works."

"Oh, I know very well how the police department works, Charlie. I know all about the secret society of white Roman Catholic officers who protect their own. I also know that Chief Cahill's trying to turn things around, clean up the department's lousy image. I have a feeling he'd jump at the chance to make an example of you, and the Prosecutor's Office would go right along with him."

A bead of sweat trickled down the side of O'Flanagan's face. "Maybe, maybe not."

"Which is why I'm not taking this to the department just yet. First, the newspapers get it. Then we see how the Chief and the D.A. react to the pressure." Platt glanced at his watch. "By tomorrow morning, the Diana del Conte story will be front page in the *Chronicle*. And your name will be right at the top, Charlie."

"That's what you say, Platt."

"You'll be out there alone, swinging in the wind. I doubt even the Police Officers Association will want to stand up for a sad sack like you. She was seventeen, Charlie. You might as well have killed her yourself."

"Who are you kidding? No colored man carries any weight with the *Chron*, except maybe one of the Willies on the sports page."

Platt glanced in my direction, talking to me with his eyes.

"On the contrary," I said. "Inspector Platt is very tight with the press. Herb Caen, for example. They're quite chummy."

"Mr. San Francisco? The most popular newspaper guy in the city?" O'Flanagan snorted derisively. "I'll believe that the day Jack Kennedy walks in here and orders a beer."

"I joined them for drinks just last night," I said. "Joe DiMaggio was there. Up at the Fairmont. They were discussing the Terrence Collier murder case."

"Actually," Platt corrected me, "I was drinking coffee. Herb and Joe had the cocktails."

"What a crock." O'Flanagan attempted a laugh, but his nervous eyes gave him away.

I slapped a dime down on the bar. "Call Caen yourself, if you'd like. He's having drinks at El Matador with the mayor and some other friends of the Inspector."

Platt's smile was cruel. "Maybe they're talking about you, Charlie, and how a mob might descend on this place from the Mission when they find out about your role in the rape and murder of a seventeen-year-old Italian girl."

"I swear I didn't have nothing to do with it." O'Flanagan swiped at the sweat with the back of his flannel sleeve. "I just found her, that's all."

"But you know how the *Chron* will write it up. You know what they'll do with a story like this. Paper never was known for subtlety."

"The guineas'll come after me with a frigging rope."
O'Flanagan's voice quaked. "They'll probably try to torch
this place."

I pushed the dime closer to him. "Call him, O'Flanagan.
Ask Caen if he knows Platt and where they were last night,
and what it was they were talking about."

"I got my own dime." O'Flanagan opened the cash register, scooped out two nickels, shut the drawer, limped to
the pay phone. He dropped the two coins in the slot, flipped
open a phone book, dialed some numbers, put the receiver
to his ear. A moment later he asked if he could speak with
Herb Caen. A minute after that, he was talking to Mr. San
Francisco himself. He explained the situation, asked a series
of questions, and got responses that caused his eyes to widen.
Essentially, he learned that Hercules Platt and Herb Caen
had indeed met over drinks the previous night, discussing
the Terrence Collier murder case, right in the Nob Hill hotel
where the murder had taken place.

When he hung up, O'Flanagan looked like a man who'd
just watched his house burn down. "I need a drink." He
hobbled back behind the bar, poured himself a generous
dose of Wild Turkey, drank it down all at once.

"Start talking," Platt said.

"I was a flunkie patrolman, just back from WW-One. A wife,
a kid, another in the oven. What did I know?"

"Tell me what you know now, Charlie."

"It's about four in the afternoon. I'm on foot patrol. I see
this fancy sedan down the alley, big car—Packard, I think
it was. Two fellas doing something, I couldn't tell what, but
it don't look right. I walk down there for a better look. I

see they're dragging this young girl from the backseat."

"Diana del Conte."

O'Flanagan nodded miserably. "They drag her over to the side and dump her. I think maybe she's drunk, that's all it is. I get closer, I see she's been roughed up. I check for a pulse; it's pretty obvious she's gone. She's got a rosary around her neck; that really got to me. I draw my weapon, tell these two Joes not to move an inch. One of 'em, the big one, he's crying. Not so much because they're caught, I think, but because of this girl, that she's dead and all. He seems real disturbed by it. The other one's cool, though, almost arrogant, the sonofabitch. Dressed real preppy, a rich kid, don't seem scared at all. The one leaking tears, he breaks down right there and spills his guts. Tells me the two of 'em was out looking for a good time, saw this pretty Italian girl walking on Strawberry Hill over in Golden Gate Park. Sweet-talked her, convinced her to go for a ride, get a malted, you know how it works. I guess the boys belted down a pint of Bushmills and the one kid, the cool one, he tries to force himself on the girl. She says no, tries to get out of the car, he grabs her, she fights back. One thing leads to another, pretty soon these two drunk college kids got a dead body on their hands."

"Funny how things can happen that way," Platt said.

"I cuff 'em both to a railing in the alley there. I got to get to a call box, you know? I take their wallets with their identification and when I seen the names, I know I'm in way over my head. The rich kid, he just laughs. Then I get my butt to a call box and a district captain's there almost before I get back to the scene. He's got the cuffs off these two kids. The three of 'em got their heads together like they're family. The captain, he tells me that he'll handle it from here on out, and says how I'm supposed to make out my report. Just say I came across the body and didn't see nothing else, he tells me. No names, no witnesses, nothing. Says I'll be taken care of down the line."

Platt glanced around at the bar. "Maybe that's how you got this place. After you won your promotion to sergeant."

O'Flanagan's eyes got shifty again. "No comment."

"Go on, finish your story."

"I start thinking what if this whole thing blows up somehow and comes back to bite me on the ass. I got some exposure here, you know? So I make out my report straight, putting down just what I seen, names and all. I turn it in that same day. Next day, my district captain, he takes me aside, tells me I need to make a few fixes, be more creative with the facts. I wanna keep my job, so I give him the report he wants, only now it's dated three days later. That's the one that goes into the investigative file. Only without telling nobody, I put a copy of my original report in the Records file, right behind the one I doctored for the captain. I figure this case is going nowhere fast, you know what I mean? It's gonna get buried, like these kinda deals do. So nobody's gonna see my two reports anyhow. But if somebody should start digging around, and this thing blows up, I got my ass covered. My first report's in there, just the way I did it before the brass twisted my balls, making me help 'em with the cover-up."

O'Flanagan reached for the bottle of Wild Turkey, unscrewed the cap. "Time went by, I didn't even think nothing about it. Not until I seen in the paper last week that this Collier fella got clocked at the Fairmont. Then his buddy Brannigan takes a tumble out at Lands End." O'Flanagan's eyes got jumpy again. "Kinda makes you wonder, don't it?"

"Collier was the rich boy who killed the girl," Platt said.

O'Flanagan nodded. "Yeah, he was the one. Back then, everybody knew who the Collier family was, that you didn't mess with 'em."

"And James Brannigan was the big kid with him."

"Brannigan, sure. Fullback for Stanford—name was on the sports page every Sunday that fall. Now both of 'em's dead, along with this rich old broad, Collier's ex. I says to myself, what the hell's going on in this city? Big shots are dropping like flies. I figure whoever solves this one gets a commendation from the Pope himself."

Platt smiled faintly. "Maybe you'll help solve it, Charlie. Maybe I can let the right people know you did the right thing after all these years."

O'Flanagan chewed his lip until it bled. "You'd do that for me?"

"I want to close this case, Charlie. That's my main objective."

O'Flanagan swallowed dryly, hanging his head a little, as if Platt was about to strike him. "I'd be in your debt, Inspector."

His hand trembled as he poured himself another whiskey.

Chapter 33

PLATT GUNNED THE Ford north along Fillmore Street between Market and Japantown while he got on his radio and ordered an all-points bulletin for Valentino del Conte.

We were passing through the Fillmore, where working-class blacks had moved in during World War II after the forced relocation of Japanese-Americans who had homes and businesses there. Over the ensuing years, as prosperity blossomed in America but left most Negroes behind, poverty, drugs, and broken families had taken their toll on the neighborhood.

"You won't find the Fillmore mentioned in most travel guides," Platt said, pushing the Ford to fifty, "unless it's a warning to stay out." He indicated an approaching side street, where Negroes hung out on stoops and black children played along the sidewalks. "My place is just down the block. Three bedrooms, nice little yard. Got it with a G.I. loan when I came home from the Big One."

"That's when you became a cop?"

Platt nodded as he swung the wheel, accelerating around a cumbersome Edsel. "I worked part-time at first, alongside a few other black patrolmen. Limited tenure they called it, meaning no benefits or pension, no job security. I was the first full-time Negro hired in '57. Now there's almost a hundred of us, nearly five percent of the force."

"Who knows? Maybe one day there'll be a black mayor."

"In San Francisco?" Platt laughed. "Dream on, Damon."

He took a hard right on Sutter Street, pointing east toward Polk Gulch.

THE lights were on in Valentino del Conte's apartment when we got there and the front door was wide open. Platt turned his wheels in to the curb, leaped out, dashed across Sutter Street and up the front steps. I noticed he had a hand on his gun.

When I caught up, he was talking to a boisterous woman with broad shoulders and short-cropped hair who wore coveralls and gripped a paint brush in one hand. Except for paint cans, a ladder, and drop cloths covering the floors, the apartment was empty.

"Valentino shipped a few large boxes Saturday morning," the woman said, in a voice that was on the deep side. "Sold most of his other belongings over the weekend. People were trooping in and out all day Saturday and most of Sunday. What he didn't sell, he gave away to friends or charity. The

Salvation Army sent a truck by this morning. That was the last time I saw him."

"You're the landlady?" Platt asked.

She grinned. "I don't know how much of a lady I am. I own the place and collect the rents."

Platt showed his badge. "I need to talk with Mr. del Conte. It's urgent."

The woman pushed back a sleeve to look at her Timex. "It's after nine. You might catch him down in North Beach, at Finnochio's."

"I thought Finnochio's was dark Mondays," Platt said, "except during the tourist season."

"Special farewell show." The woman dipped her brush in a can of white paint. "By invitation only. You know, a big send-off for Miss Valentine. I woulda gone, but I gotta get this place ready for the next tenant. So I said my good-byes this morning."

"Miss Valentine," Platt said, like he was beginning to understand.

"Hey, Valentino's one of the most popular performers Finnochio's ever had, even if he's managed to keep it private all these years. If anybody deserves a farewell send-off, it's Valentino del Conte."

Platt fingered the two names printed on the mailbox: *V. del Conte* and *D. del Conte.* "He lived alone, then."

"Depends on how you look at it." The woman raised her brush to resume painting. "Valentino lived so close to his sister's memory, the two of them kind of merged. He dressed like her, made himself up like her, whatever he could do to keep her memory alive. Even had photos taken of himself as Diana, the way she might have looked if she'd had the chance to grow older."

She paused in her brush strokes. "If you hurry, you might catch his final show."

FINNOCHIO'S was located at 506 Broadway, in the heart of North Beach between Columbus and Kearny, occupying the second floor above Enrico's. Hercules Platt had us there in five minutes flat.

We climbed five steps under a pink canopy to the door, where a heavyset Italian man stopped us with an upraised hand. "Sorry, fellas. Tonight's show is by invitation only."

"We're on the list," Platt said, and flashed his badge.

The doorman unhooked the velvet-covered rope, and we dashed inside. A wider carpeted stairway led us up another flight and into the smoke-filled club. Finnochio's had been around since 1936, run by Joe and Eve Finnochio, a married couple who touted their operation as "America's Most Unusual Night Club." To satisfy the Vice Squad, the Finnochios ran the place like a regular theater—no mingling of performers and customers allowed—with a stage up front that featured men performing in women's clothes, more than a few of them married with kids. Diana and I had dropped in once when the great female impersonator Charles Pierce was appearing; Bob Hope and Tallulah Bankhead had been in the audience that night, at separate tables—Hope with his wife and some pals, Tallulah with a few girlfriends in male drag.

Tonight, however, Miss Valentine held center stage. She had the audience in her thrall as she sashayed and shimmied before the footlights while waitresses hustled cocktails to the tables.

"Drink up!" Miss Valentine commanded. "The more you drink, the better we look!"

But Miss Valentine had no reason to apologize. She was resplendent in an extravagant gown of brilliant red satin, rather tall in her heels but padded out to create a flourishing female figure; her dusky face, carefully made up and framed by a wig of fine, dark hair, was flawless under the spotlight. There was no doubt this was the same person we'd seen hurrying from Valentino del Conte's apartment early Saturday evening, before jumping into a cab—Diana del Conte reincarnated, as she might have looked if she hadn't been murdered at age seventeen.

Miss Valentine cracked a bawdy joke that caused the audience to erupt into raucous laughter, then announced her final song. "People often ask why I always work the early show," she said. "It's to give me time to get my beauty sleep before working the breakfast shift in the morning. But there'll be no more breakfast shifts for this old broad. Honey, it's retirement time. The old gal's headed down the yellow brick road!" With a background recording crackling on the sound system, she broke into a falsetto rendition of Judy Garland's "Over the Rainbow" that immediately hushed the house. Despite Valentino's limited vocal skills, he was a born showman who sang unabashedly from the heart, investing the lyrics with genuine feeling that all the training in the world can't teach. As the song ended, with Miss Valentine giving it her all, most of the patrons were in tears, rising to their feet, calling for one more number. Platt began threading his way through the tables toward the stage while I followed.

Miss Valentine was basking in the applause, throwing

kisses to the crowd, while her fans tossed long-stemmed roses that piled up around her heels.

"I love you, I love you all," she shouted. "You've been like family! You've brought me such joy!"

Then she spotted Platt and me as we pushed our way through the crowd. She pointed a long, painted nail directly at us.

"Stop them!" She frantically signaled the stage manager as Platt mounted the steps. "Keep them back!"

Miss Valentine stepped back, throwing more kisses, as the silver lame curtain cascaded to the stage. The crowd surged forward, pulling us from the steps, swarming over us, and Platt and I went down under an avalanche of bodies.

BY the time we regained our feet and Platt backed the crowd away with his badge, the house lights were up and Miss Valentine was nowhere to be seen.

I followed Platt back through the house until we found a doorway leading to the dressing rooms, where we attempted to push past men in various stages of wardrobe and makeup, all of whom seemed to be conveniently in our way. Platt, his badge visible, demanded to know where Valentino del Conte was. A man in corseted Mae West drag draped a hairy hand on Platt's shoulder.

"No men allowed back here, Sugar. But if you should find him, you can tell him that Mae very definitely *will*."

The others laughed and we pushed on, but our path was blocked at every step: a rack of gowns, an assortment of feather boas, a magician pulling white doves from under his dress. Suddenly, we saw a flash of red just ahead—Miss Valentine, carrying a small travel bag and dashing down a narrow hallway leading to a door marked with an Exit sign.

"There he is." Platt turned in that direction, passing a small room where men sat in front of makeup mirrors, carefully shaving, affixing eyelashes, applying color to their puckered lips. We were halfway down the hall when a huge man dressed as Little Bo Peep in a hoop skirt and bonnet stepped from a wardrobe room, wielding a shepherd's staff. He wedged himself between the walls, blocking our path. Platt again showed his badge, ordering the man to move aside.

"Which way, my little lamb? Back, forward? You've got Bo Peep all flustered. She hasn't a clue which way to turn."

By the time we got past Little Bo Peep, the exit door was closing. Platt struggled down the hallway and pushed the door open, and we stepped out to a steep section of Kearny, where narrow concrete steps led us down to Broadway. As we got there, we glimpsed another flurry of red as Valentino stepped into a taxi and pulled the door closed behind him, just before the cab sped away.

Dozens of men emerged from Finnochio's, many of them in various stages of female attire. They swarmed around and past us, hailing taxis, jumping into their own vehicles, or simply racing on foot after Valentino's cab, exhorting him to make good his escape.

I leaped into Platt's Ford and yanked the door closed. The tires squealed, as he raced away from the curb.

Chapter 34

AS WE GAVE chase, tourists clogged the intersections along Broadway, moving like lemmings between North Beach, Chinatown, and Fisherman's Wharf. Hercules Platt stayed on his horn, blasting at anyone or anything in his path.

Valentino del Conte's taxi was several blocks ahead, too far for either Platt or me to make out its number or license plate. At one point, Platt pulled alongside a speeding cab, only to realize it carried three performers from Finnochio's in the backseat, each of whom extended his middle finger for Platt's benefit. We were part of a battalion of vehicles in pursuit, and most of them seemed to be ahead of us. As Platt drove, he barked into his police radio, calling for all available units to converge on Broadway westbound, approaching Van Ness Avenue, looking for a speeding cab with a woman passenger who was wearing a red gown but who was not actually female.

When Platt wasn't on his radio, he was talking to me a mile a minute, putting his case together piece by piece. "Valentino reads that copy of O'Flanagan's original report that his boyfriend lifted from records. Learns that Terrence Collier brutalized and killed his sister back in '23. Knowing how things work, Valentino figures the only way to get justice is to take matters into his own hands. He sees that old photo in the *Examiner*—Collier celebrating with Brannigan in the Gold Room, only hours after they'd dumped Diana del Conte's battered body down in the Barbary Coast. It infuriates him beyond reason. Then he sees an announcement that the Catholic Youth League is holding its big dinner dance in the Gold Room. Valentino knows it's Collier's pet charity and that he'll be there. From working other hotels, Valentino also knows that Collier has a passion for the fox-trot, always taking center stage. Valentino sees his chance to avenge his sister's death in grand style, in the same elegant ballroom where Collier drank and danced only hours after he killed her. Valentino plots Collier's demise with a theatrical touch worthy of the legendary Miss Valentine. He dresses up as Diana, tucks an ice pick into his handbag, and waltzes into the Fairmont unrecognized. Slips into the Gold Room through the back of the house, using the service kitchen passageways he knows so well as a waiter. At some point, blending in with all the other well-dressed ladies, he drops that note requesting 'Just In Time' into the bowl on your piano.

"He waits until the orchestra begins to play the fatal number, slips out, kills the lights, slips back in, concealed

by the darkness and confusion, and drives that ice pick into
Terrence Collier's heart."

"But not before letting him know why," I said. "Telling
him, 'This is for Diana.' "

"A brilliant performance." Platt's voice was hard, sour.
"Cue the applause."

"I'm not so sure Collier didn't deserve it. If Valentino
hadn't avenged his sister's death—"

"Murder's murder," Platt said, so sharply I clamped my
mouth shut.

PLATT was back on his police radio as Valentino's cab turned
right on Van Ness Avenue, then radioed directions again as
the cab swung left on busy Lombard Street, pointed west.

"It looks like he's going for the bridge." Platt laid on his
horn as he attempted to squeeze between a bakery truck and
a municipal bus.

We made it through and began to gain ground. Patrol
cars with lights flashing and sirens wailing were converging
from side streets around and behind us. It seemed only a
matter of seconds before the cabbie would realize he was
being pursued and pull over. But as we closed to within two
miles of the Golden Gate Bridge, a little Nash Rambler
convertible—top down and filled with screaming drag
queens—shot out of Divisadero Street ahead of us and
braked in the middle of the intersection. Several passengers
jumped out in their gowns and high heels, dressed and made
up variously as Carol Channing, Josephine Baker, Judy
Garland, and Carmen Miranda. They locked arms and
stood their ground like loyal soldiers guarding the Berlin
Wall, triggering instant gridlock. Sirens, blaring horns, and

screeching tires blended into a cacophony of frustration as cops in a dozen patrol cars maneuvered to get free, to no avail. Platt and I sat in the Ford, locked in among the vehicles, while Platt let forth with a string of strange words that apparently derived from the urban Negro vernacular.

In the distance, Valentino's taxi disappeared into the flow of traffic, gaining speed as it hit the stretch of Highway 101 that opened up to several lanes approaching the Golden Gate Bridge. By the time all the drivers had separated themselves to clear the intersection and Platt had us moving again, several vehicles carrying Miss Valentine's friends and fans had found routes around us and were racing ahead. As we entered the northbound lanes to the bridge, shooting past the southbound toll booths, Valentino's taxi was long out of sight.

"I hope he's not planning what I think he's planning." Platt sounded troubled, almost grim, as he pressed down once again on the gas pedal.

HALFWAY across the Golden Gate, traffic had snarled, this time so massively that vehicles came to a bumper-to-bumper standstill in both directions.

Platt and I were forced to abandon his car and trot the final hundred yards to the middle of the bridge, which wasn't easy for Platt, given his tight back. Finally, we neared the source of the pandemonium: Miss Valentine had kicked off her heels and climbed over the railing and out to a girder, where she stood twenty stories above the cold, deep waters of San Francisco Bay. A couple of dozen cross-dressers hugged each other and wailed, begging her not to jump, as hundreds of others had done so dramatically over the previous decades.

When Platt saw what was happening, he went into a sprint. By the time I caught up, he was pushing his way through the crowd, imploring Valentino del Conte to come down.

Valentino stood tall and erect, his chin raised with immense dignity, his voice strong, unwavering. "I couldn't bear to live out my life behind bars, Inspector. I broke the law, and now I must pay the price."

"Not this way, Valentino. Please."

"I'm sorry, Inspector, but this is exactly how Miss Valentine must make her final exit." Valentino smiled, looking quite at peace, as the breeze ruffled the long, dark hair framing his face. "Such a grand stage cries out for a moment of extravagant showmanship, a farewell performance no one will ever forget."

Platt lunged for the railing, attempting to hoist himself, reaching up with his free hand toward the hem of the billowing gown. But he was too late, and inches short. A collective scream rose from the crowd as Valentino leaped, throwing both hands out and upward as if in surrender. I saw Platt close his fist, grabbing air. Moments later, he clutched his lower back, sliding from the railing and crumpling to the pavement. When I reached him, his face was contorted with pain, but the look of personal defeat and sadness was etched even more deeply.

I helped him up, then pressed myself to the railing with the others. A rescue helicopter passed beneath the bridge, directing its spotlight on the water. More beams shone from Port Authority boats motoring out from the harbor. Platt and I peered over. Two hundred feet below, under the spotlights, Miss Valentine's red satin gown blossomed like a bright flower on the dark water.

"At least we know who killed Terrence Collier." Reflexively, I crossed myself, something I hadn't done in years. "May Valentino rest in peace."

"You're right, my case is closed." Platt shifted his weary brown eyes in my direction. "But we still don't know who murdered Vivian Collier."

"And we still don't know who killed Diana—*my* Diana." I stared down as divers leaped into the cold water where the red satin billowed up. "Valentino certainly can't help us, can he?"

"Damn this bridge," Platt said. "It's helped bury too many secrets."

I glanced at Platt, startled. "What did you just say?"

"I said this bridge has helped bury—"

"That's what I thought you said."

BEHIND us, more sirens pierced the chill night air, joining the mournful wails of Valentino del Conte's friends and fans.

I looked north, beyond the lights of the city, where the Redwood Highway ran like an asphalt ribbon through the fertile vineyards of Sonoma County. Platt's words had brought to mind another bridge, far less conspicuous, constructed of redwood and home to nesting bats, where Diana had once improbably ventured. My Diana.

There must have been a reason, I figured, as I stood at the railing of the famous Golden Gate, shivering with cold, saddened by the loss of Valentino del Conte, and contemplating the notion of secrets taken to the grave.

Chapter 35

IN THE MORNING, I asked Charlene if we might run up to her house in the redwoods for the day, to escape the reporters aroused by the dramatic events of the previous night.

She was agreeable, even when I asked if Lenore Ashley might join us. Charlene's attitude about Lenore had softened, in light of her role as my savior out at Lands End and the way she'd cared for me afterward. When I called Lenore, however, she seemed less than eager to make the trip. After much cajoling on my part, she finally agreed to go, and my heart beat a little faster at the thought of being with her again.

We got a late start, riding in the chauffeured Bentley into a landscape of brilliant green and gold in the sharp sunlight of late autumn. Sitting three across, we noshed on Viennese—plump sausages, vinegary potatoes, tasty kraut—that we'd picked up at Maximilian's on the way out of The City. I caught the scent of Chanel No. 5 in the car, and wondered for a moment if Lenore might be wearing it again, as she had that fateful night in the Gold Room during our first encounter. When I mentioned it, Lenore studied me in thoughtful silence, looking a little troubled, while Charlene acknowledged that she'd dabbed on some Chanel just before leaving. From there, she recalled a Ngiao Marsh whodunit she'd read a few years earlier, *False Scent*, in which the culprit puts lethal poison into a perfume atomizer. As Charlene recounted the tale, Lenore smiled and nodded politely from time to time, but I sensed a remoteness about her, as if her thoughts were somewhere else.

BY the time we arrived at Charlene's hideaway, the shadows were long and the day's warmth was giving way to the cool of an encroaching coastal fog.

I left the two women at the main house—Charlene to nap, Lenore with a collection of W. H. Auden poetry I'd brought along—and set out for Cathedral Grove alone. As I made my way through glens thick with ferns, I carried a pair of heavy gloves and a flashlight with a strong beam. When I finally reached the old wooden bridge, the golden rays of light slanting through the canopy of branches had become weak and diffuse, while wisps of fog stole among the redwoods like a ghostly army advancing on the sly.

I donned the gloves and ducked under the bridge into its shadows, flicking on the flashlight. Immediately, the reclusive bats were awake and in frenzied flight. They swarmed past me in a flutter and a rush, their broad, webbed wings

flicking at my face as the furry creatures sought escape.
Within seconds I was alone again, in a place where no human being had a reason to be. I raised the flashlight and
began to search—every beam, joint, and arch—keeping an
eye out below for rattlesnakes. As the minutes passed, and
I moved deeper into the cool darkness, I became more certain
than ever that Diana would never have entered this place
without some secret and pressing need.

Then my hand discovered something oddly out of place:
a small bundle wrapped in heavy paper and secured with
duct tape wedged deep into a crevice formed of wood and
concrete. With some effort, I was able to work it free. I set
the flashlight in the joint of two beams and went to work
under its light, unwrapping. When I had the tape and paper
off, I held a small tin in my hands. It was the kind used by
Blum's to package the candy company's cherry cordials,
which Diana used to give me each Christmas as a stocking
stuffer. Only there were no cherry cordials in this pretty tin
box. When I lifted the lid, I found—between protective
layers of cotton—five lustrous pearls, brilliant orange in
color and roughly the size of robin's eggs.

I'd finally recovered the legendary pearls smuggled out of
China by Helen Hop-Yik, the pearls that had caused so
much greed and so much grief. I placed them back in the
tin box, closed it tight, retrieved my flashlight and began
backing out from under the bridge into the twilight. Behind
me, I heard a twig snap, and froze. A moment later, finding
my courage, I turned.

"It's just me, Philip."

Lenore Ashley stood a few feet away, facing me, one hand
behind her back.

"You spooked me," I said.

"Did I? I'm sorry."

I directed my beam at her face, needing to see if her expression was as odd and distant as her voice. She squinted and put up a hand against the harsh light while keeping her other hand behind her.

"You must have followed me," I said.

"I thought I should keep an eye on you." She smiled, though it hardly looked intimate. "You seem to have a nose for trouble." Her eyes went to the tin box in my other hand. "Did you come across something?"

I lowered the beam, directing it at the tin box. "Diana must have left it here, thinking no one would ever find it. At least not until she wanted it found."

Lenore took a step forward. "She underestimated you, I guess."

"Charlene remembered seeing Diana exploring under this bridge." As I talked, I tried to look past Lenore up the trail. "She must have been looking for the ideal hiding place."

"But you figured it out. Clever, clever Philip."

The trail behind her was empty. Suddenly, I was seized with a horrible thought. "I imagine Charlene might be coming down any moment, looking for us."

"I'm afraid that when I left her, she was dead to the world." Lenore's words caused me to go sick inside. She took another step, until we were not two feet apart. "I also discovered something, Philip. May I show it to you?"

Charlene's little handgun, I thought, taken from her lifeless body—what else? So it all had come down to this, Lenore and I alone in a remote wood, and the pearls hers for the taking. Her eyes were keen, her manner intense yet entirely self-composed. Then, in one quick motion, her hand came around from behind her back, as I steeled myself for what was surely to follow.

But there was no gun. Just my W. H. Auden collection, with a bookmark wedged among the pages.

"While Charlene napped," Lenore explained, "I read some of the poetry you left with me. I can't imagine why I haven't discovered Auden until now."

"He's quite splendid, isn't he?" My head was light, spinning; I wanted to throw up my arms with relief, dance a little jig. "Diana gave me that book, years ago."

"It's wonderful. I came down to thank you for opening my eyes to it." Lenore leaned forward, gave me a chaste kiss on the cheek, then opened the book to the marked page. "Look at this one: *September 1, 1939.* He's in New York, sitting in a bar on 52nd Street, 'uncertain and afraid,' reflecting on 'the unmentionable odour of death' that 'offends the September night.' It's brilliant, the way he's able to capture a world gone mad with hate and unspeakable violence. I wonder if civilization will ever suffer that kind of horror again."

Her beauty was boundless at that moment, her eyes deep and soulful, her voice as earnest yet as comforting as a Bach sonata, tinged with a lovely melancholy. I moved to kiss her but she pulled back, not coldly but almost with a purity and innocence. She gave me her hand, though, as if we were friends.

"One never knows what lies ahead," she said. "What's that saying? Live, laugh, and love as if there's no tomorrow."

"Believe me, I try." I felt the sudden need for Charlene between us, for emotional ballast. "What do you say we go back to the house?"

We walked back slowly, talking, at Lenore's behest, of

other poets we admired, most of them European, some Japanese and Latin. Though I wanted her more than ever, I knew that something had changed between us. We were closer in a way, but at the same time, further and forever apart.

CHARLENE, of course, was thrilled when she saw the pearls. She immediately called Hercules Platt to give him the news, after we agreed never to connect the pearls to Helen Hop-Yik, sparing the Chinatown businesswoman any pointless problems in her already complicated life.

After talking to Platt, Charlene phoned Herb Caen and told him to prepare the *Chronicle* for yet another twist in San Francisco's highest profile and most complicated murder case. They even arranged for the *Chron* to shoot exclusive photographs of the priceless pearls before we handed them over to the cops.

Herb was ecstatic, but wanted more. "We still don't have a kicker," he complained, as if it was up to Charlene, Platt, and me to wrap things up as neatly as a newspaper story.

Chapter 36

THE NEXT DAY, Charlene treated Hercules Platt and me to lunch in the Garden Court at the Sheraton-Palace, known to locals simply as The Palace.

The Garden Court was possibly the most magnificent dining room in the country, its grandeur untouched from its early days preceding the 1906 earthquake and fire, from which it had been spared. Platt blanched at the prices—with dessert, lunch at the Garden Court could easily reach five dollars—but Charlene insisted he deserved it, given that he'd solved the murder of Terrence Hamilton Collier III and was now the toast of San Francisco and beyond. CBS News wanted Platt for a coast-to-coast hookup—Walter Cronkite himself was to do the interview—and *Life* had scheduled him for a cover by legendary photographer Gordon Parks.

There was even some talk that Platt might become the first Negro in the city to rise above the rank of Inspector.

"I hardly solved the case on my own." Platt lifted a forkful of fresh crab from its bed of Green Goddess salad. "You both were indispensable."

"But you uncovered the most crucial evidence at the end, piece by piece," Charlene said. "And then connected it so it all made sense."

She prodded Platt to discuss the autopsy report just back on Vivian Collier. He said there wasn't much that was new, except for traces of skin and blood discovered beneath her nails. "Apparently Mrs. Collier fought back in a futile effort to defend herself. Maybe some day science will find a way to identify suspects and victims through blood and tissue samples. For now, all we know is that someone's walking around out there with telltale wounds."

"This is *so* exciting," Charlene said. "You know, I've just started a new mystery by Dorothy L. Sayers—"

Platt and I silenced her with a shared look. She turned her attention to her Palace Court salad, picking at it while looking hurt. To cheer her up, I suggested she fill Platt in on our visit to Stinson Beach a few days earlier. Charlene immediately brightened and began relating the details of our brief encounter with Gwendolyn Sparks. By the time the dessert tray came around, Platt was jotting notes. As we finished our pastries and coffee, he'd made a list of several places or people he needed to visit: James Brannigan's children, the airfield where Terrence Collier had kept his private plane, and the San Francisco Public Library, with its excellent resources for historic research.

Charlene, of course, was itching to know what he was up to.

"All in due time." Hercules Platt thanked her for lunch as he grabbed his hat and set out on his various errands.

BY Wednesday morning, the authorities had called off their search for Valentino del Conte's body.

They'd pulled his red satin gown from San Francisco Bay within half an hour of his leap from the Golden Gate, but Valentino wasn't in it. It was presumed that he'd been separated from the garment on impact or that the strong currents had pulled him free and carried him down or out to sea. At any rate, surviving such a fall was virtually impossible. Valentino del Conte was officially declared dead.

That morning, heeding my recommendation, Platt had an appointment with George Chang, the Chinatown practitioner, and Charlene was tied up with her husband, Reinhold, on some business matters. So I walked out alone to the middle of the bridge, carrying a dozen long-stemmed American Beauties. San Franciscans, reading Valentino's story in the press, had been going out to the site in droves, leaving flowers and candles in his memory, causing terrible traffic problems that had not yet abated. Vito Panetta, the esteemed accountant for the Alioto family, had put up the money for a fine memorial down at Holy Cross, to be erected at the family plot even if Valentino's body was never found. Valentino had committed murder; no one disputed that. And if he'd been taken alive, he'd surely have ended up in prison, if not the gas chamber. But San Franciscans seem to look at things a little differently than the rest of the world, and many of them took Valentino del Conte into their hearts.

I reached the makeshift shrine at the spot along the rail-

ing where he'd jumped, and spent a few minutes perusing
the tribute notes left among the flowers and the candles, or
scratched in chalk on the sidewalk. I decided to toss my
roses off the bridge one by one, to float where Miss Valentine's soggy gown had been plucked from the chilly water.
As I leaned out and began to let the roses go, watching them
drift twenty-two stories to the channel, something on the
underside of the bridge caught my eye.

I stretched for a better look and saw a ragged piece of red
satin caught in a crusty joint of the ironwork on the underside of the bridge; torn at the edges, it was a sure match for
the fabric in Valentino's resplendent gown. The longer I
studied it, the more I thought about Valentino's youthful
exploits as a gymnast and, later, as a trapeze artist with the
circus. It struck me as entirely possible for such an athletic
showman—a member of the Flying Valentinos—to leap
from the railing to the girding lower down, catch hold, shed
his costume, then work through the maze of cables and cross
beams to the other side and back up, to disappear in the
mass confusion of traffic, or even to be whisked away by a
waiting friend.

YEARS later, returning from a South American vacation, Truman Capote would tell me about a fabulous female impersonator he'd come across in Rio—an American, who owned
a popular club there with his balding, bespectacled partner,
and who ended every show with a rendition of "Over the
Rainbow" that brought down the house.

I never spoke to anyone about that snatch of red satin I'd
glimpsed below the railing of the Golden Gate, not even to
Hercules Platt. "Murder's murder," he'd said, and I suppose

that's true. But, then, is justice also justice? Valentino del Conte had suffered quite enough punishment, I thought, as I dropped the last of my American Beauties into San Francisco Bay, long before he ever plunged that ice pick into the chest of Terrence Hamilton Collier III in the Gold Room of the Fairmont Hotel.

If I had a deep regret about Collier's death, it was that he surely died knowing the identity of my wife's murderer, while I was left to wonder. But that was about to change, as Hercules Platt prepared to put into place the final piece of the convoluted puzzle.

Chapter 37

THE MASS FOR James Brannigan was scheduled at the Italian Cathedral on Thursday afternoon, exactly one week after the service there for Terrence Hamilton Collier III. Charlene and I arrived by taxi and met Hercules Platt on the expansive green lawn of Washington Square Park, where there seemed to be as many reporters, photographers, and TV cameramen as mourners. Platt had just come from his first full treatment with George Chang and seemed to be moving less stiffly. "He wants me on a program of massage, yoga, and guided meditation," Platt grumbled, "whatever the hell that is."

"Don't expect an overnight miracle," Charlene cautioned.

"Believe me," Platt said, "I already got the lecture on patience."

The weather that morning had been clear and crisp, if not

quite balmy. By early afternoon, as we stood in front of Sts. Peter and Paul, fog had begun to drift up from the waterfront. During the previous night, alone and contemplative, I'd had a chance to sift though the suspects, motives and countless *what ifs* that made the murder of Diana—my Diana—such a perplexing tangle. In sorting it out, I'd been struck by something so obvious it should have occurred to me long before now: What if the housekeeper, Gwendolyn Sparks, had been protecting James Brannigan all along, rather than Terrence Collier? What if—by establishing an alibi for Collier—she'd indirectly been setting up an alibi for Brannigan, directing attention away from the man who'd employed her for so long and with such apparent loyalty? It was even possible, I thought, that Brannigan had murdered Vivian Collier as well, in his desperation to get his hands on the missing pearls.

I was eager to convey this theory to Platt, but the press was all over us, and he hustled us across the lawn and narrow Filbert Street to the church. Ahead of us, we could see Gwendolyn Sparks climbing the broad steps, recognizable from behind by her large, solid frame and the way she carried herself so erectly. She was attired in black from head to toe: a long-sleeved chiffon dress that was simple but tasteful and well cut; a broad-brimmed hat with falling veil; gloves buttoned at the wrist; sensible low pumps just visible below the hem of the old-fashioned dress.

As we followed her up the steps, I glanced at a line in Italian from Dante's *Paradiso*, rendered in mosaic on the façade, that Diana had once translated for me: *The glory of Him who moves all things penetrates and glows throughout the universe.* Perhaps, given the circumstances surrounding Brannigan's death—and my new suspicions about him—a line from Dante's *Inferno* would have been more appropriate.

IN the foyer, two of Jimmy Brannigan's children solemnly handed out memorial pamphlets with their father's face on the front cover. Because of the bleak events out at Lands End, I did my best to circumvent them and avoid their eyes, and hoped that Lenore Ashley would do the same, if she showed up at all.

Charlene, Platt, and I took a pew near the back, watching mourners file in, seeing familiar faces, including many who'd attended the dinner dance in the Gold Room not quite two weeks earlier: Mayor Christopher, Alfred Hitchcock, Willie Mays, Rosamund Kelly, countless others. Joe DiMaggio appeared, giving us a small wave, and found a seat on the aisle farther down that could better accommodate his long legs, directly behind Gwendolyn Sparks. Lenore Ashley also put in an appearance, offering me a sad smile that I returned with mixed emotions before she sat alone toward the far side. Herb Caen had let us know he wouldn't be there; given the media frenzy over the murders and related events, he was hanging out at the *Chronicle*, helping the news desk with his sources in its battle for exclusives with the rival afternoon *Examiner*.

While we waited for the service to begin, I leaned close to Platt and whispered my suspicions about Brannigan, suggesting Platt look into them as soon as time and circumstances allowed.

"Believe me, I intend to speak with Miss Sparks." Platt spoke casually, as if he were a step or two ahead of me. "Right after the service, as a matter of fact."

Charlene leaned into the conversation. "Is there something we should know?"

"After listening yesterday to the particulars of your visit to Stinson Beach, I got on the horn with some questions. Brannigan's children were especially forthcoming. They're not terribly fond of Miss Sparks."

"You've discovered something," I said.

"It's what I hope to learn that matters."

Charlene was fidgeting. "At least toss us a morsel, Inspector."

Platt frowned thoughtfully, then dropped his voice to a whisper. "The fiancé Gwendolyn Sparks lost in the war was William Brannigan, James Brannigan's younger brother. She attached herself to Jimmy Brannigan a year or two later, first as a friend, later as his housekeeper. As Brannigan's wife became mentally incapacitated, Gwendolyn insinuated herself increasingly into James Brannigan's life. She's been devoted to him now for nearly two decades."

Charlene leaned over. "How devoted?"

"Very," Platt said.

We shifted and pulled in our knees as a couple made their way toward the center of the pew, before Platt continued. "There's something else. Gwendolyn Sparks has a past. Two shoplifting convictions and one each for writing bad checks and fraud. All of them just after the war, before she went to work for James Brannigan." Platt fixed his eyes directly on me. "I think Gwendolyn may have the answers you're after, Philip."

Charlene's face flushed. "This is *so* exciting!"

A sharp-beaked woman in the pew ahead turned and shushed us. The three of us fell into a respectful silence until the service ended.

*   *   *

CHARLENE and I tried not to look at Gwendolyn Sparks as she
filed past, but I lost my resolve and stole a glance. Behind
her veil, I could just make out her eyes as they shifted uneasily from me to Hercules Platt.

Platt was the first among us to rise. "I'll handle this." We
stood to take positions on either side of him as he followed
Miss Sparks up the aisle. "I mean it this time, you two—
no interference."

Perhaps a dozen mourners separated us from Gwendolyn
Sparks, a number that increased as we merged in the church
foyer with others coming out from the center aisle. Charlene
and Joe found each other and began to chat, moving toward
the entrance, though Gwendolyn Sparks—with Platt on her
tail—was never far from Charlene's roving eye. I tried to
maneuver through the crowd to keep up but found myself
boxed in by shuffling mourners. Suddenly, Lenore Ashley
seized my hand and diverted me to the side, into a vestibule
that offered some privacy. After rummaging in her purse,
she found a note folded into quarters, which she thrust into
my hands. She kissed me quickly on the lips, then rushed
back into the throng moving toward the doors.

I stared after her a moment before opening and reading
the handwritten note: *Dear Philip, You won't see me again. I'm
on my way to Europe for an indefinite stay, to immerse myself in
the culture from which so much timeless poetry has sprung. I know
you think you love me, Philip, or need me, but you don't. It's what
you want me to be that you've fallen in love with. I'm not Diana.
No one can take her place. It's time to let her go, Philip. I'll
remember you always, Lenore.*

I dashed after her, pushing through the crowded foyer to

the steps outside, where fog drifted through the park. To my left, at a distance, Gwendolyn Sparks was hurrying along Filbert Street, in the direction of Telegraph Hill. She glanced back as Hercules Platt lumbered after her, as quickly as his bad back allowed. In between Platt and the church steps where I stood, Charlene was bidding good-bye to Joe, with one eye on Platt and his prey. To my right, I saw Lenore striding across the lawn in the direction of the wharf, into the billowing fog. Watching her go was like seeing Diana vanish before my eyes.

"Philip!"

I turned; it was Charlene, urging me to join her in pursuing Platt and the fleeing Gwendolyn Sparks. When I glanced after Lenore Ashley again, she was gone, into the mist-shrouded landscape. I heard Charlene again, calling me away from the woman who was now just a confusing memory, a fading dream.

"NOT a moment to lose," Charlene said, grabbing my hand as I caught up to her. "We don't want to miss the denouement."

We dashed up Filbert as Gwendolyn Sparks made a beeline toward its steepest section, followed by the pertinacious Hercules Platt.

Chapter 38

FOR SUCH A large person, Gwendolyn Sparks moved along Filbert Street at a surprising pace.

She managed the two level blocks from the church in a minute or two, then mounted the challenging incline like a seasoned climber scaling Everest. Platt was not doing as well. He passed his parked Ford on the flat, then slowed noticeably as the street ascended sharply. By the time we reached him—halfway up the steep hill, with Gwendolyn Sparks nearing the top—he'd pulled up and was doubled over, a hand on his lower back. Still, I couldn't be sure if his grimace was a reaction to his physical pain or our arrival, or both.

"What the hell are you two doing here?"

"We could see you needed backup," Charlene said.

"The police dispatcher will send backup, as soon as I call

in." Platt glanced up the forbidding hill. "I'll never make it up on foot, not in the shape I'm in."

Charlene peered up to the crest of Telegraph Hill, where Gwendolyn Sparks was entering a maze of steps. "While you call headquarters, Inspector, we'll tail the suspect. She must be headed for Pioneer Park and Coit Tower. That's all that's up there."

Platt raised a finger and narrowed his eyes. "I don't want you two messing with this lady."

I spread my hands plaintively. "But if she knows something about Diana's murder—"

"There are only two other ways down from Telegraph Hill." Platt winced as he spoke. "The wooden steps descending to the Embarcadero, and Telegraph Hill Boulevard from the north, off Lombard Street. I'll have barricades put up before she reaches the end of either route."

"There's one more way she could give us the slip," I said.

Platt straightened up, groaning. "I don't see how, Damon."

"The same way Valentino del Conte slipped away."

"Philip's right," Charlene said. "Coit Tower rises more than two hundred feet. That's a long way down, if Gwendolyn Sparks has the nerve."

"If that happens," I said, "we may never know the whole story."

Platt put up a hand in surrender. "All right—I'll let you two go after her. But just to keep her in sight." Charlene and I were already striking up Filbert. "I'll order backup, then get my car and bring it up. Remember, keep your distance!"

Charlene paused long enough to lean on my shoulder and

remove her pumps for speedier movement. Then we were climbing again, as a cool fog nipped at our heels.

THE centerpiece of tiny Pioneer Park is monumental Coit Tower, a single, fluted column of more than twenty stories that rose before us as we reached the crest. Out front stood a sizable bronze of a cloaked Christopher Columbus, gazing out past Alcatraz Island at fog-laden San Francisco Bay.

"There!"

Charlene pointed along a paved walkway where Gwendolyn Sparks was moving more slowly now, her big shoulders heaving. She kept one hand on her wide-brimmed black hat as the other lifted the hem of her long, black dress. We gave chase, but she was soon rounding the front of the tower, out of sight. Halfway down the walk, Charlene cried out, and I caught her as she was going down on a twisted ankle. She rubbed it for a moment before limping on, using me for a crutch. As we climbed the front steps into the tower's lobby, I calculated that we'd lost at least a minute, and feared that we'd lost Gwendolyn Sparks as well. Then, just ahead—across a red tile floor through marble portals—we saw a streak of black as she stepped into an elevator. A minute after that, I'd purchased a ticket to the top, placed Charlene on a wooden bench surrounded by the lobby's historic murals, and ordered her to stay there.

"Someone has to wait for Platt. Tell him I've gone up to keep an eye on Gwendolyn."

"We'll flip for it."

"You're staying here, Charlene—and that's the end of it."

"How come you get to have all the fun?"

The doors of the elevator opened, a tourist family stepped

out; I stepped in and handed my ticket to the boy operating the controls. The doors closed and the elevator began to rise, along with my blood pressure.

AS I stepped from the elevator near the top, I faced a narrow set of spiral steps to my right. I started up, knowing where they led—to a circular observation loggia of two dozen arched windows that on a clear day provided an incomparable panorama of the city and the bay. Diana and I had been up here several times on days like that. But now, as I reached the top, I saw that all of San Francisco was buried beneath a blanket of white fog, except for the downtown skyscrapers and the spires of the Golden Gate Bridge poking up into the late afternoon sunshine.

To my surprise, the loggia was empty. I was alone.

I crossed to one of the open arches to peer out, worried that Gwendolyn Sparks might have somehow eluded us, fleeing from the park far below. As I scanned the greenery for escape routes, I heard the click of heels on tile behind me. Charlene, I thought, ignoring my orders to stay put.

As I turned, prepared to scold her, I faced a moving cloud of black chiffon and a mask of fury beneath a lifted veil. Gwendolyn Sparks came flying at me from the stairwell, and I realized too late that she must have hidden around the stairs below, waiting to see who came up. She was on me all at once—two hands at my throat as I felt the full force of her mass and strength. Before I could react, she thrust me straight back toward the open arch and a plunge to certain death. I fought desperately to keep my footing, grasping for anything that might save me from going over. I felt my feet leave the floor and the sensation of falling back against the ledge until my upper body was suspended, with nothing but the sky above and the hard ground far below. I clutched at the folds of her billowing black dress, pulling her with me, hearing a growl through her clenched teeth as she summoned a final effort to fling me from the tower. Together, we struggled, locked in a death grip, as she desperately tried to choke the life out of me. I felt her hands tighten on my throat, and the hideous growling grew louder until it filled my ears like a scream. Then it slowly grew distant and small, and I knew I was on the verge of blacking out, and going over.

A moment later a different sound pierced my panicked brain: the scuffle of running feet, Hercules Platt shouting, a last moment of terror as I fought to keep my balance. Then I felt Gwendolyn's weight coming off me and her hands leaving my throat. I saw Platt slam her against a wall as he reached with his free hand for his gun. Charlene appeared, grabbed me, and pulled me back from the brink. I stood upright on wobbly knees, my heart pounding furiously while I fought back nausea and tried to understand exactly what was going on.

For the past minute, I'd perceived everything as if in slow motion, with crystal clarity. Now I was back in real time, yet my perception seemed fuzzy, muted, feverishly bright. Across the loggia floor, as I regained some focus, I saw Platt aiming the muzzle of his snub-nosed .38 at Gwendolyn Sparks's chest. She sat down heavily on the floor with her back to the wall, pulling her dress over her knees to properly cover her legs. After that she stared blankly, as if receding behind the dull glaze of her eyes, away from us and into her own world. Platt opened a set of handcuffs. Without looking at him or speaking a word, she held her hands out submissively.

He ordered her to unbutton and remove her gloves and push up the long sleeves of her dress. She complied, revealing hands and forearms that were deeply scratched from her lethal struggle with Vivian Collier. Platt slipped on the handcuffs and locked them tight.

Below us, distantly, we heard sirens as police vehicles raced up Telegraph Hill.

"I need to know what happened to my wife." I knelt beside Gwendolyn Sparks as she sat mutely against the wall, her eyes dreamy and lost. "I'm appealing to your decency, if you have any."

Nearly a dozen cops crowded the loggia around us—officers, detectives, a district captain, Police Chief Thomas Cahill, and one of the department's five policewomen. Cahill kept the other cops at bay, letting Hercules Platt run the show. He was taking his time, but Gwendolyn Sparks still had nothing to say.

"She's not the type who feels she owes anyone anything, not even remorse," Platt said. "She's the kind who always blames someone else for her troubles, and doesn't care who she hurts to get what she wants. The technical term is sociopath."

From her purse, Charlene handed me a gold-plated flask filled with good French cognac that she always kept on hand for special occasions. I took a long sip. My heartbeat had slowed and my head was clearing. Yet I felt, if anything, more anxious than before, aching inside for the knowledge that had eluded me for two agonizing years.

"Miss Sparks is not at all what she appears," Platt went on. "She comes from East Coast money and good breeding, a family that was once socially prominent. A father profiled in *Who's Who*, if one goes back far enough, looking through the old directories. It was a life of comfort and privilege, until the Crash of '29 and the Great Depression that followed. The Sparks family lost everything. Mr. Sparks took his life and Mrs. Sparks slowly drank herself to death. The children scattered to live with relatives or to get by however they could. Then, just before the war, Gwendolyn met William Brannigan, the brother."

Gwendolyn reacted slightly as the name was mentioned, but she still said nothing. Platt continued the story.

"Thanks to James Brannigan's connections, his brother Bill had done reasonably well for himself. He and Gwendolyn were to be married the moment the war was over. Only William died at Normandy, derailing Gwendolyn's plans. So she turned to crime—fraud, bad checks, theft. Feeling some responsibility, James Brannigan took her on as a housekeeper, in charge of the family home in the Parkside district. As his wife deteriorated mentally, Gwendolyn made herself available to him emotionally. Eventually, Brannigan became dependent on her for companionship. He set her up at the house in Stinson Beach, still in the guise of his housekeeper. In truth, they were secret lovers, though Brannigan's children were never fooled.

"Then things started to fall apart financially for Brannigan. Terrence Collier's spending was driving the company toward ruin. Through Jimmy, Gwendolyn learned of the pearls, although they couldn't be sure who had them—Diana Damon or Vivian Collier. Two years ago, someone flew to New York—someone Diana knew and trusted enough to let in that night. Gwendolyn was to be the alibi—the house-keeper who would tell the New York police that both Collier and Brannigan were out at the beach house all weekend, deep in business matters, should the detectives ever ask."

I shook my head furiously. "It wasn't Collier. He'd assaulted Diana physically. She wouldn't have let him in." I seized Gwendolyn's wrist, just above the bracelet of the handcuffs. "It was James Brannigan you were protecting, wasn't it?"

Platt kneeled and removed my hand from her wrist, silencing me with his calm eyes, which he turned again on Gwendolyn Sparks. "Jimmy Brannigan was a decent man—a gentle man, according to everyone who knew him. No, Jimmy would never hurt anyone, not even to save his business and protect his wealth. But Miss Sparks would. Wouldn't you, Gwendolyn?"

She raised her eyes briefly, said nothing, then gazed out at the reddish orange sunset spreading across the western sky.

"By being the one who provided the alibi for Brannigan and Collier, she very cleverly created an alibi for herself, deflecting suspicion at the same time."

Tears stung my eyes. "*You* killed Diana?"

Her eyes remained fixed on the colorful sky, her mouth shut tight.

"Miss Sparks and Mr. Collier planned it carefully," Platt explained, "keeping it secret from Brannigan until the police investigation forced them to bring him in on it. She couldn't fly commercial to New York—the chances of being found out were too great. So Collier's personal pilot flew her in his private plane, without logging it. We took the pilot's statement this morning. Faced with a choice of being charged as

an accessory or granted immunity, he became quite talka-
tive."

Charlene could no longer restrain herself. "After Valentino del Conte murdered Collier, and Brannigan faced financial insolvency, finding the pearls took on a new urgency.
That's why Gwendolyn went after Vivian, suspecting she
might have them or know where they were."

"She might have gotten away with it," Platt said, "except
that her car's engine was still warm when you and Mr. Damon stopped by the house at Stinson Beach. If you recall,
she told you she'd been in all morning, baking in the
kitchen."

"But there was no aroma of baking in the house," I recalled. "Behind her apron, instead of house clothes, she was
dressed as if to go out. And she kept her oven mitts on the
whole time, to hide the fresh scratches on her hands and
arms." I stared into the impassive face of Gwendolyn Sparks,
feeling sick, revolted. "For a few pearls, you killed my wife,
our unborn child, and another woman."

Gwendolyn Sparks finally looked at me, breaking her silence.

"You kids today." Her voice was curt, dismissive. "You
have everything you want. Cars, clothes, money whenever
you need it. But no concept of what it's like to do without."
She fixed me with her soulless eyes. "Yes, I killed your wife,
Mr. Damon. And I killed Vivian Collier, and I might have
killed you, too, if Inspector Platt hadn't stopped me. Do you
know why, Mr. Damon? Because I'm a survivor. I know
what it's like to lose everything, to face utter destitution. I
vowed that I'd never go through that again—that I'd hold
on to whatever I had, no matter what."

I rose and backed off, needing to get away from her. Platt

signaled two uniformed officers, who stepped forward and lifted Gwendolyn Sparks to her feet. The policewoman frisked her, then two detectives moved in and took charge, turning their suspect in the direction of the stairs. I kept my back to her, watching the sunset deepen into lavender above the vast plain of fog, relieved to know the truth at last but feeling crushed by the weight of it just the same.

"Mr. Damon."

I turned at the sound of Gwendolyn Sparks's voice, which was now almost friendly.

"Did I ever tell you how much I enjoyed hearing your father play?"

"Yes, Miss Sparks. You told me."

"Some evenings, my beau and I would tune in your father's show on the Philco. Roll back the carpet, dance right there in the living room. He was such an elegant man, your father, so sophisticated. Didn't he often wear a red carnation in the lapel of his tuxedo?"

I nodded. "I often wear one when I play."

She beamed, clasping her cuffed hands under her chin. "How grand! One rarely sees a man wearing a red carnation these days."

Then she sighed audibly, seeming to deflate. "Such a shame how the world has to change. Wouldn't it be nice if things could just stay just the way they were?"

WHILE Hercules Platt and I made our exit from Coit Tower, Charlene used a phone in the office to call Herb Caen, which is how the *San Francisco Chronicle* scooped the *Examiner* on the biggest local story of the decade, with the kicker Herb was hoping for.

Platt's Ford was parked at the top of Filbert Street just behind the park, which was now shrouded in the rising fog. As we walked in that direction, he told me that on the advice of the police department orthopedist, he'd decided to put in for early retirement.

"It's either that or take a desk job until I get my 25/50." Platt shrugged plaintively. "I don't see myself shuffling paper. I'd rather find a spot on the sidewalk in North Beach, put out a cup and play my horn." He figured the timing was right to take his pension, he said, since he'd just closed the books on three high-profile murder cases in two major cities, and another from forty years ago that he considered just as important.

"They're all important, every damn one," Platt said, "if folks could just get that through their thick skulls."

I was feeling pretty good about things again. We'd finally found Diana's killer, which was certain to help me come to terms with the whole dreadful experience. Soon, when our gig at the Venetian Room was up, I'd be heading home to Manhattan, and my friends there. It even looked like I'd be providing the music at the next Presidential inaugural if John Kennedy were re-elected, which seemed likely. Jackie had told me she wanted to get together to discuss it late next month, after she and the President returned from their scheduled trip to Dallas. My life felt like it was finally back on track, moving smoothly forward, in a world that was whole again.

I asked Platt if he was still interested in working as a sideman, now that he was retiring from police work. He said that he was, although he intended to keep a private investigator's license to fall back on. I told him my alto sax player was quitting the band to play rock and roll, even though I figured rock music was a passing fad. Platt acknowledged how that was an interesting development.

"We're on the road a lot," I said. "Palm Beach to Palm Springs, most major cities in between. Even an international date now and then."

"I've always wanted to travel."

I asked him if he knew how to play "As Time Goes By," since it was our most requested tune.

Platt smiled a little, shrugging. "Just name the key."

I slipped an arm around his shoulders as we walked deeper into the swirling fog.

"Hercules," I said, "I think this is the beginning of a beautiful friendship."

LOVE MYSTERY?

From cozy mysteries to procedurals,
we've got it all. Satisfy your cravings with our monthly
newsletters designed and edited specifically for fans of who-
dunits. With two newsletters to choose from, you'll be sure to
get it all. Be sure to check back each month or sign up for
free monthly in-box delivery at

www.penguin.com

Berkley Prime Crime

Berkley publishes the premier writers of mysteries.
Get the latest on your
favorties:
Susan Wittig Albert, Margaret Coel, Earlene
Fowler, Randy Wayne White, Simon Brett, and
many more fresh faces.

Signet

From the Grand Dame of mystery,
Agatha Christie, to debut authors,
Signet mysteries offer something for every reader.

Sign up and sleep with one eye open!